TRUE NORTH

AMY KNUPP

*G*etting dumped sucked, even when you weren't that wild about the guy to start with.

Getting dumped two days before your sister's wedding, being left dateless… That was an altogether different level of suck.

Sierra Lowell shut the back door of her business harder than she meant to and let out a quiet but heartfelt stream of swear words.

"Everything okay?"

She turned from the door to see Cole North, her foreman, sticking his head into the room.

"Fine," she said, brushing off the irritation from her personal life and slipping back into business mode. It probably revealed a lot about her relationship—*former* relationship—that she so easily got her mind back on the subject of her meeting with Cole. "Sorry about the interruption."

"You sure?" he asked as she approached him from across the kitchen of the cute Cape Cod house, built nearly a century ago, that served as the headquarters of Dunn & Lowell Remodeling. They'd been about to start a two-person evening meeting when Kevin, her ex, had interrupted.

"Yep," she said, not having to fake the optimism in her tone. "What I want to discuss is important." She led Cole back into her office, originally one of the two cozy bedrooms of the house, and retook her place in front of her notebook, laptop, and coffee at the round table in the center of the room.

Before sitting again, he pulled his gray hooded sweatshirt over his head to reveal the black T-shirt with the small Dunn & Lowell logo on the chest and tossed the sweatshirt on the chair between them. Both were dusty after their regular workday at the jobsite. Sierra wouldn't call herself clean either, but that was status quo and a sign that they'd worked hard. "So what's up?" he said as he sat down across from her.

She flipped back several pages in her notebook to some notes she'd jotted down late last night. "Chances are good you're going to think I'm crazy."

"Sounds like a normal day." Cole wasn't one to smile a lot, but the tips of his lips tilted up slightly now as he pulled his legal pad and carpenter pencil closer.

Sierra leaned back in her chair and pulled her cargo-pants-clad legs up to sit cross-legged, took in a deep breath as she chose her words carefully. "Are you familiar with William Eldridge?"

"I've heard the name. Is he the guy who owns a bunch of TV networks?"

"Networks, newspapers, magazines, websites, who knows what else," she said, brushing back a long strand of hair that'd come out of her ponytail hours ago. "Originally from Tennessee."

"Richer than God if I remember right."

"You do. Also egotistical, from what I've heard, and loves being in the spotlight. Anyway, I saw something on his home remodeling network last night between shows. He recently bought a mansion in town, south of here. An old Italianate-style house built in the early 1900s. He got it for a steal because it's a mess—"

"And he needs a remodeler," Cole said.

"He needs a remodeler, but he's not going about finding one in the usual way. He's holding a competition and putting it on a TV series."

"You've got to be kidding me." Cole sat back in his chair.

Sierra's heart sank the tiniest bit at his tone, but she reminded herself it was exactly the reaction she'd expected from him. "When you own one of the top networks devoted to remodeling, what else are you going to do?"

"And you want to get into the competition, just like that? Because you saw an ad on TV?" Cole said, his eyes narrowed at her.

"Of course I do. But I wanted to get your opinion on it."

He studied her with the look in his eyes that she'd expected—as if she hadn't given it enough thought. Yes, it was sudden, but how could she not try? As soon as she'd gone to the website and read the details, she'd known she had to enter.

"This is your company," he said. "You make the calls."

"Yes and yes." She kept her voice firm. She would do this, would go for it, because winning the competition would propel her company to new levels and give her a new platform. The thought had excitement pulsing through her again. But the project would be a lot smoother if Cole, her right-hand guy, was on board.

Dunn & Lowell was doing well, always had a lineup of projects, the vast majority of which were remodels of historical buildings. They received most of their business through word of mouth because Sierra personally did everything possible to ensure her customers' complete satisfaction and she employed an excellent crew with remarkably little turnover.

She was blessed in so many ways—to have inherited the business from her grandpa, Roger Dunn, to have learned the industry from him, one of the best in the field, and to genuinely love what she did for a living. Beyond the basics of carpentry and construction, her grandpa had instilled in her a passion for uncovering and bringing out an old building's soul. Quality and authenticity were valued above shortcuts and cheap solutions, and his tenets were what she continued to build the company's reputation on. But lately she'd been thinking a lot about how to make the business even more. She was at a crossroads, where she could either decide this was the pinnacle of Dunn & Lowell or she could work on taking it even higher. Her vote was for pushing it higher. The timing of this opportunity couldn't be more perfect.

"What would this entail?" Cole asked, tapping his flat pencil on the table.

She lowered her legs, sat up straighter, and referenced the bullet items in her notebook even though she knew them by heart. "There are three stages, and at each stage, the field of competitors narrows. Application, interview, and the final one is a full-blown, in-depth, multimedia proposal for the mansion."

"It's a circus parade just to get to the proposal stage," Cole said, tapping away.

"That's the spirit of TV, I guess." Truth be told, Sierra would thrive on the chance to be in the spotlight. She wasn't shy, and she knew her stuff. Being a woman in a man's field had always been an uphill battle and she continually had to prove herself and then prove herself again. Making it past any of the contest rounds and appearing on Eldridge's network would increase her credibility as an expert and show that women could run a renovation company just as well as a man—and better.

"So the prize is the job?"

"That's just the beginning." She took a sip of her coffee—vanilla caramel in her mug that said GIRL BOSS—before continuing, to slow her thoughts and her speech, which were both ramping up with her enthusiasm. "The remodel would be featured in detail on the network for a full season, and after that season, we'd get our own show for a year, where we basically go about our business as usual and they film our work, interview us, show what we're doing and how we do it."

"So a typical home network show."

"Yes, with a focus on century-old-home renovations."

"Our bread and butter," he said.

"I know we could compete."

Cole sat up taller, a cocky look on his handsome face. "We could do more than compete. We could win it. But are you sure you want all the bullshit that would come with it? The show, the attention, the bureaucracy, being accountable to someone besides yourself and the client?"

She nodded, loving that he felt comfortable enough to speak his mind. That's what she wanted. Not some yes man. "I thought about all of that, thought about it practically all night long, and it's a lot. To me, the benefits outweigh the negatives, but it will affect everyone who works here to some extent."

"Sure as hell will." He said it with conviction, and Sierra's mind spun with how to bring him around, how to get Cole's support.

She didn't want to hard-sell this. She wanted Cole to be in favor of it without her persuasion, because he'd become important to her business, almost like a partner in some aspects. He was highly intelligent, had above-average skills and knowledge, and worked as hard as she did. In the years he'd been in the industry, he'd gained immeasurable experience in solving whatever problems arose—and because they dealt with decades-old, sometimes centuries-old buildings, they'd had some real headaches.

"When's the deadline for the application?" he asked, doodling designs along the margin of his otherwise-blank yellow legal pad.

"We've got a week and a half."

"What would my role be?"

"I can do the app. I went through some of it last night, the short answers and financials. There's a few essay-type questions, like why I want to win, what's the most challenging historical renovation we've done, that kind of thing."

"What about the other stages?" Cole asked, interrupting his doodling to look her in the eye, and it hit her that that was where his hesitation lay. While she loved the idea of being on camera, being the center of attention, being hailed as an expert, Cole wouldn't. He would detest it.

"How about this? If we get past the application, you can stay behind the scenes. I'll handle the interview and the proposal."

Cole's body language changed, telling her she was on to the key. "What if they want a second person involved?"

"Someone else can do it. Troy, maybe. Demetrius. They're both extroverts who never shut up. Even Carlos. With a little coaching, he'd do great, and probably gain a few female fans in the process."

"That's the last thing he needs," Cole said. "It all sounds okay, but what if we win? There's no way you can guarantee I can stay behind the scenes then."

"I'll tell them you're off-limits. Maybe I'll tell them you have a speech impediment," she said, grinning.

"Next thing we know, they'd want to do a feature on the tongue-tied foreman. Hell no."

"There'd probably be times when you might be on screen, but I'll do whatever I can to keep them from interviewing—*if* we get that far. It's a long shot and you know it."

He set his pencil down, crossed his arms over his chest, and sat there pensively, silently. Sierra had more than a little practice with sales techniques, as she was the primary salesperson for the company, so she knew it was time to shut up, to not jump into the heavy pause as she had the urge to do, and to let him think through things.

She sipped her coffee and flipped to the next page in her notebook to double-check the deadline schedule for all three stages, which she already knew, but she was fighting to seem nonchalant.

"You really want to be a TV star?" he asked as he leaned his elbows on the table, his biceps flexing from under the ends of his T-shirt sleeves.

"Not a star," she said, because that wasn't the end goal. "But if this is the way to teach more people why old buildings are important, why we should bring them back to life instead of knock them down and throw up a brand-new cookie-cutter version, I'm all in." She was itching to spread the knowledge and the passion she'd gotten from her beloved grandpa. And this, she believed, was the best way to do exactly that.

Cole met her gaze, his hard-edged caramel eyes giving no hint as to his thoughts, and she raised her brows in a silent *Well?*

"Yes, you're crazy as a loon, and yes, I'll stand behind you on this, do whatever you need, as long as it's off camera."

She didn't have a chance to celebrate before her phone dinged with a reminder. She picked it up and read the note to pick up her sister, Kennedy, for the bride's and bridesmaids' pedi/mani, and with that, she was plunged into the wedding to-do list that would only intensify tomorrow, which was why she was taking a rare day off. Now she needed to call her mom and tell her she didn't have a plus one after all—that or find one. She'd be much better off finding one, but at this late date…

"Dammit," she muttered to herself as she set the phone down hard on the table and started packing her things in her bag to take home with her.

"Okay," Cole said, already standing, his legal pad and pencil back in his work bag, ready to go. "What did what's-his-name do to you?"

"How do you know it's what's-his-name?" She stood and picked up her Dunn & Lowell fleece jacket from the back of her chair and put it on.

"You were fine all day, even with the wedding stress. He shows up, you slam the door, I find you swearing a blue streak after him… Are you going to tell me it's not?"

Cole was the kind of guy who didn't say too much but who paid attention, sometimes more than she wanted him to. "He screwed me over for a wedding date," she said.

"He canceled on you?"

"Broke up with me. Which wouldn't be a big deal if not for Kennedy's wedding. We were never that serious but had agreed to at least get through the wedding."

"What changed?"

She blew out a breath as she pulled her ponytail out from under her jacket. "He met someone he really likes. Wants to see her this weekend."

Cole watched her, assessing, and then he said, "That blows."

"I'd be okay with it if it didn't leave me in the lurch for the wedding."

"Do you really need a date?" he asked skeptically.

Such a guy.

"I really do. My mom is militant about RSVPs and head counts for the hotel caterers. If I don't show up with a plus one, I'll never hear the end of it."

There was more—as the youngest Lowell sibling, Sierra

always felt she had to prove herself, in every arena, justified or not, and both her siblings had found their person, were settled or settling, and she was so far from it, it wasn't funny—but it wasn't worth going into with Cole. She fully acknowledged it was at least partially in her head, but it wasn't likely she could resolve twenty-some years of mental crap in the next forty-eight hours.

"Plus there's the bridal party dance..." She shook her head, realizing how woe-is-me she would sound to admit out loud she didn't want to be the odd girl out.

"What kind of dance?" Cole said, lowering his bag to the chair he'd been sitting on.

"Just a slow song. Standard partner dance. Nothing special, but it's a thing." She looked away, pressed her lips together as she started sorting through options, because the other single attendant—the groom's brother—was bringing a date, and they'd already decided their dates would join them for the bridal party dance. If Sierra didn't find someone, she'd either look like a dumb ass out there by herself or be conspicuously absent for that song. She disliked both options.

"It's Saturday night?" he asked, looking pensive.

"Five thirty. I have"—she picked up her phone and pushed the button to check the time—"forty-seven and a half hours to find someone. I'm not going alone."

She unlocked her phone, opened her contacts, and was about to tap on her brother's name, hoping he'd know someone he could set her up with, as pathetic as that was, when Cole said, "I can stand in for your date."

With her thumb hovering over her brother's name, she froze and met his gaze, surprised and more than a little afraid he was joking. When she saw only sincerity in his eyes, she said, "Really?"

"If you need me to," he said.

"You'd be my fake date?"

"No fancy dance steps I have to learn?"

"No fancy dance steps."

He broke eye contact and picked up his bag. "Text me when and where and I'll be there."

Sierra let out a breath of relief and resisted the urge to throw her arms around him. Because on some level, she hadn't lost sight of the fact that he worked for her and there were lines they couldn't cross. But he was offering her a solution, and she'd be stupid not to jump on it. "Thank you, Cole. I'll make sure you don't regret it."

CHAPTER TWO

$\mathcal{I}$t took Cole approximately thirty seconds—long enough to walk out of his meeting with Sierra and get into his truck—to regret his offer.

Fifteen minutes later, after belittling himself for the entire drive home, he hit the brakes harder than necessary as he whipped his truck up along the curb near his apartment. Leaving his tool belt and his work bag on the floor, he burst out of the vehicle into the cool October evening and slammed the door. The drive hadn't calmed him down. He was still just as pissed at himself as he'd been when he'd walked out of the office.

After thirty-two years on this planet, he had one good thing in his life, one thing he valued—his job. So naturally he'd just gone and endangered the shit out of that.

At the nondescript wooden door that led to the stairs to his second-story apartment, he stopped with his hand on the knob and eyed the next door over—the dark-tinted glass door of Sunshine's, the hole-in-the-wall bar below his place. He chose the dingy, stale-smelling tavern over the comforts of home and headed inside. It would take his eyes a minute or two to adjust to the darkness, but that didn't matter. He could find his way to the counter of this dive with his eyes closed.

As he strode across the 1970s-era black-and-white-checked linoleum tiles to his usual spot at the far end of the bar, he took a quick inventory—five tables occupied, mostly men, two women at the bar, pool table in use, Winona behind the counter. He didn't make eye contact with anyone, was nearly at his stool when some asshole plowed back-first into him from the side.

"Son of a bitch!" the guy yelled as he turned and glared at Cole. "The fuck you doing?" He was about as tall as Cole, but Cole had twenty pounds of muscle on him and was in just the right mind-set to use that muscle. The bastard had beady hazel eyes and one of those dumb-ass overgrown beards that made him look like a lumberjack. Cole raised his chin as he scowled, his knuckles begging for contact with the guy's ugly mug.

"Evening, Cole," a familiar female smoker's voice called out. "Got your usual ready for you." Winona's way of saying, *Get your ass over here and stay out of trouble.*

She was right. This guy wasn't worth the trouble.

After three more seconds of stare down, Cole turned away and resumed his path to his duct-taped black-vinyl stool, second from the far end.

"Smart," Winona said as he took his seat. "You look like you had a shit day."

"Not my favorite," Cole said as he pulled the glass mug of beer toward him. "Johnnie kind of day, matter of fact."

Winona took the hint and pulled the Johnnie Walker Double Black bottle down from the shelf and filled a tumbler, skipping the ice. The somewhere-over-fifty black-haired bar owner, who was also his landlady, knew him better than most, which wasn't a lot. Some people would say that was pathetic, but it was how Cole preferred it.

"I'd ask you about it, but I know better," Winona said. "You want food?"

"Got sourdough today?"

"You betcha. Roast beef and cheddar? Barbecue chips?"

"Yes, ma'am."

"Don't ma'am me," she muttered as she went to the compact kitchen. She only offered cold sandwiches and chips, but they were freshly made and served as Cole's dinner multiple times a week.

Left alone, Cole swigged down half the whiskey as his mind went back to the meeting with Sierra and his ace move.

One weak moment. One bone-headed sentence out of his mouth.

What the hell had he been thinking when he offered to stand in as Sierra's fake date for her sister's wedding?

Offered, for fuck's sake.

He knew damn well what had made him do it though. He hated to see Sierra upset, especially for this wedding that he knew for a fact she'd been spending hours upon hours working on every evening, all to make it memorable and low-stress for her sister, Kennedy. After all her selfless hard work, she deserved to spend the evening not worrying about whatever the hell she would worry about by going alone. Though he didn't get why it was so important, he did understand it was, indeed, important to her, so he'd opened his mouth.

Sierra had firm boundaries in place between herself and her construction crew, and Cole had always respected that, had liked that about her and saw the wisdom in it. He wasn't out to make friends himself. But in the three years plus that he'd worked for her, his brain had taken to thoughts about his boss that were inappropriate. Inappropriate and scorching hot. He shut them down as much as possible during his waking hours, but the truth came out in a guy's dreams, and apparently his truth was that he wanted to do wicked, dirty things to his boss. Things he would never, in reality, allow to happen. Not with her.

Spending an evening with her outside of the office, close by her side, dancing with her, was the worst idea ever. Touching her politely when he wanted to do so much more privately would be torture. And yet that's what he'd signed his stupid self up for.

The asshole who'd rammed into Cole earlier planted himself on a stool at the other end of the bar, next to the two blondes, but Cole barely noticed. The guy wasn't worth the oxygen he breathed in.

Winona emerged from the kitchen with a plain white plate with a double-decker sandwich cut diagonally in half and a heap of barbecue chips. She set it in front of him, then went to take an order halfway down the bar.

Cole emptied the whiskey glass, then headed to the back hall, where the restrooms were, to wash off the remaining grime from work. He'd washed his hands at the office after coming in from the jobsite, but his clothes were still full of construction dust and he wouldn't feel clean until he rinsed it all down the drain in his shower.

When he came out of the men's room, he heard a feminine voice to the right, outside the ladies' room, saying, "I told you I'm not interested."

"I saw you looking at me."

Two feet away, with his back to Cole, the bearded asshole was blocking the way of one of the blondes from the counter who'd apparently gone to the restroom and was trying to get back to her friend. Cole met her eyes and saw wariness in them, verging on fear.

"She said no," Cole said, taking a step closer.

"Mind your own business," the guy threw over his shoulder.

"Leave her alone." Cole got in his space, forcing the guy to face him.

"Make me."

"Be easier for both of us if I didn't have to," Cole said in warning.

They stood eyeing each other, every muscle in Cole's body taut and ready to spring into action. At last, the bastard sagged back a step, his chin dropping in acquiescence, opening up enough space for the blonde to get through. She did so without a word as Cole relaxed a degree.

Cole shot a glance after her as she reached the open area by the counter. As he turned back, he saw movement out of the corner of his eye and tried to dodge it. Pain exploded above his right eye and he swore. He shoved the asshole toward the back door that was a few feet away. He had a deal with Winona not to fight in her bar, but this douchebag wasn't getting away with punching him.

Cole pushed the back door open and the guy stumbled out

into the alley, then threw another punch at Cole. Cole ducked it and hit him with an uppercut and a hook that had him staggering.

The back door to Sunshine's slammed open behind Cole, and he whipped around just as another scrawny dude, apparently the bearded bastard's sidekick, lunged at him. Asshole Number Two's punch missed its mark, but Cole's didn't. Cole whipped around in time to avoid Asshole Number One's next attempt, then sent him sprawling with one more well-placed hit. Within a few seconds, Cole had both of them laid out, conscious but not moving much, crying for their moms.

Cole tried the back door, but it was always locked from the outside and had latched. He left the two and walked down the block to the next opening between buildings to get to the front door of Sunshine's. As he made his way back to his place at the counter, where his roast beef and cheddar was still waiting for him, he felt the eyes of the two blondes on him, but he kept his gaze pointed forward.

Winona must have been back in the kitchen, which allowed him to sit down as if nothing had happened and shove a chip in his mouth. That's when the adrenaline slowed down and he realized his knuckles were torn up and his head was bleeding right above his brow. He grabbed a stack of napkins from the counter and pressed them to the gash. When he pulled them away, the napkins were soaked with blood, but he didn't worry much. Head wounds always bled a lot.

Winona came out of the kitchen, walked in his direction, and tossed an ice pack on the counter in front of him without a word. She traced her steps back to the center of the counter, took a guy's order for two draws, filled two mugs, served them, and collected the guy's cash.

"Did they take off?" she asked Cole, and it took him a couple of seconds to figure out who she was talking about.

"They weren't moving much," he said, holding the ice to his head.

"Do they need an ambulance?"

Cole shrugged. "Not that I know of, but I could go check—"

"No. You're done," she said. "I'm not saying they didn't deserve what you gave 'em, but the fun's over."

Holding the ice pack with one hand, he used the other to pick up the sandwich and take a bite. Winona shook her head at him, as if to say, *How can you eat after that?*, then came out from behind the counter and headed down the hall toward the back door. She returned shortly and resumed her place behind the counter.

"They're gone," she said matter-of-factly. "Let me see your head."

Cole shoved another bite of sandwich in his mouth, every movement of his jaw throbbing through his whole head, then lowered the ice pack for Winona's inspection. She leaned across the bar, peering over the top rims of her glasses.

"He caught you just right," she said. "I don't think you need stitches but that's quite a cut. Maybe a shiner on the way too."

Hell. His "date" with Sierra was only two days away. If he had a black eye, that would draw the wrong kind of attention to him and Sierra.

He couldn't go back on his offer. That would put him in a class even lower than what's-his-name, her ex. He'd just have to buck the hell up, cross his fingers his eye turned out okay, and try not to fuck up her evening in any way.

Long shot and he knew it.

CHAPTER THREE

When Cole walked into the historical church in downtown Nashville Saturday evening, there was a scattering of people in the outer room, none of whom he knew, as expected. He checked his watch—his trusted jobsite-worthy Timex that was completely out of place with his suit—and realized he had twenty-five minutes before the ceremony started.

Dumb ass. You should've killed some time in the truck.

He hovered along the outer wall near the door, uncomfortable for so many reasons, the least of which was not that he was wearing a suit and tie. It was random luck that he owned one. He'd bought it four years ago for his uncle's funeral and hadn't worn it since. He tugged at the collar as movement in the sanctuary caught his eye through the open doorway. Walking closer, he spotted the bride, Kennedy, at the altar, facing out, toward him, posing for a photo with Ivy Gibson, one of the bridesmaids, who Cole knew through the bakery on Hale Street. Dunn & Lowell had done a months-long full renovation of the historic Wentworth Hotel at the end of Hale, and he and the rest of the crew had become regulars at the bakery.

Kennedy made a beautiful bride. Her copper-colored hair was swept up in a complicated style under a veil, and she wore a simple column of a white gown with cut-outs at the neckline, a cinched waist, and a train. Cole didn't see Hunter or any of the men in the bridal party, but he would bet his pickup truck the groom would forget his own name as soon as he saw his bride.

A dozen or so people sat in the front two rows watching the photo shoot. Cole skimmed his gaze over the backs of their heads, looking for one in particular. He spotted Sierra at the end of the first bench, identifying her by the rich russet color of her hair, which was also pinned off her shoulders. He couldn't see much more from here, but he had time and nothing better to do than watch the bride's half of the wedding party finish up photos.

After Ivy's turn, Violet Morello, the brunette bakery owner, posed next to Kennedy, then Asia, who was engaged to Kennedy and Sierra's brother, Jackson, took her place next to the bride. Then it was Sierra's turn to pose with her sister.

Cole's gaze stayed glued to her as she stood and made her way up the three steps, saying something he couldn't hear, throwing her head back and laughing. When she turned around, Cole forgot how to breathe.

Her attention was on the photographer, and she hadn't spotted Cole, which allowed him to drink her in at his leisure. She wore a long navy-blue gown that went over one shoulder and left the other bare. As she stood next to Kennedy, she angled slightly to the side, treating him to a view of her slender, toned leg, revealed by a high slit in the side of the dress. Her sparkling sky-high heels wrapped around her ankles, and just looking at them, at her legs in them, could short-circuit a guy's brain. His eyes trailed upward, over the curves of her hips, her sexy bare shoulder, to her stunning smile, highlighted by pink lipstick. Her eyes, he could tell from this distance, were accented with makeup, which she normally skipped for work. And her hair… It was a complex mix of braids and knots and wisps framing her face, all held together, he would bet, by a hundred pins.

He could take those pins out for her, one by one, run his fingers through her hair as it cascaded over her bare shoulders.

Jesus. Get a damn grip.

She was his boss. And he was in public. Another ten seconds

of that line of thought and everyone around him would be able to see proof of what she did to him below the belt.

He leaned one shoulder against the doorframe, his hands in his pockets, trying to rein in his thoughts but unable to tear his gaze away. *This* was why he'd volunteered, he admitted. He'd remember how stunning she looked for as long as he lived.

The next group up for pictures turned out to be the Lowell family—Sierra, Kennedy, Jackson, and their parents, he guessed. It was evident, as they posed and reposed and smiled and the photographer shot a couple dozen pictures, that their family was close-knit and loving. They stood near one another without being told to, joked among themselves, smiled real smiles. They were a Christmas card photo in everyday life, he could tell from here.

Unlike his family. At least when he was around. Maybe his brothers and mom were as carefree and affectionate as the Lowells, but he knew full well he brought a tension with him anytime he was in the same place as the rest of the North clan. He shrugged. It was what it was, and he was who he was. He didn't do close relationships, family or otherwise.

The photo shoot ended momentarily, and as Sierra descended the altar steps, her gaze met Cole's and she flashed him a smile of acknowledgment and, he suspected, relief that he'd shown up. She gestured toward her sister and the side door, where they were heading, and he made out the word *sorry* on her lips. He shook his head to let her know he didn't expect to talk to her until after the ceremony, and she smiled again as her mom sidled up next to her and started talking, gesturing with her hands, obviously conveying some crucial details about something, and then the whole group disappeared through the side door.

Cole backed away from the main doorway and glanced around, realizing he'd been riveted to the front of the church for the past ten minutes and oblivious to anything else around him. More guests had arrived, including an elderly couple emerging from the coat room and a family with four kids bursting noisily through the outer door.

When he glanced at the sanctuary again, two guys in tuxes emerged, the ushers, he assumed. One of them he recognized,

Hudson Bennett, a lawyer who Sierra had used for some business contracts. Bennett nodded at him as the other usher handed the lawyer a stack of programs. Several of the guests started forward at the sight of the programs, and the ushers began seating them.

Cole fell into the short line, his mind skipping forward to the reception, when he would dance with Sierra, touch Sierra. Dancing wasn't his thing, but it did have its benefits, and he was damn sure it would be the highlight of the night, torture or not.

In his peripheral vision, he noticed someone heading his way, and he turned to find the man he assumed was Sierra's father. The guy, in his early sixties, he'd guess, was just about as tall as Cole and had a full head of brown hair. He wore a black tux and had a commanding presence, as if he owned the place—or was paying for this party.

"Cole?" The man held his hand out as soon as Cole nodded in acknowledgment. "Wayne Lowell, Sierra's dad. I understand you're accompanying her to the reception."

"Yes, sir." As he gave the guy a firm handshake, he wanted to tell himself this wasn't important, that he wasn't really "with" Sierra, and therefore there was no pressure in meeting her parents, but he couldn't quite convince himself of that. Even though they weren't a couple, he worked for her, and he didn't want to make Sierra look bad in any way. Cole's shoulders tensed as he endeavored not to say anything stupid. He wasn't good at small talk or meeting a girl's parents, avoided both as much as possible.

"She asked me to come check on you and apologize for her not coming out to say hello. Those girls…" Mr. Lowell shook his head. "They look breathtaking to me, every last one of them, but they're in there adjusting their makeup, checking out their hair for the tenth time, fussing over every last thing. As women do."

"As women do," Cole said, not that he'd know personally. His mom had always been practical about her appearance, taking care of it but never fussy. He had no sisters, only one female cousin, and when it came to the women he spent time with, he never let it get that intimate that he'd know how they lived.

"I understand you agreed to come last minute," Mr. Lowell said. "Appreciate you helping her out." Cole listened for some kind of judgment or disapproval in the man's voice but didn't detect any.

"No problem," Cole said, then reached deep for his rusty conversation skills. "How long are you in town for?"

"We fly back to Arizona on Monday. We've been here for a week and I'm going to need a month's vacation to recover from all the wedding prep."

"Seems like a lot of work," Cole said, thinking how stressed out Sierra had been all week. She'd taken the day off yesterday, as well, which she didn't do often, if ever. It seemed to him, if you wanted to get married, elopement was the way to go.

They discussed the October weather and the elaborate historical features of the sanctuary, Cole wondering to himself what the chances were of it bursting into spontaneous flames when he walked in to be seated. Sierra's dad seemed like a decent enough guy who'd made Cole relax a degree or two in the five-minute conversation—that was, until he shook hands again, preparing to find his older daughter to walk her down the aisle, and threw out there, "I trust you'll keep it business with Sierra tonight. Nice meeting you."

Mr. Lowell walked off, summoned by his wife, before Cole could reply. There wasn't much to say to that anyway. Of course he'd keep it as business as he could. He wasn't stupid. But the message was clear and hard to ignore anyway—Wayne Lowell had determined, accurately, within minutes what Cole already knew. Cole would never be right for Sierra, even if he wanted to be.

CHAPTER FOUR

"That's a wrap, folks," the photographer said to the rowdy, happy wedding party after finishing the last of the formal post-wedding shots. "See you at the reception."

"Head directly to the Wentworth," Sierra said to the group, conveying what the wedding coordinator had asked her to before heading off to the hotel ballroom to make sure everything was as it should be. "The party's already started, so don't waste any time."

"Need help with anything, hon?" Sierra's mom asked, her dad hovering next to her, all smiles.

"Just get to the party and make sure everything's good."

Her mom nodded as she retrieved her bag from the front pew. "I'm sure Burke's people have it under control—"

"They better," her dad said good-naturedly of the owner of the Wentworth Hotel—and one of Hunter's groomsmen—with a hint of *for what we're paying them* in his voice.

"We're on it," her mom said, her cocoa-colored eyes radiating happiness as she linked her arm with her husband's. "We'll leave right away."

Behind Sierra, Kennedy swore softly, and Sierra whirled around to see her fiddling with the clasp of her necklace at her nape.

"Language," Ivy sang out from halfway down the aisle at her fiancé Burke's side, on their way out. "You're in a church."

"Oops," Kennedy said. She dropped her arms to her sides and appealed to Sierra. "My damn necklace is caught in my hair."

"I've got this," Sierra said to Asia and Violet, the other two bridesmaids, who'd swooped in to help. "You guys go ahead." To Kennedy, she said, "Turn around."

"Good luck," her sister said as she turned as ordered. "There's so much spray my hair is concrete. Do you still have those scissors somewhere?"

"I'm not cutting your hair," Sierra said calmly. She stretched up to get a good look and had the hair loose within seconds. "There." She guided Kennedy back around to face her, met her sister's hazel eyes, her makeup still perfect and more pronounced than usual. "You're gorgeous. Still. The limo is outside waiting for you and Hunter. Your bag is in the limo. Everything is taken care of."

"You, sister-in-law," Hunter said as he sidled up behind his wife, both his hands winding around Kennedy's waist, "are a godsend for keeping my beautiful wife mostly calm. Thanks for all you've done."

"This is calm? I don't feel calm," Kennedy said, her pitch rising.

"Did you see Violet two months ago at her wedding?" Hunter asked. "This is calm."

"I heard that," Violet called as she and her new husband, Nick, headed out.

Sierra nodded, having been a guest at Violet's wedding. "He has a point. Between sister duty and maid-of-honor duty, I've got you covered."

"Thank you." Kennedy pulled Sierra into a hug. As they held on, Hunter pressed a kiss to the top of Sierra's head and moved away. "Someday I'll return the favor," Kennedy said.

"It'll be a while," Sierra said dryly. "Like, decades."

"Whenever." Kennedy backed away and discreetly swiped at her eye. "These damn tears…"

"You're still in a church," Sierra said, laughing. "Let's get out of here before your mouth gets you struck down. I need to find Cole."

"I'll meet you in the narthex," Hunter told his wife as he hurried out the side door. "Two minutes."

Sierra grabbed her bag and her purse from the pew, which the wedding coordinator had brought out after the ceremony, and as she and Kennedy made their way back down the aisle, they could see—and hear—the rest of the wedding party gathered near the outside doors, getting ready to leave.

"Everyone looks amazing," Kennedy said, gazing at her group of friends from afar. "I'm lucky to have these people in my life."

"They're good ones. What'd you think of the ceremony?"

"I barely remember it," Kennedy said.

"They got video, right?"

"Hope so. It's the only chance I have of experiencing the details." Kennedy wove her arm through Sierra's.

"The vows were awesome. You definitely need to hold Hunter to the no-dirty-socks-on-the-floor thing."

"I'd try to get it in writing, but saying it in a church has even more power, right?"

As they hit the doorway from the sanctuary to the outer room, Sierra darted a glance around, searching for Cole. When she spotted him to the right, leaning against the wall, reading something on his phone, oblivious to their entry, her step faltered and her eyes popped wide open.

Kennedy, still holding on to her, paused as well and followed Sierra's line of sight. In a voice that only Sierra could hear, she said, "He cleans up well."

That was an understatement.

"Who knew?" Sierra muttered. Yes, she'd spotted him briefly right before the ceremony, but she'd been sidetracked and certainly hadn't had a chance to linger over him and appreciate the pretty picture he made.

"You should. Don't you work with him every day?" her sister said.

"He wears a T-shirt and old jeans." And as a rule, she didn't allow herself to think about his appearance beyond that. He was her employee, and she didn't consider the men she worked with to be dating prospects, period. While she and her BFF, Hayden, did plenty of looking and sizing up and even sampling when they went out, Sierra's agenda at work was altogether different, her mind-set that of the day's goals, to-do lists, and challenges.

Now she took a moment to really look at him. Cole wore a black suit with a white shirt and a gray and black tie, one shoulder supporting his weight on the wall, his gaze zeroed in on his phone. He was good-looking in a rough, hard-living way, with dark hair he kept cut military short, caramel-colored eyes that had an edge to them most days, and a seriousness it was sometimes hard to break through. From here, she thought she spotted a cut above his eye, not fresh, but he hadn't had it Thursday at work.

His body was chiseled and solid, the kind earned from a physically demanding job instead of a gym. The suit smoothed out some of the rough edges, but even though Sierra had registered his appeal on some superficial level in the past, this was the first time she'd seen him in this context—as the guy who'd be at her side all night, the guy whose arms she'd be in for dancing.

He looked up and met her gaze, his normally scruffy jaw clean-shaven, and when his lips slid into a slight grin, she felt it in her chest.

He straightened, slid his phone into his pocket, and Sierra stood there not moving, not taking her gaze off him, momentarily stunned stupid, like a bird that flew into a window and found itself on the ground, trying to figure out what had happened.

"Are you ready to go, Mrs. Clayborne?" Hunter's question to Kennedy as he approached them pulled Sierra out of her stupor, and she held her sister's arm out to him as if hand-delivering his bride.

"Kennedy Clayborne," Sierra said, thinking it sounded just right, as Hunter swept in and took Kennedy's hand. "I'll see you two lovebirds at the Wentworth."

When she turned toward Cole again, he was only steps away.

"Hey," he said, walking toward her, and again, that half grin flirted with his lips—lips that she'd never really noticed but that now she couldn't help wondering how they'd feel…

Sierra shook the thought away. "Hi, Cole." She tried extra-hard to put some business-as-usual into her tone.

"You look stunning," he said, and business-as-usual took a hard falter.

"Thank you. You look good yourself. Are you ready to go?"

"You're the boss." He paused, blew out a short, amused breath. "In more ways than one."

That was something she definitely needed to keep in mind, but then, as they turned toward the door, he pressed his hand to her lower back, trailed it lightly to the outside of her waist, and she was hyperconscious of the feel of him through the thin material of her dress. Her body reacted deep within, her hormones clicking into the *yes, please* position, and then, as they walked, he was so close that she caught his scent—clean, masculine, with a hint of spice to it.

Cole was turning her inside out without even trying, and that was a big, fat problem.

"You made it through the ceremony," she said, and she was pretty sure it was the lamest thing she could've come up with.

"Nothing to it. Pretty short and sweet."

He opened the heavy outer door and held it for her, his hand still on her waist, and they went out into the cool fall evening.

"My truck's over there." He pointed to a coveted spot along the curb, halfway down the block, unnecessary since she knew his bright blue Ram extended-cab pickup well.

Sierra gathered her long dress in one hand so she didn't trip —she didn't often wear heels and was much happier in her sturdy work boots—and as they made their way down the front steps, she held on to his arm with her other hand. She couldn't miss the strength of his corded forearm, even through the material of his suit and shirt, and she silently scolded herself for noticing.

Cole was off-limits. She did not fraternize with the men on

her crew. Black-and-white issue. It was hard enough to be taken seriously as a woman in the construction field without opening herself up to any kind of romantic ties with someone who worked for her. Her grandpa, who'd mentored her from the time she hit double digits and was allowed on jobsites, had drilled that into her head even before she'd had the slightest interest in the opposite sex. Not once had she veered from the advice, either back when she worked for his company or after his death, when he'd left the business in her hands.

Tonight, of course, was the single exception to her rule, and it had been a frantic decision made without enough thought at the end of the stressful pre-wedding week, when she'd worked so hard to shoulder a lot of her sister's burden. She was grateful Cole had stepped in after Kevin let her down, and she'd lain awake last night pondering the ramifications of going out with one of her employees but had told herself she could handle it just fine. Maybe she'd been wrong.

They didn't speak on the walk to the truck. When they arrived, he helped her up into the passenger seat, and she almost succeeded in not noticing his strong, calloused, capable hands.

Once he closed her in, she took a deep, shaky breath and got things straight in her head. They weren't a couple. This was a one-time thing that would end up with her going home alone. Cole was merely doing her a favor. She shut her eyes for a moment and summoned her construction boss self, forgetting about the long column of silky material that said otherwise.

The driver's door opened, Cole climbed up, and the space shrunk, but Sierra was determined now. Determined not to act awkward and determined not to make Cole uneasy. They had several more hours together, and it would be rough enough for Cole, having to meet extended family and longtime friends. She strived to act normal, as if they were working together on a project.

"Did you check out the architecture in there?" she asked, eyeing the majestic bell tower as he started the engine and pulled out.

"It was impressive." He gave a half laugh. "I wondered if you had time to eyeball it. Bet you were itching to run your hands over those rails around the altar."

"The details were incredible. And the columns…"

He nodded. "Did you notice the detail on the main doors?"

"The ones that must have weighed a hundred pounds each?"

"Had to be original. Mortise-and-tenon construction."

"Agree," she said as her phone dinged from inside her purse, signaling a text message. She dug it out as Cole turned into the parking garage at the Wentworth, a five-minute drive from the church.

The message was from Hayden, who'd been invited to the wedding but was out of town for a trade show on the East Coast.

Know you're busy but I need a full report on the wedding when you can.

Sierra typed out a reply. *You caught me between the ceremony and reception. Kennedy is officially a missus!*

Hayden replied with a bride and groom emoji and *Tell her congrats from me and I hate that I'm missing it.*

I will, even though she won't remember it.

More importantly, how's your date?

Sierra texted, *Fake date. Next to me.*

Send me a pic please. And drink champagne for me too.

Demanding wench! But okay times two.

As she pushed send, Cole parked the truck and killed the engine. "Ready?" he asked.

"I'll leave my big bag here."

Cole got out and came around to her side. She was stuffing her bag behind the seat when he opened her door. He held out his hand to help her down, and Sierra took it, trying not to think too hard about it, forcing her mind to reception details.

"As soon as we get inside," she said, "I need to take a selfie of you and me for Hayden. Remind me or I'll never hear the end of it."

"I'll take a photo of you."

"Nice try but nope."

They entered the historical hotel and made their way across the marble-floored lobby toward the ballroom. She waved at

Mariana, the night manager, who was behind the check-in desk helping another employee. As they approached the ballroom door, the din grew louder.

Sierra paused just outside the closed door. "You ready for this?"

"Scared shitless," he said with that semi-grin again.

"Smart man." She grabbed the handle and opened the door and the sound of a couple hundred people all talking at once washed over them.

They stepped inside and Sierra stopped to take everything in. Even though she'd been here earlier this afternoon and seen it when it was nearly ready, it still took her breath away.

The sprawling ballroom looked almost unrecognizable and had become a lot smaller and more intimate with so many people inside. It had been transformed into a midnight-blue and silver wonderland, with dim, blue-tinted lighting and strings of white fairy lights everywhere. White floral centerpieces surrounded by multiple silver votives contrasted with the dark blue tablecloths on the round dinner tables, where some guests were already seated. The dessert and gift tables to the left of where they stood were skirted with dark blue velvet and tasteful decorations in silver and white, and though she couldn't see the two bars because of the hordes of people, she knew they matched. The whole thing was romantic, under-stated, classy yet unpretentious. It fit Kennedy and Hunter perfectly.

She scanned the room for the bride, and there, across the way with Hunter, near the bridal party table, Sierra spotted her, thanks to her own towering shoes. Shoes that were likely to kill her before the end of the night. She exhaled in relief that her sister was here and things were underway just as they should be. As she stepped forward to head into the crowd, Cole grasped her arm and stopped her.

"You wanted a photo?" he said into her ear so she could hear him, and something about his deep voice that close sent a shiver through her.

She ignored it and pulled out her phone, relieved he'd

reminded her before she found a place to put her tiny sequined purse, out of sight and out of her way.

"How are you at selfies?" she asked him.

"Never done one."

"What?" She looked to see if he was serious, and it appeared he was. Cole was usually serious, and he never mentioned any kind of social life, though surely he had one. She figured he just wasn't the type to share personal details.

"Novice," he confirmed. "Sure you don't want me to just take your picture?"

"Nice try again." She opened the camera app and turned it to selfie mode, then handed it to him. "It's easier to use the side button."

Cole took the phone from her and started to hold it out directly in front of them.

"Wait," Sierra said. "Angle from above, and see if you can get a little of the background in too."

"Yes, ma'am."

She nudged him lightly with her elbow. He held the phone up higher, and as they looked at the perspective on the screen, they moved closer together to fit in the shot. Then she felt Cole's hand at her side, grasping her at the empire waist of her dress, just under her breasts, and his touch… Once again, it did something to her, heated her blood, jolted her heart into high speed, made her lady organs deep inside contract. Trying to blow her reaction off, she angled her head toward his, and he leaned into her as well, until the sides of their heads touched. Though he'd obviously shaved, when his cheek brushed against her temple, she could feel its rough texture, and the intimacy of that momentarily stole her breath.

"Hold on," she said. "Selfie basics. You have to smile."

Cole laughed quietly and eked out a grin, and then he clicked it several times. A group of people had just entered, so he was still pressed to her side in the crush as he handed her phone back.

"Thank you," she breathed out near his ear, hoping he couldn't detect the effect he was having on her fickle body. "I need a drink."

As they headed toward the bar in the far corner with the shorter line, she thought to herself she would need more than a drink. Maybe six drinks and a cold shower and willpower of steel to blow off the way her body had reacted when Cole pulled her close.

CHAPTER FIVE

*C*ole would be lying if he said the evening sucked.

Meeting dozens of Sierra's relatives and family friends wasn't his favorite thing, but he could stand at her side, offer a firm handshake, and say *nice to meet you* till he was blue in the face. Faking smiles was a tougher task, but he found he didn't have to fake it much when Sierra sidled up so close he could feel the heat of her body along the side of his.

He could do all of that and more for the chance to touch her, pull her into his arms, hold her for three or four minutes straight as they danced.

The last notes of a ballad filled the ballroom, and since the deejay had announced it was the final slow song of the night, Cole soaked in all the details of the woman in his arms—the silky wisps of russet-brown hair that framed her face and teased her shoulders, the curves at her waist, where her muscled torso flared into modest hips, the bewitchingly feminine scent that brought to mind seduction and those curls and braids draping over high-thread-count sheets.

As they eased apart, she flashed him a smile, her slightly bowed lips revving his pulse like they did every time she smiled, whether on a jobsite in her standard cargo work pants and T-shirt or here, looking like a dream in midnight-blue. "I've had you out here for every single slow song tonight," she said, leaning close to be heard. "You're a saint."

He nearly snorted at that and gripped his tie to keep from holding on to her too long. "A saint would dance to *all* the songs, slow or not. You got stuck with the wrong guy."

She raised a teasing brow. "You say you can't dance to upbeat songs, but I bet you have secret moves," she said generously.

He had moves, all right, but they weren't dance floor appropriate.

"My sister should make her exit soon," Sierra said, glancing around for the newlyweds.

As she and Cole turned to walk off the dance floor in the center of the Wentworth ballroom, she hooked her hand around his forearm and his focus once again zeroed in on the contact. There'd been touches throughout the night, innocent touches outside of the dance floor as she guided him, directed him, introduced him, and Cole had noticed every single one of them, felt the hum in his blood from her proximity. He'd have to spend tomorrow forcibly putting all of it out of his mind so he could work by her side on Monday morning without battling a perpetual hard-on.

They reached the maze of tables surrounding the dance floor as an old-school disco tune started up and a loud quartet of women in their fifties rushed out to get their groove on.

"Sierra, honey," came an elderly female voice from a couple of tables away.

"My great-aunt Lucy," Sierra said as she veered them to the left toward her aunt. Sierra angled a chair to face the elderly woman and sat down in it. Cole followed suit like a good date.

He'd not yet been introduced to this woman. He'd remember the slightly lavender hair that matched the decidedly lavender dress.

"How are you doing, Aunt Lucy?" Sierra asked her. "Are you having a good time?"

"It's a beautiful evening," the woman said. "A beautiful event. Your sister and her beau make a breathtaking couple."

"They do. They'll make gorgeous babies." Sierra took her

aunt's frail-looking hand in hers. "Can I get you some more cake or another drink?"

The woman, who looked to be in her eighties, shook her head distractedly. "Pete's getting me more cocktail nuts. I want to meet your boyfriend," she said with an adamant nod toward Cole.

"Oh." Sierra laughed graciously and placed an innocent hand on Cole's knee that made him think anything but innocent thoughts. "Cole's not my boyfriend. He's my employee, who was kind enough to be my fake date for the evening."

Those were all facts, but her easy denial stung anyway. Up until now, no one had asked outright what Cole's role was, and Sierra had skipped over the details when she introduced him.

"Cole North," Sierra continued, "my great-aunt Lucy Hanson."

He gave her hand a gentle shake.

"Pleasure to meet you." Lucy turned back to Sierra. "A girl like you shouldn't need to get a fake date," her aunt said with the bluntness of someone who didn't worry much what people thought.

"You might be surprised." Sierra shot a self-conscious look to Cole, and damn if he couldn't stop wondering what those lips, glossed in that bright pink, tasted like.

Aunt Lucy was scrutinizing Cole, as if she could read his thoughts, and then she turned her gaze back to Sierra. "Well." The old woman grinned boldly, and mischief sparked in her eyes. "You certainly danced like he's your boyfriend."

Sierra sent Cole an apologetic glance, laughed, and said, "That's just how people dance these days, Aunt Lucy."

"If you're certain," her aunt said.

"Grandpa taught me early on not to get involved with the crew," Sierra said. "Cole and I work together every day."

"That brother of mine," Lucy said, "he could be a pest, but he was smart about his business, that's for sure."

"He was the best." There was no mistaking the affection in Sierra's voice.

Though Cole had never heard Sierra voice her no-involvement policy in so many words before, there'd never been any question. She was well-respected by the men who worked for her, and though she joked around with them and fostered a friendly work environment, she kept a certain professional distance in place during work hours.

It didn't matter if she had a strict policy or not though. Cole wasn't dumb enough to think he was the right man for her, no matter how many nights she popped up in his sweaty, X-rated dreams. He didn't want to be the right man, for her or anyone. He was more cut out to be a right-now guy.

"I need to remind the newlyweds that it's time for them to make their getaway," Sierra said, standing. "Aunt Lucy, I see Uncle Pete wending his way back to you. I'm so happy you two could make it tonight. It was wonderful to see you." She bent down and kissed the woman on the temple.

"You too, sweetie. If you ever get down to Memphis, you stop by and see Pete and me."

"Promise," Sierra said.

"Nice to meet you," Cole said as he stood. He grasped the woman's hand loosely and received a wide smile and a wink.

"This will only take me a minute," Sierra said to him as they walked away from her aunt. "The hotel people are taking care of all the cleanup, but I need to say some goodbyes. Then I swear we can leave."

"Take your time," he told her. The thought of going home, back to his apartment, alone—and he would be alone—didn't appeal the way it usually did.

He spotted Kennedy's veil-covered copper hair across the way and pointed, then they walked toward the elated couple, who were surrounded by the other three bridesmaids and the four groomsmen. As Sierra spoke to her sister, Cole turned to Hunter and offered his hand.

"Congrats again. Hope you have a hell of a honeymoon," Cole said. He knew Hunter fairly well, had been the main contractor for his bar's renovation around the same time as the Wentworth project, and he'd been in Clayborne's on the Corner for a drink or a sandwich multiple times since then.

Hunter shook his hand, grinning so wide his face nearly split. "My sexy wife and Key West. I don't see how I can go wrong."

"Are you ready?" Kennedy sidled up next to her husband. "I'm told it's time for us to go to our suite."

"Already?" Hunter said dryly, and the smile on his face left no doubt that he was more than ready for their wedding night.

As Sierra appeared at Cole's side, he registered the sound of spoons clinking against glasses—again—throughout the room.

"Kiss!"

"One more kiss before you go," Ivy ordered. "Make it good, Hunter."

Hunter took the challenge seriously and dipped his wife, which elicited a happy squeal from the normally subdued Kennedy, and then he took his sweet time, drawing out the lip-lock before returning her to vertical. The crowd howled and clapped, and a male voice from across the ballroom hollered, "Get a room!", making everyone laugh.

"I'm on it!" Hunter yelled back. "Thank you, everyone!" He waved to the room at large, and Kennedy blew a kiss, and then they ducked out of the ballroom.

Cole stood by Sierra's side as she talked to various guests, said goodbye, hugged, talked some more, and the guests eventually started to file out in clumps.

"After-party at Clayborne's," Violet shouted when the crowd had thinned down considerably. "Everybody's welcome."

Hunter's bar was a short walk down Hale Street, at the other end of the block.

Cole looked down at Sierra, and her eyes were lit up with unmistakable interest.

"You want to go?" he confirmed.

"Do you mind?" she asked, her arched brows shooting up over the large brown doe eyes that could convince him to do just about anything tonight.

"I don't mind."

The lights got brighter, and the cleanup crew appeared at the opposite end of the room, unobtrusively and efficiently picking up glasses and crumb-covered cake plates and removing the centerpieces table by table.

"Guess our time's up here," Sierra said as they retrieved her purse. "I've never been so happy not to have to clean. My feet are screaming."

"We can stop at your apartment on the way so you can change," he said, knowing she lived across the street from the hotel.

"You not only look good in a suit but you're brilliant." There was a sparkle in her eyes as she said it, and an image flashed in his head of her with that look, naked, peering up from beneath him…

As they turned toward the ballroom door, her mom, who Cole had met at the beginning of the reception, approached, effectively chasing the thought away. "Are you and Dad going to join us at Clayborne's?" Sierra asked her.

Tammy Lowell, slender like all three of her children and dressed in a flattering floor-length dress of silver and sparkles, blew out a sigh that said she was exhausted. "I don't think I have it in me. We need to touch base with the hotel people, and then I think making it up one level to our room is the last thing I can handle."

"You've had a long day," Sierra said. "Everything turned out perfect, don't you think?"

Her mom nodded with a tired smile. "Kennedy thanked us several times. As long as she's happy, I'm happy. Thanks for all your help, honey."

The two women hugged, and then, before Cole knew what was happening, Mrs. Lowell threw her arms around him and squeezed. "Cole, we hope to see you again, whether you're a fake date or a real date."

He forced an obligatory laugh. The glaring truth was that he wasn't the kind of guy any mom wanted her daughter to bring home. "Yes, ma'am. Pleasure meeting you. Have a safe flight back."

When their embrace ended, Mr. Lowell, who'd shot Cole

covert suspicious looks throughout the reception, was at his side, hand extended. "Cole."

"Mr. Lowell, great party tonight. It was good to finally meet you after hearing Sierra talk about you for so long." Fake date or not, it was smart to stay on this man's good side. The man who was giving him *that* look again. The look that accused Cole of imagining his daughter naked.

Guilty as charged, sir.

"You get my daughter home safely, Cole."

Yep, Cole heard the *and say good night at the door while you're at it* buried in his tone.

"Will do, Mr. Lowell." *But not because you told me to.*

A few more minutes and a couple of goodbyes later and they were on their way, out of the ballroom, across the marble-floored lobby, and into the temperate October night.

Hale Street was a lively, block-long street not far from the heart of downtown Nashville that had gone from deteriorating, mostly deserted buildings to a thriving neighborhood in the past couple of years. Businesses lined the ground floor—a boot store, dress shop, music store, bakery, and more—and the second and third floors contained newly remodeled apartments. Historical details had been preserved from one end to the other, including the old-time streetlamps and the brick sidewalks.

Sierra lived on the second floor above Bliss, the type of spa place that was a mystery to most men, Cole included. They wandered past the green space on the Wentworth side of the spa. He noticed some of the leaves had started to change, and there was an edge to the breeze tonight that said colder weather was on the way.

As they walked, Sierra seemed to blow off steam by chattering on about all the details of the wedding and the reception and her sister's dress and the people who'd showed up... Cole found if he replied with an *mm-hmm* whenever she paused, she was happy, and that worked for him because he was swept away by the lilt of her voice.

When they reached the staircase to her place, he followed her up, held the door for her as she stepped into the hall that had a single apartment on each side, waited while she fished out her key from her sequined evening bag.

He followed her inside, more than a little curious to see the place she called home. To the left of the door was an open kitchen and dining area with white cabinets, butcher-block countertops, and a large farmhouse sink below the window at the opposite end. He could tell, at a glance, that Sierra had had a hand in choosing the historically appropriate finishes that gave the place the feel of a 1940s kitchen—the era of the original building—but brand-new.

On the right was the living area, with the narrow-planked wood floor carried in from the kitchen, a gray sectional with a chaise on one end with a dozen or so turquoise, white, and dark gray throw pillows, and a door on the wall on the Hale Street side that he would bet led to a wrought-iron balcony. The place was well-decorated, homey, welcoming. It fit her perfectly.

Sierra kicked off her shoes and left them next to the kitchen island, emitting a little moan of relief that had his dick taking notice. "Something to drink?" she offered as she padded toward the refrigerator. "I need water, but I've also got beer, wine, vodka…"

"Water's good." Cole had skipped alcohol altogether tonight. He'd needed all his faculties to navigate the formal affair—and his attraction. Plus, he still had to drive across town to his apartment, which was in a neighborhood that was a far cry from the trendiness of Hale Street.

Sierra took out two glasses from the cabinet and filled them with ice cubes and water from the dispenser on the fridge on the far side of the kitchen. He joined her, took the glass from her when she offered it, did his best to ignore the flare of heat when their fingers brushed. They both took a long drink, then he leaned against the cabinet next to the fridge and let himself really breathe for the first time in hours, now that they were away from the hordes of people.

When she'd emptied her glass, she stuck it back under the dispenser and refilled it. The hem of her long dress pooled on the floor now that she'd removed her heels. He roved his eyes upward to the band that cinched around her middle, just under her breasts, and he couldn't help noticing how delicate she seemed. He knew firsthand the extent of her physical strength—she could hold her own on almost anything with the men, big men, on her crew. Her bare arms were firm and muscular but didn't take away from her femininity. The single strap that held the dress up showed off a lot more flesh than he was treated to at work, and he decided on the spot that those were the sexiest shoulders he'd ever seen in the thirty-two years he'd been alive. Distinctly feminine, with curves and dips in all the right places and smooth, soft-looking skin that made him want to run his lips over every inch. Her necklace was nestled just below the hollow of her throat, verging into the valley between her palm-sized breasts.

Cole's mouth went dry, and he sucked in another full breath and forced his mind to baseball stats. Cardinals, of course.

"So," Sierra said as she faced him fully again.

"So," he repeated, then cleared his throat because his lust-coated voice barely came out. So much for baseball.

She stood close, near enough he could catch her scent again, facing him, and she reached out and grasped his forearm. Even through the two layers of clothing, he could feel the burn of contact. "I know that wasn't really your thing tonight, and that makes me appreciate it double. So thank you, Cole, so much."

Her gratitude flustered him for a moment, and he didn't know what to say, so he blurted out the first thing that occurred to him. "Wouldn't do it for just anyone."

It was supposed to come out as light, humorous, but when Sierra peered up at him, the lightness failed, and there was only a pulsing tension between them as their eyes met and held for two seconds…three. Finally, she opened her mouth, as if to say something, but no words came out. Then she laughed lightly on an exhale, lowered her gaze, and dropped his arm. "I better change my clothes so we can go."

Cole swallowed and nodded, worked at stuffing down his attraction to her yet again, took half a step to the side at the same time she turned toward the private part of the apartment. He was still leaning for all he was worth against the cabinets when she reached the hallway to her bedroom, paused, and looked back toward him. She smiled distractedly, and he could swear her eyes narrowed a fraction, as if she'd seen more than he wanted her to see. As if he'd given away too damn much.

CHAPTER SIX

Sierra closed her bathroom door and leaned her back against it. Her head was spinning, and not from the three partial drinks she'd had—and unintentionally abandoned before finishing—over the course of the reception.

What the heck had just happened?

That look from Cole… It had stolen her breath, and God's truth, if she'd stood there staring into his eyes for one second longer, it would've been impossible not to step closer to him and…

She exhaled hard, tried to gather her wits and regain some perspective on the man in the other room.

Cole had worked his way up to foreman quickly, as he had a lot of experience and was unquestionably intelligent. So intelligent that she'd wondered more than once how he'd ended up doing construction, suspected that it was something he'd settled for, but she didn't question it too hard because she was glad to have him, lucky to keep him. She'd never seen any sign of anything besides boss-employee between them.

But that look out in her kitchen—and if she was honest, it was more than a look, more like crackling sexual tension—that had blindsided her and she didn't know what to do about it. She tried to wrap her head around the idea that Cole might feel something for her. *Might*. Or maybe she'd just misread him.

She stepped toward the mirror to take off her jewelry.

The only thing to do was to ignore those five seconds in the kitchen and finish out the night on a friendly note. She would've hesitated to label Cole a friend before tonight, because that was muddying up the lines, and frankly, she didn't know much of anything about him outside of job-related traits. But she liked him, respected him, wanted him to enjoy the rest of the evening. She hoped he could relax and unwind after enduring a family-filled formal affair that she was certain was way out of his comfort zone.

"Sierra?" Cole's voice reached her from the kitchen, so she turned away from the mirror and her struggle to release the clasp of her necklace and opened the bathroom door, still fully dressed in the dark blue gown.

He sat on the end stool at the island, and it struck her again how well he wore that black suit. His tie was folded neatly on the counter in front of him, apparently retired for the evening, and the top couple of buttons of his white shirt were undone.

"Your phone's exploding with texts," he said. "I thought it might be something important."

"Thanks." She crossed the room to the island and took her phone out from her evening bag. "Two from Ivy, one from Violet, and one from my brother, wondering why we aren't there yet," she said.

She was about to reply when another text notification sounded. Not on her phone this time.

Cole pulled his phone out of his pocket. Read whatever was on the screen, stood abruptly, and went pale. Sierra stepped closer, studying his face.

"Is something wrong?" she asked.

He tapped his phone, unlocked it with his fingerprint, and she could see a long text message that filled the screen. He remained silent, reading, his distress climbing. His eyes widened, his fist covered his mouth, and his breathing seemed to stop.

"Cole?"

"It's my mom," he said, his voice sounding choked with uncharacteristic emotion. "Oh, hell, my mom." He tightened his fist and squeezed his eyes closed. "She's being rushed to the hospital. Possible heart attack."

"Here in town?"

He swallowed, nodded. "I have to go."

"I'll take you."

He shook his head distractedly. "You have a party to go to."

"Cole, I'm taking you. My truck is out back. Yours is two long blocks away in the garage, and you don't look like you should drive." Without hesitation, she jammed her feet back into her heels. "Let's go." She grabbed her purse and keys, pulled him out the door, locked it in a rush, and they hurried down the hall to the back.

He was silent down the two flights of stairs, didn't argue again when she led him to her Ford F-250 parked in a spot off the alley. As she walked, she typed in a message to her brother, telling him they wouldn't make it and why.

Once they were in her truck, she started the engine and asked him which hospital his mom was en route to. He swore, as if he hadn't yet thought of that, and his large thumbs fumbled over his phone screen.

She studied him across the darkened cab as they waited for a response. She'd never seen him like this. Shaken to his core. Never seen him anywhere close to it, as he was generally an even-keeled guy who kept his emotions locked out of sight. Without thinking about it, she reached out and put her hand on his forearm, wishing she could comfort him somehow.

"He's typing," Cole said, his eyes locked on the screen.

"Who's he?"

"Gabe," he answered absently, then seemed to realize she had no idea who Gabe was. "My brother."

"I didn't know you had a brother." He'd worked for her for more than three years. How did she not know he had a brother? Or a mother who lived in town?

"Head to Oliver Medical Center."

They were silent as she pulled out of the alley and into Saturday night traffic.

"Older or younger brother?" she asked.

"Both. Gabe is five years older." He checked his phone every few seconds, as if willing it to give him more information.

"And the younger one?"

"Zane and Drake. Twins."

"Four boys." His mother must be a saint.

"Five. Mason's the oldest. None of them like me much," he said. "So you know." He said it with zero emotion, but the fact that he said it at all conveyed more than his tone.

Sierra couldn't help being curious about his family—and that he'd never before mentioned a single one of them. Though she made a point of not calling him or the rest of the crew her friends, he knew plenty about her family just through her mentions over the years. He'd met both her siblings multiple times and knew a lot about her parents, even though they lived in Arizona.

"What about your dad?" she asked hesitantly.

"He died when I was seventeen," Cole said in a monotone, his gaze glued straight ahead.

She was not making anything better. "I'm sorry."

"Long time ago."

His phone sounded with another message. "Gabe made it to the hospital. The ambulance just pulled up."

They were still about twenty minutes out, and she pressed harder on the gas pedal. Cole wouldn't be able to do a thing to help his mom right now, but maybe he'd be able to see her soon.

They were quiet for the rest of the drive. The quiet came to an abrupt end the second they stepped through the ER doors. Saturday night. Close to eleven o'clock. Worst time ever to have an emergency because that was apparently when everyone else did.

The bright lights of the waiting room beat down on them as they made their way inside. The room was crawling with people, from a screaming baby being held by a stressed-out girl who couldn't be more than twenty, to a family with three kids clustered in the corner and looking like they had some kind of plague, to a loud, obviously drunk guy who was being handled by security. Dressed formally as they were, she and Cole received more than a few curious looks.

After a brief hesitation, Cole headed toward two men standing near the hallway to the rest of the hospital. She could tell in a glance they were his brothers. Both had dark hair like Cole's, and one of them was wearing a suit. The other wore khakis and a button-down shirt. The suit guy glared at Cole, and if she had to guess, going by looks, he must be the oldest, Mason if she remembered right. Sierra followed, her shoes officially reaching the torture stage, but that wasn't important right now.

"Hey, Cole," the khakis brother said. "Glad you're here. They took her to the cath lab."

Sierra saw Cole swallow hard as he absorbed that news. "Sounds bad," he said.

"She's in the best place to get help," the suit guy said in a low, authoritative, not-really-warm voice. "We're lucky she was able to call for help on her own."

"What happened?" Cole directed the question to the brother in khakis, barely sparing the suited brother a look.

"I talked to her around six because she wasn't feeling well earlier in the day. She insisted she was fine, just had some indigestion." The khakis brother shook his head, gritting his teeth. "I wish I would've asked more questions. She texted me around ten thirty that the pain was worse and she'd called 911. I was at a thing downtown, so it was faster for me to meet her here."

Though Cole didn't say anything more, his body was tense and worry radiated off him. Feeling helpless, Sierra grasped his forearm lightly, squeezed it once, just to remind him she was there for him, then let her hand fall to her side. The action seemed to catch khakis brother's attention, and he looked at her for the first time.

"Hello," he said to her, his eyes roving up and down over her gown. "I'm Gabe North." He extended his hand, all manners in spite of the circumstances.

"Sierra Lowell," she said as she shook his hand.

"This is our oldest brother, Mason," Gabe said, pointing his thumb at the guy in the suit.

Mason was reading something on his phone, and he lowered it and gave Sierra's hand a firm shake. "Nice to meet you," he said, sounding on autopilot.

"Likewise," she replied. The tension in the air was thick, and she didn't think it was only because of their mom's grave situation, though that would be more than enough to make anyone unfriendly and pensive.

"Were you two out on a date?" Gabe asked as Mason went back to his phone.

"Sierra's my boss," Cole said emphatically. "She owns Dunn & Lowell Remodeling."

Gabe nodded, raising his brows as if surprised to learn what she did for a living, which Sierra was used to. There was a hint of admiration in his expression as well, which she wasn't used to. Mason shoved his phone in his pocket and directed his attention —his somehow commanding, hard-to-ignore attention—at her.

"I've heard a lot of good things about your company, not just from Cole," Mason said, and she couldn't help liking him a little. "We considered getting a bid from you when we renovated our eastside store, but Cole said you specialize in historical renovation."

"We do, but we'll take on just about any kind of remodeling project." She glanced at Cole, wondering why he'd shut down their chances for what sounded like a decent bit of business.

"It was a few months ago, when we were already juggling the theater reno, the Preston project, and the Meyers project," Cole said to her.

"Ahh. In the middle of which we were also short-handed," she recalled. It had been a stressful couple of months, for sure, but she still would've bent over backwards to see what she could do to win Mason's business—whatever that was.

"We had a limited turnaround time for the store renovations," Gabe said, smoothing things over for Cole.

Interesting dynamics between these three, and her mind raced with questions about Cole's family and their relationships and the business that at least two brothers were apparently involved in.

"It would've been a challenge, but we're good at handling challenges," she said to Gabe and Mason, smiling to show she had no hard feelings. She had to literally bite down on her tongue to keep from saying she would love the opportunity to help them if they had remodeling needs in the future. The ER, with a mother whose fate was in question, was not the place or time to do business.

"Good to know," Gabe said diplomatically. "So you two were at a business function tonight or…?"

Sierra stole a look at Cole, whose jaw was taut, eyes hard as he peered toward the doors that led to the emergency department.

"Her sister got married tonight. Sierra needed a plus one. You think we'll hear something soon?" He glanced toward the doors again, leaving no question he didn't want to talk about their fake date.

"Not as soon as we want," Mason said.

"They'll talk to us as soon as they know something," Gabe said.

"Is Drake coming?" Cole asked.

"I texted him multiple times. Called him twice but can't get ahold of him," Gabe said, his frown deepening.

Cole scowled as he glanced around the waiting room. He nodded toward the other side. There were two available chairs in a corner, adjacent to each other. "We're going to sit. Sierra's been on her feet all night." Without another word to his brothers, he put his hand on the small of her back and guided her away.

This time, Sierra didn't give any thought to all the lines they were blurring. Cole needed someone, and it was crystal clear he didn't want that person to be one of his brothers. After what he'd done for her tonight, she was more than willing to step up.

CHAPTER SEVEN

ole had gone emotionally numb a good twenty minutes ago. He was aware, at some level, that was probably his brain's way of coping with news he couldn't otherwise handle.

He wished he could go deaf to the chaos and noise around them. The corner he and Sierra were sitting in was anything but private, and his head throbbed in time with the toddler two seats away who was pounding an old-fashioned toy hammer on a mini workbench that had eight plastic pegs sticking up at varying heights. The tyke's father was bent over his own knees looking like death warmed over, and Cole couldn't help but wonder if he was ill or if he had a loved one behind those looming automatic ER doors.

Easier to think about other people's problems right now.

"Want me to grab some coffee?" Sierra asked, leaning close to him to be heard over the racket of three or four dozen people stuffed into a too-small room.

"You should go home," he said, a little surprised she was still here. He appreciated the ride, barely remembered the drive, in fact, so it was good that he hadn't been behind the wheel, but she didn't have a horse in this race, didn't know his family, and sure didn't need to endure the nightmare of this Saturday-night ER waiting room.

Sierra glanced over at his brothers, who were still leaning

against the same wall across the way, not talking much, checking their phones periodically as they waited for more info on their mom. "I'm fine."

"It's your sister's big day," he said. "Everyone's waiting for you."

"I'm staying. Kennedy's not even there," she said, and he didn't miss the thread of *don't argue with me* laced in her tone. He knew it well from work.

She was crazy to sit here any longer than she had to, but he could admit to himself he was glad to have someone around besides Mason and Gabe. She served both as an excuse not to hang with them and as someone to keep him from getting lost in his head.

"Let's go to the cafeteria, get the hell out of here for a few." He stood without waiting for her to answer, and she rose with a nod.

They had to walk by Mason and Gabe to get to the elevators to the lower-level cafeteria.

"Can we get you guys something to drink?" Sierra asked as they approached. She was nicer than him, as he wouldn't have asked.

"No, thank you," Mason said.

"I'm good," was Gabe's response.

"Text me if there's news," Cole said and then he ushered Sierra away with his hand on her waist. He didn't know if he'd ever touched her in a personal way before tonight, and all the previous ones, at the reception, were required, but this one was for him. He needed the contact.

The elevators were down the hall and around a corner, and when they turned, the noise and cacophony faded by several degrees. Cole breathed in the relative calmness as they waited for the car to arrive.

"It's a madhouse back there," Sierra said.

"One of the nine circles of hell. Not sure which one."

The doors opened to an empty elevator and they stepped in. When they exited one floor lower, it was immediately evident that the cafeteria was closed. Though there were no doors and all the seating looked to be accessible, a metal gate blocked off the area with the stainless-steel food service counters, and two thirds of the lights were off. The remaining third illuminated the route to the attached vending machine haven. They walked toward it, her heels clicking on the hard floor.

There was a vending machine that brewed coffee, and they went directly to it. Cole took out his card. "My treat."

"Vending machine coffee is my favorite," Sierra said lightly, then tilted her head slightly, as if struck by an idea. "They should make one of these for wine."

"Or beer," he said as he handed her the first paper cup of "freshly brewed" coffee. The machine dispensed his, he grabbed it, and they walked by the other vending machines. "Want something to eat?"

She homed in on the machine that offered every kind of candy under the sun. "I got this," she said, opening her purse. "You like Peanut Butter M&Ms?"

"No."

"What?" She paused with her card halfway to the machine and looked at him, jaw gaping, as if he'd said babies weren't cute.

"Plain or peanut are good. Almond is okay. But if you want peanut butter, there's Reese's."

"Blaspheme. Peanut butter cups are one of my favorites, but if you want hard-shelled candies with peanut butter, M&Ms hands down."

She punched in the number for Peanut Butter M&Ms, and then she hit another number, and he watched the Plain M&Ms fall to the trough. She bent to retrieve both, then handed him the plain. His appetite was in negative numbers, but he took them anyway.

"Let's sit," she said, and she led him down one of the aisles of tables to a booth with high backs in semidarkness.

They seemed to have the whole area to themselves, and he couldn't think of a better place to wait for news. The thought of returning to the circus upstairs made his stomach hurt.

"Your brothers seem friendly," she said as she slid onto one bench, careful with her dress, and he sat across the table from her. "Well, Gabe was friendly. Mason seemed preoccupied and upset, which is understandable."

"Gabe's okay. He gets along with everybody." He was the one Cole was closest to, though the word *close* was misleading.

Sierra nodded. "What's Mason's story?"

"Uptight oldest-brother overachiever syndrome, I think they call it."

She smiled as if she knew what he was talking about as she tore off the corner of her candy package.

"He's the one who always does the right thing. Well, Gabe mostly does too, but Mason thinks he's better than everyone because he does."

"Jackson's an overachiever too," she said of her brother, who he knew was the oldest Lowell sibling. "You probably have to be to be the CEO of a large, fast-growing company."

Cole gave a halfhearted scoff. "You might be on to something. Mason is the CEO of the family business."

"Family business?" Sierra asked, her brows dipping in confusion as she popped a handful of M&Ms in her mouth.

He took a swallow of hot, over-strong coffee that would surely burn a hole in his gut if he had more than one cup. When he set it back on the table, he said, "North Brothers Sports."

"What?" Sierra's eyes doubled in size and she leaned forward. "*The* North Brothers Sports? On Hopkins Road?"

"Hopkins on the west side, Gateshire on the east, plus stores in Memphis, Knoxville, and Chattanooga," he recited.

"And those North brothers are yours."

"Originally, the North brothers were Harrison and Hamilton North, my dad and uncle. Now it's Mason and Gabe and some cousins."

"But not you," she said. "Why not you?"

The answer to that was long and convoluted, but he simply said, "Not interested."

"So Mason's the CEO. Sort of explains the suit." She checked the time on her phone and he could see it upside down—11:42 p.m. "Sort of not. Does he sleep in it?"

That was the closest Cole had come to smiling since Gabe's first text tonight. "I suspect he might but there's no proof."

"And Gabe does what?"

"VP of Human Resources."

"What about your other two brothers?"

"Drake works part time in the Hopkins store by choice. He's also a personal trainer and somewhat of a flake. Zane is in the military."

Sierra crunched on another handful of candy. "I never once put together your last name with the sporting goods chain."

That was just the way he liked it. "It has nothing to do with me." He'd made sure of that when he graduated from high school and made an adamant point of signing away his rights to his financial share of the company. He didn't want to talk about it anymore, although the subject was slightly better than thinking about what might be happening upstairs with his mom.

A wave of fear washed through him at the thought. Cold, black, nauseating fear centered in his chest. He picked up the unopened plain candy package from the table, gripped it hard, shoved it in the pocket of his suit jacket. He fought to get back to the inane chitchat of sixty seconds ago, to put the fear out of his head, but he couldn't escape it this time. It was as if the numbness defense was wearing off, like some Harry Potter spell. Suddenly burning up, sweating, he whipped his jacket off, set it aside on the bench. He unbuttoned his shirt sleeves and pushed them up, his heart hammering with anxiety.

"Cole? Are you okay?"

He rotated to the end of his bench, feeling trapped in the small booth. "Yeah," he lied. He stood, free of the booth now but finding no relief. He paced deeper into the labyrinth of booths and tables, seeing nothing but the images in his mind of his mom, her warm smile, her love and concern for her sons that shined in her eyes, always.

He tried to think whether she'd looked tired or pale or unwell lately but—*fuck*—the truth of the matter was that he hadn't seen her for a few weeks. That was on him. Son of a bitch, that was all on him.

Sunday nights were family dinner night, every week, without fail, and Faye North cooked her heart out for her boys every single time, but Cole hadn't made the effort to show up for at least a month. Not for any reason other than spending time with his family was not something he enjoyed, and he hadn't felt like dealing with it.

"Is there anything I can do?" Sierra was right behind him, and her closeness startled the shit out of him.

"I just… Give me a minute."

His phone vibrated in his pocket and he pulled it out, fear hammering through him. Gabe's name was on the screen, and Cole unlocked his phone to read the whole message.

Mom had a severe blockage. When they were doing the cath, her heart stopped and they had to shock her back. They're prepping her for bypass surgery now, moving us to ICU waiting area on third floor.

Physically reeling, Cole leaned against the closest table.

He managed to type, *Can we see her before surgery?*

Three dots appeared and then *No. Condition is critical.*

He felt Sierra move in close.

"What's it say?" she asked gently.

He didn't know if he could speak, so he held his phone out to her. She angled his hand so she could see the screen, read the message, blew out a breath without dropping his hand. Cole pulled it away from her instinctively, so used to handling everything alone. This, though… He wasn't sure if he could handle this at all, alone or with someone by his side.

The images flashed through his mind again, of his mom, his loving mom. He loved her, respected her, admired the crap out of her. She was everything Cole wasn't—devoted to her family, giving, unselfish, forgiving… She was the glue that held their family together, before and after their dad's death. Cole was the opposite, doing his best to keep his distance, to keep himself separate.

The backs of his eyes burned. Bypass surgery was serious shit —he didn't need a doctor to tell him that. Heart stopped? Did that mean she'd momentarily died? His mom had always seemed strong and unbreakable, but now that seemed like an illusion. A heart attack could break the hell out of a person. Could kill her just as easily as a car wreck had killed his dad.

Acid bubbled up in his throat, sheer, burning fear that was on the verge of leveling him. He wasn't ready to lose his mom. Dammit, he couldn't lose her.

Sierra hoisted herself up on the table right beside him and brushed her fingers up and down his forearm. "She's going to be okay, Cole. The doctors know what they're doing. She's getting the medical expertise she needs."

All of his fear tangled up with all of his love for his mom and formed a big, painful ball in his throat that was doing its best to suffocate him. He didn't pull away from Sierra this time because it was a relief to have someone there. He hadn't let his family be there for him for years and years, maybe most of his life, but he allowed himself to take strength from Sierra's presence, to lean on her this once. Because he wasn't sure how else to get through the darkness that was clawing at him from the inside.

"She has to be okay," he said, his voice a low, unrecognizable rumble.

"The doctors are taking care of her."

The bitterness of regret pulsed through every last inch of him, constricting the air out of him, and his inhales felt like big, ugly gasps. He was losing his shit and he knew it, couldn't even begin to care that he had an audience. He shot away from the table and started pacing again, rubbing his hands up and down his face, feeling as if every breath was a fight. He'd never experienced such an overwhelming, panicked blackness before. Its grip on him was all encompassing—physical, mental, emotional. He couldn't process a coherent thought. It was as if his skin was suddenly too small, tight and suffocating, and he couldn't do anything about it except try to walk the sensation off.

He didn't know how many times he'd passed Sierra when she reached out and grabbed his wrist, halting him.

"Cole. Stop for a minute. Breathe."

He hadn't seen anything at all as he paced, but he did stop, focused on her, registered that she hadn't moved from before. She kept a grip on his arm, and though he could've easily pulled away, he didn't. Because he needed grounding. Calming. Something.

"Sit," she said gently, scooting over so her feet rested on the bench, butt on the table, making room for him next to her.

He was suddenly so bone-tired that he couldn't imagine standing any longer, and he sank down onto the table, pulled his feet up to the bench, tried to shake off the mental paralysis. He realized he was sweating and swiped a hand over his forehead.

Sierra thankfully said nothing more, just sat next to him, her body up against his, and entwined her arm with his. He did as she'd said and tried to get a couple of deep breaths in, willed himself to stop being carried away by the vortex of black fear.

A thought was scraping at him, the words pulsing to get out. He hated to give them any power, but they wouldn't let go of him. "What if she dies?" he finally let out in little more than a whisper.

Instead of giving him some bullshit line that she wouldn't, Sierra merely held tighter to his arm and leaned her head against his shoulder. He allowed himself to breathe in the scent of her hair, taking comfort in the femininity of it, in having someone to lean on for once.

Several minutes ticked by with them not moving other than to breathe in and out, for him to stop losing his shit to the point he couldn't form a thought. The thoughts that finally filled his head were ugly, harrowing, painful as fuck. He'd never, ever been a talker, was the opposite of a sharer, but now, as the pressure inside of him built, he was compelled to let some of it out, desperate to get it out into the light, so to speak, to sort through it, try to find some kind of relief. Any relief.

"I don't know…" he started, his voice full of gravel and grief. "I'm not a good son. She might not know I love her."

"Ohh, Cole, she knows. Moms know."

"I haven't told her for years. Haven't showed her." Anytime he stepped foot into her house, the house where they'd all grown up, he set his defenses sky-high, determined not to let anyone in.

"I've never met her, but I still bet she knows," Sierra said, her voice like a soothing balm in the middle of a walk through shards of glass.

That didn't mean he believed her.

Cole buried his face in his hands, and the images he normally blocked out filtered into his mind against his will. His dad, back when Cole was a teenager and a thorn in the old man's side. Harry North had been a good man, a hardworking man, involved in his sons' lives to the nth degree, from baseball games to grade reports to girlfriends, as much as they would let him. Cole had done his best not to let him, had argued with his dad over pretty much everything. Argued to the end.

The regret that lived in every single cell in his body, no matter how hard he worked to push it down, roared to life, flooded his system as if it sensed his weakened state and was moving in for the kill.

"I…" He swallowed hard, again feeling the burning need to spill the bad shit out, as unfamiliar as that was to him. "I told you my dad died when I was seventeen," he managed, and he felt Sierra nod against his shoulder. "The last time I talked to him, we had an argument." He pushed air out of his lungs. "The last words I said to him were hateful. I stormed out, and the very next day, he got broadsided on his way home from work. Died at the scene. I never got to make peace with him," he forced out.

He'd never told anyone that secret. Had held it close for all these years, fifteen years, so close that on most days it was buried too deep even for him to think about it. But it was always there, that awful truth. And now Sierra knew.

"God, that sucks," she said, and he braced himself for whatever she would say next, needing it to be something other than the loathing he deserved. "That must have made his death so much harder to come to terms with."

He didn't answer. He felt her head lift from his shoulder, sensed her peering at him from the side, but he couldn't meet her gaze.

"You were a teenager, and teenagers are hard," she said, and he blew out a scoff. "Your dad knew you loved him, just like your mom does. They know, Cole." She squeezed his hand as if she thought she could force that supposed truth in through his skin if she applied enough pressure.

He wished it was that easy.

"He couldn't have known," he said.

"Did you love him?"

Cole nodded, squeezing his eyes shut.

"He knew." Sierra said it with so much conviction that he wanted to believe her, but fifteen years was a long time for his doubts to burrow in.

They sat in silence for a while, a long while, watching across the way as a middle-aged woman shuffled to the vending machines and purchased several items, then walked back out in a daze, without noticing them. Cole breathed in Sierra's shampoo scent, focusing on it as if it were a security blanket, drawing what comfort he could from it and the quiet sounds of her breathing.

It was well after midnight when he straightened, ready, finally, to head up to the third floor to face his brothers and his mom's fate.

CHAPTER EIGHT

he ICU waiting room was an upgrade from the ER, and thank God, because Cole and three of his brothers had been there for hours. Instead of hard plastic chairs, there were couches and recliners, and a nurse had offered them blankets, though Drake was the only one who'd taken one. The youngest North brother was with Gabe and Mason when Cole and Sierra had finally come upstairs. Their family had had the smaller, dimly lit waiting room to themselves the whole time, so it was impossible for Cole to distance himself from his brothers, but oddly, he found he didn't want to. Crisis situations brought out some weird shit sometimes, he figured.

They'd persuaded Sierra, who'd looked close to collapsing with fatigue, to leave not long after they'd found the ICU waiting room. It'd taken all four of them to convince her, and she'd scrutinized Cole's face until she'd apparently seen the truth—that he was okay with her going. She'd pulled him through his personal shit storm of a reaction with the patience and understanding of a saint...and that thought reminded him of her use of the same word, *saint*, at her sister's wedding. Hard to believe that was only a few hours ago. His whole world had gone ass over elbows since then.

It was after three in the morning when Drake, fully reclined in the chair in the corner, said, "Someone should offer pizza delivery at this hour. It's time for fourth meal."

"Only you could think of your stomach at a time like this," Mason said from a couch on the opposite wall, and Cole realized one side of his own mouth was tugging upward in a hint of a grin. They didn't have reason to feel lighter, no cause for relief, but there was something about the hour and the extreme circumstances, the isolation of the waiting room, that made everything feel surreal. Surreal beat the hell out of cold fear, Cole thought.

"Wrong. If Zane was here, he'd agree with me," Drake said from his nest of blankets. "Probably could even be convinced to go out and find some food for us. And beer. I could use a beer."

He was probably spot on, as the twins' united goal in life had always been to eat the family out of house and home. Cole figured that's where the majority of their dad's life insurance had gone—toward feeding the three active, athletic sons who'd still lived at home. Drake and Zane seemed to have an ongoing competition for who could eat the most.

"Anyone talk to Z yet?" Cole asked. Last he'd heard, their brother was deployed overseas somewhere, but he wasn't sure how up-to-date his info was.

"I sent him an email," Mason said. He'd staked a claim on the other couch, next to Cole's chair. "There's not much else we can do at this point." The truth hung heavily over their heads that if they needed Zane home for a funeral, their options for contacting him would increase. "I haven't heard back yet."

It was almost funny how, even now, with all of them in their thirties or late twenties, the brothers still fell into their usual roles. Mason was the leader, acting as the spokesperson with medical personnel. He couldn't *not* take the lead in anything in life, Cole was pretty damn sure of it.

Drake was the baby, the one who got by on charm alone, who'd managed to convince a good-looking nurse to share a piece of the chocolate cake the medical staff had behind closed doors in celebration of a fellow nurse's birthday.

If Zane were here, he'd probably fill the hours by talking their ears off about his passion—planes and flying—just as he had since he was a grade-schooler.

Gabe was the quintessential peacemaker, the guy who made sure everyone was okay, or as okay as they could be with their mom currently under the knife.

And Cole, he was the asshole brother, the keep-to-himself guy, the black sheep. Tonight, he'd mostly just sat quietly, pensively, consumed by thoughts of his mom and brothers and his relationships with each of them. His conclusion? He sucked at relationships. Always had.

These were his brothers, the people he'd grown up with. With their mom's condition in question, it was clear that they needed to pull together, that his distancing was stupid.

Or maybe he was over-fucking-exhausted. Delirious.

The TV mounted up high in the corner of the room was off, and when his brothers weren't talking, it was eerily quiet in the alcove that was removed from the main hallway. As footsteps approached their waiting room, the likelihood that someone was coming to address them was high, and Gabe and Mason both straightened on their separate vinyl-upholstered couches. Drake opened his eyes and raised his recliner a few degrees as a willowy woman in green scrubs entered the waiting room.

Cole searched her face for a sign of what news she brought, but her expression gave nothing away.

"Faye North's family?"

"That's us." Mason stood, took a couple of steps toward her, looking intense as always with his suit jacket still on, eyes direct, business face intact. His only concessions to the hour and situation were the tie he'd taken off and tossed on a side table and the uncharacteristic five o'clock shadow. "How is she?"

"I'm Dr. Beacham. Let's sit down."

Cole's alertness doubled and he watched her face to see if her refusal to answer that question meant there was bad news. The doctor still gave nothing away as she lowered herself to the coffee table in front of Gabe's couch. The four of them gathered around her, the tension in the room stretching taut for the few seconds it took them.

"The surgery was a success," the doctor finally said, and there was an audible collective exhale in the room. "Faye is holding her own."

Cole was fairly certain he remained sitting at attention between Gabe and Drake, but inside he went limp with relief and heard only a fraction of the rest of the doctor's report—it'd take their mom a while to wake up, they could see her in a couple of hours, she'd likely be in ICU for two days...

He stared at the doctor's face as she spoke but was lost in his own thoughts, knowing Mason was paying full attention and could fill him in later if necessary. All that mattered right now was that she was okay and her heart was fixed.

After the doctor had answered a dozen questions from Mason, Gabe, and Drake, she left them alone again. The four of them remained where they were—Cole in between Gabe and Drake on the couch, Mason on an adjacent chair he'd pulled close, all of them with their long legs stretched in front of them— and they talked, all four of them. They shared Mom stories, laughed, predicted what kind of patient she would be for the next week plus, started discussions of post-hospital care, joked about who could cook Sunday dinners that would meet her approval. Easy answer was no one.

For those minutes that stretched into a couple of hours, Mason stopped directing, Gabe quit worrying about everyone, Drake turned off the eternal charm button and was just their brother, and Cole managed to quit acting like an asshole. They rehashed dozens of times they'd gotten into trouble over the years, reminiscing about their mom's reactions to the shit five boys could pull. She'd never hesitated to discipline them, both before and after their dad's death, and there were times when she'd lost her cool, so many times, but what it came down to was that she was the best mom anyone could ask for. As different as the North boys were, they could all agree on that.

Mason brought up the time in grade school when Zane and Drake had pulled off keeping a squirrel from the yard as a pet in their walk-in closet for nine days. They'd fashioned a litter box out of a shoebox, fed it Planters nuts from the family snack stash in the pantry, and only gotten caught when their mom had gone in their closet to put something away and discovered that squirrels do not take to litter boxes. She wasn't sure what kind of critter infestation they had until the squirrel, who'd been nesting down under a pile of dirty clothes, dashed out of its hiding place and scared the daylights out of her. The hours-long attempt to get the animal out of the house had elicited their mom's most creative, epic streams of swear words that any of them had ever heard. As the four brothers held their abs and wiped their eyes from laughing, a tall, built male nurse came in to tell them they could visit their mom one at a time. That sobered them up quickly, and Cole straightened, his mind filled with images of breathing tubes and wires and IVs and all the other crap the doctor had warned them about.

Mason stood, obviously thinking to go first, as was his way, but Gabe moved forward to the edge of the couch and held up a hand. He eyed Cole, then addressed Mason. "Let Cole go first."

Mason's brows crinkled together at Gabe, then he looked at Cole and shrugged. "Sure. Don't wear her out, Cole. The nurse said two minutes."

Cole didn't understand what had prompted that, and he didn't care. He let Mason's directive—the guy just couldn't resist —roll off and stood, nodded. As his brothers discussed the order of visitation, Cole followed the nurse through the maze of hallways to a private room with a large bank of windows to the outside. The curtains were drawn and the room was illuminated dimly.

His heart lurched when he laid eyes on his mom, intubated, surrounded by a dozen machines and monitors, her eyes closed. When he came up next to her, they slowly opened, met his gaze, took him in. Though she was drowsy, his mom was in there.

He'd been warned she couldn't talk because of the breathing tube, but he would swear one corner of her lips twitched slightly upward when she recognized him. He took her cool hand in his and leaned down and kissed her forehead, that baseball-sized lump lodged in his throat again. He cleared his throat, willed the lump down.

"You scared the ever-loving crap out of us," he said. His voice was hoarse, thick. "Everybody's here, well, except Zane. We only have a minute each because you need to rest but…I love you, Mom."

She gave his hand a weak, almost imperceptible squeeze, and despite her condition, her love was there in her cloudy eyes. After several seconds, her lids lowered, as if she couldn't hold off the drowsiness any longer. Still holding her hand, he took in the room, the equipment, the wires, the sounds, and it struck him again how close they'd come to losing her.

But she was okay. They were lucky as fuck. And he was going to do his best to remember that. Not just today or this week or over the next few months as she recovered. This was his wake-up call to get his head out of his ass and be a better son, a better brother, a better person. He didn't know how to do that, exactly, but as he stared at his mother's lined, pale face, he vowed to figure it out.

CHAPTER NINE

Monday morning, Cole was nearly running late for his seven o'clock meeting with Sierra at the office. The thought of sitting across the table from her and acting as if nothing had changed, as if he hadn't revealed shit he never, ever revealed, turned his stomach, but that was exactly what he would do.

After the harrowing all-nighter Saturday and an emotional, exhausting Sunday split between seeing to his mom, interacting with his brothers, and fighting off thoughts of his boss, Cole felt raw. His energy reserves were bottomed out, his defenses down. Just when he needed them most.

He locked his apartment and thundered down the narrow interior stairs to the street. He climbed into his truck, which was parked at the curb out front, started the engine, switched the music from country to the loudest, hardest metal he could find, and cranked it up until his windows rattled. That was his only hope of keeping his mind blank on the drive in, and he needed blank like a deployed soldier needed a blow job.

At this hour, traffic wasn't an issue, and he was pulling up behind the office in no time, ready or not.

He allowed himself thirty seconds once the engine was off to close his eyes, consider the Draper project, where they'd be replacing the plumbing of the 1920s French-revival-style home later today. The day's work was sure to turn up yet more challenges, as hundred-year-old buildings always did, but that sounded preferable, by far, to facing the woman who'd taunted his dreams all damn night.

"Nothing to do but do it," he muttered as he gathered his bag and his travel mug of strong-ass coffee from home and left his tool belt behind the driver's seat.

He entered through the side door into the kitchen area and instantly discerned two things—Sierra had already brewed her god-awful more-sugar-than-caffeine "coffee," and she'd cranked up the furnace. He could see from the entryway that she was in her office with the light on. He went there directly.

"Morning," he said from the doorway, taking in the sight of her sitting, as usual, at the table instead of her desk, dressed in her standard cargos—dark gray today—a fleece quarter-zip Dunn & Lowell pullover, and scuffed dark brown work boots. Her silky hair was in a high ponytail, and her pretty face radiated her typical early-morning optimism with a bright smile as she looked up at him and returned the greeting.

He shoved down the zap of lust when their eyes met and averted his quickly as he crossed the room to the chair opposite her.

"I didn't expect you to make it this morning," she said.

"We have a meeting, don't we? Seven o'clock?"

"We did, but your weekend—"

"Everything ended up okay," he said dismissively. She'd texted yesterday for a report on his mom and he'd filled her in, so she knew the emergency element was past and what was left was a lot of healing and life revamping for his mom.

He set his canvas bag on the table, yanked his sweatshirt over his head, because, shit, she must have the heat set at about eighty degrees, and then took out his notebook and sat down. "How's that application coming along?" he asked. The Eldridge competition was the reason for their meeting.

She narrowed her eyes at him—he didn't look up from searching for a pencil to see it, but he could feel it—and paused for a second, as if she was debating with herself whether to force talk about the weekend and his mom or jump to business mode.

Business, he urged silently. He was grasping to it by a thin thread himself, fighting off images and memories of Saturday night.

Another few seconds ticked by before she made up her mind. "It's done. I finished it late last night so you can go over it." She held out a packet of multiple pages.

"Deadline is a week away?" he asked as he took it from her.

"Yep. We can submit it online, though I'd prefer to do it early."

"Lot of pages," he said as he sat back and leafed through them.

"Multiple essay questions. It was worse than a college app."

"Wouldn't know. Didn't go to college," he said, maybe trying to highlight a difference between them. The first part was a lie though. He'd filled out multiple applications, essays and all, just never sent them in.

"See, I know that but I don't get it," Sierra said, and he realized his error in bringing it up. "You're smart, Cole. Wicked smart. I've never seen you use a calculator on bids, but they're always correct. I check," she admitted.

He glanced up at her because he hadn't realized that—that she'd noticed or that she double-checked his math.

"It's my name on the door," she said with an unapologetic shrug, proving that she, too, was smart.

He nodded in acknowledgment, turned his attention to the application, ignoring her probe for more info.

The first few pages were short answers, facts, dates, numbers, records, and then there were a couple of pages of three-line answers, and then the long ones. "You handwrote it all?" In turquoise ink, no less.

"I think better that way. I'll type it in after you've read through it."

"S. Lowell," he read in the first response. "You think they'll hold your gender against you?"

"Always a possibility. They'll figure it out soon enough if we advance."

That they would. While Cole could work up a good panic attack at the thought of being on a weekly TV show, Sierra was born for it in every way—with her confidence, her knowledge and experience, and her looks. But he'd seen firsthand more than once where she'd lost a bid because of those looks, because someone didn't think a woman could do this job. Dumb fucks, every one of them.

Cole read over the basics quickly, more interested in the longer answers, as those would be what the people judging the entries would focus on. A lot of the questions in the middle section were about past projects, gathering information on the company's breadth and length of experience. Then it got serious with the essay questions, and so had Sierra. He leaned back in his chair to read while she worked on something on her laptop. Most of the questions were about problems and challenges and how they'd overcome them, with some asking for details on successful renovations as well. She'd exceeded the space given for multiple questions, her precise, left-tilting, scripty print spilling onto the backs of the pages.

"Your content is spot-on," he said a good twenty minutes later after reading every word.

"Thanks," Sierra said, sitting up and closing her laptop to give him her full attention. "It sounds like there's a but."

"Is there a word limit? Either stated or constrained by the online form?"

"Not stated. I didn't check the form for limitations. You think I rambled too much?"

"I wouldn't call it rambling." He blew out a breath, considering how to say what he wanted to say. "What you wrote is straightforward. The details are good. They show you know your stuff."

"But? Cole, just say what you're thinking. You're not going to hurt my feelings."

"What's missing is the marketing."

Her brows dipped. "It's not supposed to be marketing. Just facts."

"Marketing is facts presented in a different way," he said. "You know this."

Though she'd hired Kennedy, who freelanced as a marketing consultant in addition to being part owner of Sugar Babies bakery on Hale Street, Sierra was still closely involved in all the promotional work. Kennedy helped her set budgets and choose which media to focus her time and money on and guided her in overall branding, but the nitty-gritty of the content still fell on Sierra, who regularly garnered input from Cole. It was a team effort, and they were the experts on their business, something that Kennedy wasn't. Cole had zero formal training in marketing, but he'd read books on it from the first time Sierra had asked for his assistance. That's how he operated—need to know something? Read a book. There was always a book out there that could teach you what you needed to learn, and he was a fan of knowing what he talked about, whatever the topic.

"It's an application, not an ad," Sierra said, running her hands over her face, which told him she was trying to understand his point instead of arguing outright.

"You can present the facts while highlighting your strengths. You want to win, right?"

"You know the answer to that." Her voice teemed with frustration.

"Let me take this home. I'll take a stab at it."

"You want to rewrite them?"

"Not rewrite. Refine. You've got the meat in there. It just needs a little subtle, strategic horn tooting. If you don't like what I do, you can go back to what you have."

Sierra exhaled loudly, nodding. "Have at it. If you really want to try, I'm open to changes. I trust you."

The way her eyes pierced into him with that statement felt suddenly personal. Too personal for comfort. He'd fought hard to become what she needed on the job since the day she'd hired him, had given it more effort than just about anything, because, as his history showed, he could fuck things up with the best of them, and he was loathe to let her down. He strived to be her go-to guy at work, but anything beyond that would be unwise on her part.

"I'll make a copy," Cole said.

He launched out of his chair and headed into the front room, where the copier was. He flipped the lights on as he entered, stuffed the packet of paper in the copier, set it to duplicate the whole bundle, and leaned against the wall to wait, relieved to have a couple of walls between them. Normally he enjoyed being with Sierra, working with her, solving problems at her side, but everything felt different today. Their normal had been shot to shit.

The copy machine was behind the desk, which was seldom used and more for show and storing their various promotional pieces. Sierra's friend Hayden, who owned an interior design company, had helped her set up the rectangular room, originally a living room, to welcome customers and potential customers.

It was cooler in here due to an ancient HVAC system that didn't distribute heat evenly. A relief today, between the air temperature of the office and the underlying tension between him and Sierra. She was itching to ask about his mom and probably his brothers too, he was sure, but he needed to keep it business as usual.

He let out a scoff, because his thoughts Saturday at the reception, his dreams last night, they were anything but business as usual. You'd think his mom's health emergency would be enough to override his lust for his boss, but it seemed his lack of sleep and the resulting edginess had only made him more incapable of getting her out of his head.

Once the copier stopped, he took out the new pages, found a stapler in one of the desk drawers, and stapled the packet. He picked up the originals and headed back into the office.

"Anything else?" he asked. It was a little early to leave for the Draper site, but that's exactly what he was going to do.

"Tell me about your mom. How's she feeling? When are they moving her out of ICU?"

He stacked the papers on top of his notebook and slid them into his bag, threw his carpenter pencil in.

"She's tired and weak but upbeat, all things considered."

"Any idea when she might get to go home?"

"Maybe this weekend. Depends."

"And she's still in ICU?"

"Until tomorrow."

"Are you in a hurry?" she asked, eyeing him as he stood there while she still sat across the table from him.

"Ready to get started on the day's work is all."

"Cole." She shot out of her chair and came around the table.

He crossed his arms and leaned his butt on the table, which put him closer to eye level with her but also added a little extra space between them. Much-needed space, because her feminine fragrance filled the air, and it was nearly impossible for him not to be affected by it, not to let it take him back to holding her in his arms as they danced, close enough for her wisps of hair to tickle his cheek, her breath to flutter over his ear when she spoke. He'd told himself he'd be back to strictly professional today, that he'd shove Saturday night aside by now, but that was turning out to be a monumental struggle.

She blew out a frustrated breath. "This is dumb."

"What's dumb?" As if he didn't know.

"This. Us. Acting like we barely know each other."

"Just keeping it professional." Or trying.

Failing, if you counted his thoughts or his body's reaction to her being so close.

"You're guarded. Uptight." Standing face-to-face with him, she reached over and squeezed both of his shoulders, as if to check how tense they were.

"Monday morning. Back to boss-employee," he managed to say in a mostly matter-of-fact voice, even though it was turning out to be a lie. "Fake date," he continued. "You said it yourself."

She snapped her gaze to his, narrowed her eyes, studied him. He tried to keep his expression blank.

"It was supposed to be a fake date," she said pensively. She pressed her lips together as she continued to size him up. "And by saying that Saturday night, I was trying to keep things straight in my head, trying to justify going against my own policy of not getting involved with anyone at work. But that made it seem like I didn't want to be with you, huh?"

"You were keeping boundaries in place. I got that."

Her gaze dropped to the floor, and she shoved her hands in her back pants pockets. "That was the goal. Boundaries. But after everything that happened, those boundaries are history."

"They don't have to be." He needed them not to be. He needed to put about six feet between them so he couldn't see the flecks of gold in her brown eyes or the sheen of uncolored gloss on her lips. So he couldn't extend his arm, touch her, pull her closer the way he was dying to.

"I call bullshit." She stood up straighter, lifted her chin. "I had fun with you, liked being with you. And then later, with your mom—"

"I'm sorry you had to deal with that. I should've driven myself."

"Stop it. You needed a friend. I'm glad I was there. Glad I got to meet your family that I didn't know existed." Her lips quirked up, eyes sparked with a hint of teasing, then she went serious again. "I get the impression you don't let a lot of people in, but guess what? I'm in. We're friends. No going back."

He didn't know much about friends, didn't really have any, but this didn't feel quite like *friends*. Not the way his blood was pounding through him.

Sierra's gaze slipped downward, to his lips, and she moved closer, mere inches away, those doe eyes locked to his again. He couldn't get himself to look away, couldn't break the sudden connection. He dropped his arms to his sides, gripped the table behind him, fighting not to touch her or put a hand at her waist or brush that stray lock of hair from her cheek.

A heartbeat later, she closed the rest of the space between them, grasped his upper arm, and pressed her lips to his.

He froze. For a split second, his brain said no, but then the synapses connected and he received the message from his lips, and everything in him said hell yes. He couldn't stop himself from gripping her hip, holding her to his body as he soaked up the feel of her lips on his—soft, pliant, feminine but unwavering. She let out a sexy satisfied moan, and her hand landed on his chest, gripped his T-shirt, pulled at him. Instinct and need had him taking it deeper, sliding his tongue over her lips until she opened to him, let him in, and he lost all ability for rational thought.

She tasted of coffee and mint, smelled of oranges, felt diminutive and feminine as his hands landed on her lower back, pulling her into his body, showing her he was hard as a steel beam. She moved her hands to his neck, one of them roving over the back of his head, her fingers digging into him, as if she couldn't stand the thought of letting him go, letting this end.

The outside door to the kitchen opened and then slammed shut, and Sierra jumped away from him at the same moment he snapped to attention and stood up tall, stepped away from the table. Sierra swiped a hand over her lips as if she could erase any evidence of what they'd been doing, and he turned around to face the table, pulled his bag close, struggled with the zipper, his hands shaking.

"Morning," Reggie said from the office doorway mere seconds later.

Cole picked up his sweatshirt, grabbed his bag, hoped like hell his face was blank, and turned around. "Hey, Reggie. See you on-site," he said to Sierra, and then he walked out of the office and out of the building at a normal pace, as if his heart wasn't about to pound right out of his damn chest.

CHAPTER TEN

*S*ierra had managed, nearly nine hours ago, to shove that kiss into a mental lockbox. Nine everlasting hours. She'd had to in order to get through the grueling day with Cole at her side, a day when they'd only gotten half as much done as they'd planned due to a crap ton of unforeseen challenges with the century-old house.

As she drove toward home, in the relative privacy of her truck, she let out a semi-hysterical laugh-howl she'd had bottled up all day because *she'd kissed Cole.* One of her employees. She'd broken her own rule, done something she'd never done before, and it'd been impulsive—she could own that—and crazy and spectacular.

She hadn't planned it, but when he'd walked in so closed-up this morning, acting like none of Saturday night had happened, she'd wanted to shake him up, pull him close, scream in frustration, hug him… And she'd ended up kissing him.

"Got his attention anyway," she muttered, still unsure whether it was good attention or bad.

She and Cole hadn't spoken a single word about it. There hadn't been an opportunity, and for that she was grateful, because she didn't know what to say, didn't know if she should say *anything.* It might be ludicrous to think they could just carry on without ever acknowledging that lip-lock, especially since it wasn't just a run-of-the-mill kiss. No, in roughly two minutes and two seconds, Cole had pretty much raised Sierra's baseline for kissing for the rest of her life.

At last, she drove her truck down the alley behind her apartment and parked it in her spot. Without hesitation, she got out and strode past the stairs that led up to her place. Instead, she headed toward the green space that bordered her building and went through it to get to the sidewalk on Hale Street.

It was nearly five o'clock, and multiple people were making their way toward Bliss carrying yoga mats, probably for the five-p.m. power yoga class that Sierra usually worked too late to make. She crossed the bustling street toward the flower shop, the dress shop, and Frank's Diner, where the dinner crowd was already starting to pick up. Monday was the fried chicken special, and nobody did fried chicken like Frank Dole. But she walked on by and kept going past the recording studio as well, though she gazed in the windows, checking for familiar famous faces who might be recording today. The front lobby was empty.

The next storefront was her destination—Henry Interiors—but it wasn't the one-of-a-kind furnishings or decor she was after. She needed girl time, decompression time, and a big-ass glass of wine, and Hayden Henry would handle all three.

An old-fashioned bell announced Sierra's entry, and she spotted Hayden in the back half of the sales floor, fussing over some funky textured gold and white throw pillows on a pure white comfy-looking couch flanked by an end table and a floor lamp. As usual, her friend was wearing a cute, professional outfit —black pants, silky white tank, light pink open cardigan with matching pumps, and a chunky but feminine necklace.

"Hey, you," Hayden said when she glanced up, pushing her shoulder-length espresso-colored hair out of her face. Then she did a double take, as if all of Sierra's angst was written on her face. "Ooh. Bad day?"

Sierra glanced around to make sure they were alone. "Weird day. Wine day. Whatcha got?" She kept walking toward the back room, understanding that Hayden might or might not be able to join her right away, as the store was open for another hour.

"There's a Pinot Noir and a Malbec on the counter, or help yourself to the wine cooler."

"Goddess. Pinot Noir will do. Where's Elena?"

"Day off. She had a thing to do," Hayden said distractedly, still eyeing the layout of the white-couch area, one of several furniture groupings scattered throughout.

Sierra slipped behind the curtain that covered the extra-wide doorway between sales floor and back room, the contrast between the two areas jolting her as it always did. The public room was impeccable, exquisitely designed, with every detail well thought out and executed. It was the kind of showroom that made you itch to buy something, to make your home as beautiful as the store, the moment you walked in.

The back room, on the other hand, was overfilled with merchandise stacked to the high ceiling in places. Some of it was in boxes, but most of it was one-of-a-kind treasures that Hayden had found or created from other pieces. She was a genius at repurposing anything from an old chair to an antique cabinet, but the fact was, she'd outgrown this space within months of opening. The landlord, Burke Wentworth, who also owned Sierra's apartment building, had allowed her to construct a sturdy storage shed in back, and it was stuffed to the gills as well. In addition, Hayden's two-car garage at her home was her work area, where she refinished, reconstructed, redesigned the pieces she picked up at shows, estate sales, and antique stores. It, too, was overflowing with "treasures." The girl had a knack for visualizing some stunning pieces, but it was a messy, large-scale endeavor. The retail aspect of it was young but successful so far.

In the far-left back corner was a tiny sort-of break area for Hayden, her assistant, and her two employees. There was a sink and a three-quarter-size fridge next to a microwave and a cabinet, all situated behind a short counter that fit two barstools. The stools barely cleared the doorway to Hayden's minuscule office, which was too small for storing stock and contained only an antique desk that Sierra rarely saw her use.

Sierra went behind the break area counter, located the Pinot Noir, and made quick work of the cork. She reached up to the hanging wineglass rack and took down two glasses, then filled them, Hayden's to a moderate level and her own to the top, knowing that Hayden wouldn't drink much, if any, until after she locked the store doors for the day.

Hayden came into the room as Sierra set the bottle back down, and her eyes widened as she noticed how full Sierra's glass was.

"Okay, let's hear it. What happened to you?" Hayden said as she tossed two apparently rejected pillows into an open-topped bin where she stored the spares.

Instead of answering, Sierra lifted her glass and took a big, socially inappropriate gulp of the deep burgundy liquid. "God yes. That's good stuff."

"Want a shot glass instead?" Hayden asked dryly.

Sierra took a more restrained sip, letting the hints of berry linger on her tongue before swallowing it. She went around the counter and slid onto a barstool, and Hayden took the other one, pulling her glass closer. Waiting.

When Sierra still didn't speak, because she was trying to figure out what to say, how much to tell, Hayden said, "Let me guess. Cole?"

Sierra snapped her gaze to her friend. "How the hell could you know that?"

Hayden took out her iPhone from the pocket of her tailored pants, unlocked it, swiped several times with her thumb. She held the phone up, and Sierra recognized the selfie of her and Cole from the wedding. "Look at you two."

Sierra did, for the dozenth time since Saturday night. It was a good picture, if she did say so herself, but then she'd been fancied up to within an inch of her life, her makeup profession-ally applied by Harper, the esthetician at Bliss, and her hair by one of Violet's friends. And Cole...the guy didn't need profes-sionals to make him look good in a suit and tie, even with the cut above his eye. There was something about a normally rough-around-the-edges man cleaning up and dressing up. Something irresistible, apparently, as she'd proven this morning.

"Mr. Foreman looks gooood," Hayden said.

"Yeah," Sierra said in an exhale, taking an extra couple of seconds to study his face. In spite of his uptightness as they'd arrived at the reception, his smile in the pic was real and wider than his usual reluctant half grin. It did something to his whole face, and that, in turn, did something to her heart rate, even now, even though it was just pixels on a screen. "You had a good trip?"

"My trip was fine," Hayden said of the trade show in Boston. She'd returned late last night, texting Sierra she was home and exhausted and they'd catch up today. "Back to you. And this guy. I want to know everything about Saturday night."

"Saturday night ended in the wee hours of Sunday morning—"

"Hello. So much for not banging the boys who work for you."

"I didn't bang anyone," Sierra said. "I'm not going to bang anyone." The second sentence was less sure than the first, and she swigged some more Pinot.

She launched into a play-by-play of the wedding, the reception, her time with Cole, that moment in her apartment with him. She told Hayden about the hospital, his brothers, and how worried sick he'd been about his mom, keeping the parts about his dad to herself. That felt intensely personal, was Cole's secret.

"It was a whole different side of him," Sierra said. "All of it. The brothers, their weird dynamics, and his concern for his mom. He usually keeps himself locked up tight at work."

"It must be terrifying to have your mom rushed to the hospital," Hayden said. "It's good you were there for him."

Sierra nodded, thinking back on his shakiness, the sheen of sweat she'd seen on his forehead, the stark fear in his eyes. "His mom basically died on the table for a few seconds."

"And he chose to be with you instead of his brothers," Hayden said, her look turning speculative.

"Like I said, weird dynamic. He says they don't like him. His oldest brother was kind of distant to him, but I didn't get that from the other two so much." She told her friend what she knew of the brothers and the fact that his family was the Norths of the largest sporting goods chain in the area. "Good-looking, every last one of them," she said. "Well, the ones that were there. One's in the military and apparently deployed somewhere. I could set you up." The last part she said to get a reaction out of Hayden, who'd sworn off relationships almost a year ago.

"Don't you dare," Hayden said. "So how did the night end?"

"I left him with his brothers, waiting for surgery to be over. I felt bad deserting Cole, but it was pretty awkward once we went upstairs to the ICU waiting room with them. It felt like it should be family only."

"And it was the middle of the night by this point," Hayden said, as if reinforcing she'd made the right decision in leaving. "His mom made it, I take it?"

Sierra told her the basics, which was all clammed-up Cole had given her between yesterday and this morning.

"That's a high-drama night for sure," Hayden said.

"It pales in comparison to this morning at the office," Sierra said.

"Oh?" Hayden leaned closer, planting her chin on her hand, elbow on the counter. "Do tell."

"He was back to reserved Cole, business-only Cole, but even worse than usual. Really buttoned up and he didn't want to talk about his mom at all."

"Like an awkward morning after, and you didn't even get the sex," Hayden said.

"Sort of like that." Sierra spun her glass round and round, her fingers at the base of it, a repetitive, almost subconscious movement as she went back to the morning in her head. She'd been able to tell, from the second he walked into her office, that he was guarded and she was going to have to smack him, figuratively speaking, back to the reality that Saturday had changed things. "I kissed him," she blurted out.

Hayden had raised her glass for a drink, but she froze with her hand midway to her mouth. "What? Like, an *I'm sorry your mom is unwell and I'm here for you* kind of thing?"

Sierra grinned. "More like a *damn, you look good and I need to kiss you to remind you that we practically spent the night together two nights ago* kind of thing."

"Okay." Hayden sat up straighter, lifted her glass in a toast. "Here's to going after what you want."

Sierra laughed, raised her glass, drank. As she set it back down, she said, "Do I want him though?"

"Seems like a resounding yes from here."

"Shit, Hayden, I kissed one of my employees. How many ways is that wrong?"

"How many ways was it right?"

Sierra glared at her, then eyed the bottle, starting to think there wasn't enough wine for the evening. "What if he thinks I harassed him?" she asked, trying to break through her friend's lack of concern.

Hayden's perfectly groomed brows went up. "Harassment would mean he didn't welcome the attention. Did he seem like he didn't want it?"

"He didn't want the personal talk, but the kiss?" She remembered every second of him pulling her closer, his strong hands on her back. "He took control of the kiss."

Hayden let out a quiet sigh of longing.

"You don't want a guy," Sierra reminded her.

"I don't want a boyfriend, but being ravaged by the right guy wouldn't suck."

"Slut," Sierra said, grinning as she went for another healthy swig of wine.

"I haven't had sex for almost a year," Hayden reminded her. "If I'm a slut, I'm failing."

"Mason is the CEO of North Brothers Sports—"

"No."

"Gabe? Friendly guy, good-looking—"

"No."

"Drake is the baby. I got the feeling he can charm the pants off any girl he wants—"

"God no. We're talking about you. What are you going to do about Mr. Foreman?"

Sierra grasped the base of her ponytail and slid her hand down the length of her hair, then threw her head back, gazed at the ceiling. "I don't know. My rule is to not get involved with employees."

"Sounds like you're already involved."

"I could stop it." Sierra's voice sounded a lot more confident than she felt.

"So stop it."

Sierra narrowed her eyes at Hayden.

"You don't want to stop it," Hayden said insightfully. "What's the worst thing that could happen if you and Cole started seeing each other?"

"I lose credibility with the guys. I turn into a female instead of the company owner, their boss, someone they don't think of as a woman."

"I'm pretty sure they think of you as a woman, no matter how much they respect you. You have boobs," Hayden said.

"When things go south with Cole, then there's drama. With him—how do we work together after that? With the rest of the guys—'ooh, maybe she'll sleep with me now that North's out of the way'…"

Hayden, sitting sideways on her stool, leaned her back against the wall, staring at Sierra expectantly.

"One of us, at least, would get hurt," Sierra continued, "and how do you work with someone in that situation?"

"Could be awkward," Hayden admitted. "My take on it? Those are good reasons to not get involved with the guys who work for you. Your personal policy is smart."

"Thank you." She'd never doubted the wisdom of it, never had a problem adhering to it before now.

"But…" Hayden straightened again, her face animated, and Sierra recognized that her BFF was about to tell it like she thought it was. And Sierra welcomed it, because she herself sure as hell couldn't figure out what was what.

She waited while Hayden took a sip of wine.

"But," Hayden said again, "maybe that policy has outlived its usefulness."

Sierra deflated. "Not helpful."

"No, hear me out. How long have you worked at Dunn? Since you were a kid."

"Grandpa let me start as an apprentice when I was ten."

"That's twenty years. And how many times, Cole not included, have you gotten involved with someone who works there, whether you were the owner or not?"

"Zero," Sierra said easily.

"So it's worked. For twenty years. You've never talked about any of your employees in terms of their looks or their date-ability—"

"Because I don't think of them that way," Sierra insisted.

"My point exactly. You don't think of them that way, until Cole. Which tells me that Cole might be special. He broke through."

"It's because he went to the wedding with me."

"It doesn't matter why. Something made you say yes when he offered."

"Desperation," Sierra said with a scoff-laugh.

Hayden slid down from her stool and walked around the mini-bar, planting herself across from Sierra, peering into her eyes. "All I'm trying to say is, maybe Cole could be important to you on a personal level. All these years, maintaining your anti-involvement rule has worked…until this one guy. So maybe you should see where it goes."

"And just throw out twenty years of rules?"

"Why the hell not? Maybe Mr. Foreman is worth it."

"What if he's not?"

"You won't know until you try."

Sierra closed her eyes, a hundred thoughts spinning through her head. "You make it sound so easy."

"Maybe it is."

"But what if it's not? This is my company, my livelihood, my way of life, and I don't want to do anything to screw it up."

"You're being overdramatic."

"I'm being smart," Sierra said. "Or trying to."

"Maybe smart and heart don't go together."

"I need to be smart right now. Things are starting to line up for the company. The Eldridge Mansion thing could be life changing."

"It could be," Hayden said, who'd listened to Sierra ramble about the pros and cons of the competition a few days ago. "But so could Cole North."

"Now who's being overdramatic? I'm talking about sleeping with him, not marrying him."

Hayden shrugged. "Either way. I'm just saying Cole broke through the barriers you lived by for two decades. Maybe you need to see where it goes. Otherwise, you'll always wonder."

Sierra blew out all the air in her lungs, thinking. "I don't even know whether he's interested. The point could be moot."

"Maybe so. Maybe not. At the very least, I think you should kiss him again."

At those words, the memory of kissing him came flaring back, and Sierra couldn't lie to herself. She wanted to feel that way again, wanted to explore that sizzling chemistry that had risen between them suddenly. She wanted to know what it would be like to get closer to him, to be naked with him, to have him on top of her, bearing down on her, inside of her...

Sierra reached for her wineglass, tipped it back, poured more than a delicate sip down her throat.

Maybe she was getting ahead of herself, making it more complex than it needed to be. Maybe Hayden had some good points. Maybe she would always wonder if she didn't pursue him now, assuming he was interested.

Maybe to all of that, but...something told her it wasn't quite that simple.

CHAPTER ELEVEN

Tuesday morning, Cole woke up before his alarm. Long before it, thanks to a never-ending shitty night of tossing and turning and trying to get Sierra out of his mind. Tito, his grumpy cat who looked like a black cat that had had a sack of flour explode nearby, had given up on snuggling hours ago and moved to the spare pillow, where he was currently glaring at Cole.

That kiss yesterday had blown every single fantasy he'd ever had about Sierra to pieces. His fantasies had been enthralling, absorbing, and sexy as hell, but the reality of her was so much more. That kiss, those curves, the sweet taste of her... The memories were visceral, driving him to an ache that was more than physical, that pounded relentlessly through every cell in his body and then some. Nothing would dampen it—not Johnnie Walker Double Black, not an ice-cold shower, not his hand. He'd tried them all.

Though he sometimes hit the office before heading to the day's jobsite, today he was planning to go straight to the Draper home. He was going to time his arrival to be as close to eight a.m. as possible and not a minute earlier. Get there and get straight to business, with no time for small talk, no time to check out Sierra as she climbed down from her badass truck, definitely no time to rehash what had happened in her office yesterday morning.

He didn't know how to cleanse his mind and his body of her, but he had to do something, and soon. Maybe he'd hit a bar and try to find a woman who was interested in a few dirty, sweaty hours between the sheets and nothing more. He didn't do it often, because sometimes it was more trouble than it was worth, but if it would get his boss out of his mind for a night—

His cell phone rang from the nightstand, and Tito darted off the bed, out of the room, probably to lobby near his food bowl. Cole rolled over to see who the hell was looking for him before seven in the morning, and then almost immediately, the thought crashed into him that maybe something was wrong with his mom. Seeing Mason's name on the screen didn't help, because Mason didn't tend to call him unless there was good reason.

"Yeah," Cole answered, breaking into a sweat.

"Hey," Mason said, "can you be at the hospital this morning between eight and ten? That's when the doctor is supposed to make rounds, and one of us needs to be there."

"She's okay?"

"As far as I know," Mason said, and Cole relaxed a degree.

"I thought Drake was doing it," Cole said.

Their youngest brother was the only one who didn't have an eight-to-five. He split his time between being a personal trainer and working part-time shifts at one of the North Brothers Sports stores on the retail floor. He had brains enough, plus the requisite college degree, that he could've worked in just about any department at the corporate office, but Drake showed no interest in it. Whereas Cole's aim was to avoid the family, Drake seemed more against taking responsibility in general.

Yesterday, Drake had said on the brothers' group text, which had started up the day after their mom's heart attack and focused solely on navigating Faye North's health crisis, that he could be at the hospital today to get the doctor's full report. Their mom insisted she could handle it herself, but she was medicated, she was weak, and she was tired. She needed her sons, even if she couldn't admit it, and that's the one thing they all agreed on— they'd be there for her and with her.

"He's not answering his phone," Mason said. "Calls or texts. Gabe and I have the annual management retreat today, otherwise one of us would do it."

There were all kinds of insinuations wrapped up in that one sentence, and Cole resented every single one of them—that their responsibilities with North Brothers Sports were more important than his with Dunn & Lowell, that they were only appealing to him because they had a big management spank-off, that he could just drop everything to pick up the slack for Drake...

For his mom, he would do it.

"Yeah. I'll be there," Cole said.

"They might move her out of ICU today," Mason said unnecessarily.

"I know," Cole said. "Hope so," he added, belatedly remembering his goal of getting along.

"Fill us in on what the doctor says. Thanks, Cole."

"She's my mom too," he said, but Mason didn't hear, as he'd already disconnected. Mr. Important had important things to do.

Now Cole had a legit reason to avoid Sierra today. In the three years he'd worked for her, he'd never called in sick and had taken very little personal time, maybe a couple of hours here and there when it couldn't be helped. Sierra had told him, more than once since Saturday night, to do whatever he needed to do for his mom. Guess he was going to take her up on that offer.

He pulled up her contact info on his phone and shot her a message. As expected, she replied within seconds to take the whole day, more if he needed it, and not to worry about work.

Anything I can do to help? she texted as he was crawling out of bed.

Get out of my damn head was what he wanted to say, but instead, he typed, *Keep a close eye on Barrett. His skills with this type of insulation are untested.* He was still working on trusting Lee Barrett, the new guy, even though he'd been with the company for a couple of months now.

On it, she replied, adding a smiley emoji at the end.

Cole shot out of bed and headed for the shower, which was

approximately five steps away from his bed in his small but adequate apartment. He opened his music app and set it to a metal station, turned on his Bluetooth speaker, and stepped into the shower without letting the water heat up, forcing his mind to his mom and away from a particular brunette.

———

FAYE NORTH'S face had more color today, her short platinum hair looked as if it'd been combed recently, and her brown eyes had a hint of her usual sparkle back in them when Cole sauntered into her ICU room. The head of her bed was angled up to about thirty degrees, and the television was on, though she hit mute as soon as he walked in.

"Hey, Mom. How are you feeling today?" he asked as he hugged her. He slid one of the visitor chairs up next to her and sat down.

"I'm feeling pretty good," she said, smiling. "A little tired, but I managed to get some sleep. Kind of a feat in this place."

"You look better than you did last night," Cole said. He'd stopped to see her on his way home from work, sat with her while she ate her bland dinner, and had taken off when Gabe showed up. "Has the doctor been in yet?"

His mom glanced at the institutional clock on the wall. "It's not even eight yet."

"So no?"

She shook her head and held her hand out in a silent plea for him to grasp it. He did, then rested their interlocked hands on the narrow mattress.

"What happened to your forehead?" she asked.

Another mark of her feeling better, as she hadn't previously noticed the cut from last week's altercation with the asshole at Sunshine's. It was healing well but still impossible to hide, especially from a mom who normally didn't miss much.

"Cole, not another fight?"

"Guy had it coming. It was no big deal."

She exhaled, aggravated with him, as she'd done no less than a hundred thousand times in his life. "Violence doesn't solve anything," she said, also not for the first time.

He could argue that he'd stopped some jackass from continuing to harass a woman, but he knew it wouldn't sway his mom. She hated fighting, always had, and he wasn't a big fan of disappointing her.

"You've always been my rebel," she said.

He let out a quiet, self-deprecating laugh. "If by rebel you mean pain-in-the-ass troublemaker..."

"You had your moments." Her smile was closer to a grimace, but there was no mistaking the understanding in her eyes. "You didn't handle your dad's death well."

Cole pulled his hand away and lodged his elbows on his knees, rubbed his hands over his face. "Let's not tiptoe around things," he said. "I didn't handle much well."

His mom was pensive for a few seconds. "Your troubles started early," she acknowledged. "I've always suspected it was a result of your spot in the family. Mason and Gabe are close in age and have each other. Then came you in the middle, but you were too much younger to bond with the older two. Then the twins came along and had each other. You've always been the odd guy out, and I hated that for you."

He whipped his gaze to hers, surprised at her insight and even more shocked that she'd never mentioned it before. Everything she'd said was spot on. He'd been four when Zane and Drake were born, and he remembered how he'd anticipated being a big brother to someone, instead of the little brother who was too young to do anything with Gabe and Mason. He'd had it in his little-boy mind that the new babies would be his playmates. He hadn't foreseen how the twins would have an instant best friend, hadn't understood the twin bond. He could fully admit—now, and only to himself—he'd grown up feeling like he didn't fit anywhere. Too old for his younger brothers, too young for his older brothers, his own little island in the middle of the family. He'd never fared any better with the kids at school either. He should've known his mom recognized the issue.

"Natural order of things, I guess," he said, trying to blow off something that had unquestionably played a big part in his screwed-up psyche.

His mom reached over and rubbed his head. "I never wanted that for you. Your dad used to accuse me of spoiling you a little extra to compensate. He was probably right. Then when he died, I had my hands full with just getting up in the morning and taking care of you and the twins and handling the business."

"I didn't make it easy on you." And wasn't that an understatement. "I'm sorry for that," he said for the first time ever. "For all the crap I caused. You didn't deserve any of it."

She shook her head, as if he didn't need to apologize, which was bull. He'd caused this woman so much angst and heartache that he would never be able to make it up to her even if they both lived another hundred years.

"It's been good to see you more these past few days. I just wish I hadn't needed the heart attack to get you here." She grinned, and he knew she was giving him shit, but her words cut at him anyway. His doing, hundred percent.

He sat up straight, grasped her hand again. "I'm going to do better. Going to make a point of coming to Sunday dinner once you're well enough. But first we have to get you recovered, and I'll be here for that too."

His mom never got a response out, because at that moment, his loud-ass youngest brother blew through the doorway.

"Hey, how's my favorite lady in the whole world?" Drake said with his full-of-shit factor fully engaged. He wore his usual gym shorts and a wine-colored T-shirt from one of the honky-tonks on Broadway.

"Morning, Drake." Their mom held out her other hand toward him and sent him a warm smile.

"What are you doing here?" Drake said to Cole. "Thought you had to work today."

"I had to make sure someone was here when the doctor comes in," Cole said curtly.

"I'm here," Drake said. "Like I said I would be."

"Ten minutes late. You could've missed him," Cole said.

"You boys..." Their mom had dropped both their hands and

was raising the head of her bed more. "Would you believe, after sixty-four years on this earth, I can talk to the doctor myself?"

"You're medicated," Drake said.

"You might not think of all the questions to ask," Cole added.

"I have a heart condition, not brain damage," she said. "But I know you mean well, and I appreciate it."

"Good morning." A tall, thin nurse who looked to be in her fifties entered and glanced from Drake to Cole to Faye. "You've got a room full."

"My boys take up a lot of space," their mom said with a note of affection in her voice.

"You didn't tell me you breed 'em big and handsome."

"We didn't come out this big," Drake said, his charm setting on high, and Cole shook his head.

The nurse laughed, as Drake had been aiming for.

"I'm Drake." He held out his hand, glanced at the whiteboard on the wall with all the medical staff's names, and said, "You must be Nurse Angelica."

"I am. Nice to meet you, Drake. Would you two mind giving your mom and me some privacy for a few minutes?"

"You got it," Drake said.

Cole nodded once as he pushed out of his chair and followed his brother out to the hallway.

"What the hell, Cole?" Drake said once they were in the wide hallway. They wandered past a couple of patient rooms, the wide glass doors keeping patients visible to medical personnel and everyone else. "I said I'd be here."

"You should've answered Mason's texts or calls this morning."

"My phone is busted. Shattered it at the gym."

Cole swore to himself. "If you were better at showing up when you say you will, he wouldn't assume you'd blow it off."

"You should talk," Drake said.

Cole halted as they came to an intersection in the hall. He leaned his upper body against the wall, the doorway to their mom's room in his line of sight. "If I say I'll be somewhere, I'll be there." He was smart enough most times to not promise much, but if he did, he followed through. Drake, on the other hand, had a rep for overpromising.

Drake took up a similar position on the opposite wall and shook his head. "This is Mom. I wouldn't skip out."

At the sudden rawness that rang through his brother's voice, Cole backed off. "You know Mason," he said with a shrug.

"Directing a multimillion-dollar circus isn't enough. He's got to micromanage the family as well."

"Hit the nail on the head," Cole said. "He was about to flip his shit by the time he called me."

Drake smirked and shook his head. "It must suck to be him."

"It must," Cole said, cracking half a grin himself. Their high-strung oldest brother had always been something they could agree on.

"Mom seems more like herself today," Drake said.

"She gave me the *fighting doesn't solve anything* lecture, so yeah."

Drake laughed. "Maybe one day you'll take that one to heart."

Cole scoffed. "You should talk." He checked the time on his watch, saw it was crawling toward nine a.m. "You need to go buy a new phone?"

"As soon as I'm done here," Drake said. "I don't have my next shift at the gym until this afternoon."

Cole glanced toward their mom's room again, where the nurse still hadn't come back out. "Go ahead. I got this."

"Don't you have to get to work?"

"I took the day off. You might as well take advantage of it." Cole straightened, seeing the nurse emerge from their mom's room.

Drake's gaze followed his. "You sure? I could stand to get some food too."

"Goes without saying," Cole said. "I'm here. If I didn't want to stay, I'd say so."

Drake nodded. "I'll slip in and tell Mom bye, come back tonight between the gym and my date. Thanks, man," Drake said as they started back down the hall toward her room. "I owe you one."

Cole didn't point out that Drake was already doing him a favor. While their mom was unquestionably the priority, it sure as shit didn't suck to have a legit reason to avoid Sierra for the day.

CHAPTER TWELVE

It was almost quitting time Friday afternoon, and the crew was finishing up for the week at the Draper home, cleaning the site for the weekend, loading up what equipment they wouldn't need next week. Sierra was pondering important questions as she secured her laptop and some papers in her truck: Red or white wine? Happy hour solo in her apartment or out at the bars with Hayden?

One way or another, there would be a happy hour.

It'd been a hell of a week, between the challenges of a hundred-year-old house with an attitude, getting her ducks in a row on the Eldridge app as she waited for Cole's input, and, well, personal stuff. Personal Cole stuff. Stuff she shouldn't let bother her, but dammit, it was bothering her.

Since Monday morning, when she'd swan-dived over the line and kissed Cole in her office, he'd managed to avoid spending any private time with her. After his day off on Tuesday, which she fully understood and supported, he'd made a painful point of not starting or ending the day at the Dunn & Lowell offices, as he normally did several times a week, and he showed up at the Draper site as close to starting time as he could get without being late, giving them zero opportunity to discuss anything but the day's work. Which was his objective, obviously.

She didn't need to hash out the kiss or their feelings, but

she'd thought they were past the stiff, impersonal professionalism stage. Long past it. Clearly, kissing him had been a mistake. Message received. But what had happened to the companionship, the camaraderie they'd built up over, oh, either three years or, at the very least, last weekend?

Red wine it was. She needed the mellow relaxation…plus the ability to stop picking apart every interaction—or lack thereof—with Cole. Though it was getting chilly as the sun lowered in the sky, maybe she'd see if Hayden was up for red wine on the balcony with a warm blanket or two this evening.

Sierra shut the door on her truck, intent on one last trip inside to make sure the guys had cleaned their work area to her standards. As she made her way past the back end of the truck, toward the house, and tried to step up on the curb, she somehow misjudged and stepped wrong and—

Shit!

She went down in excruciating pain, biting down on a stream of swear words as her ankle bent in ways it wasn't meant to. Tears burned in her eyes as she sat there at the side of the street, trying to figure out what had happened, but then she couldn't think around the pain. It radiated out from her ankle, up her leg, down into her foot. She sat there frozen, dumbfounded, the breath squeezed out of her by the pain.

As she gradually came out of her stupor, her first thought was to get up before someone discovered her. She got her left foot under her and tried to baby her right foot into following suit but —No. Hell no.

Shit, this was bad.

With a slow, shaky inhale, she tried to maneuver to the curb, with the intent of pulling herself up to it to evaluate the situation. With some effort and a shit ton of determination, she made it and sat there on the concrete curb, panting.

"Sierra?"

She closed her eyes at the sound of Lee Barrett's voice behind her, several dozen feet away. Her instinct was to brush off her injury and stand up to face her most recent hire, but the truth was, she was barely managing to get oxygen in and out of her lungs over the throbbing pain.

"Sierra!" he called again, concern creeping into his voice, and she heard his steps quickening to a jog across the grassy yard behind her. "You okay?"

"Yeah," she managed. "Sort of. I twisted my ankle."

"Let me help you up," he said kindly.

As much as she was wired to do it herself, she couldn't deny she needed a hand, so she let him grip her arm as she got her left foot solidly under her again and tried to get her right one in position just for balance if not for support. Right foot was having none of it though, and she swore before she could stop herself, sitting back on the curb hard.

"That's not good," Lee said as Sierra squeezed her eyes shut against tears again.

"Hey." Cole approached from behind, and she could tell he, too, was moving faster than a walk, and she hated that she was causing a scene. "What's going on?"

"She hurt her ankle," Lee said since she couldn't get her voice to work, mainly because she was fighting so hard not to cry like a damn girl. "It seems pretty bad. I was just trying to help her stand."

"She shouldn't stand," Cole said, aggravation in his voice. "I've got this. You go close up after the others."

"You sure? I can—"

"Go," Cole barked out. He came around to the front of Sierra, studying her face instead of her ankle, and she reluctantly met his gaze, trying to hide how much she hurt.

"I think it's just a sprain. I somehow missed the curb—" Emotion crackled through her voice and she bit down on it, shook her head in sheer frustration with herself.

"It's okay," Cole said in a quiet, gentle voice. "Let's get a look. I'm going to take your boot off, okay?"

She nodded as she blew out another shaky breath. "I hate this."

He let out a low sort-of laugh, but instead of irritating her, it soothed with its understanding. "Most people don't like pain too much."

Oh, she hated the pain, but even more, she hated being laid out, useless, weakened.

Her entire lower leg pulsed with pain as Cole rolled up her loose cargo pants leg and unlaced her work boot. When he eased it off, she bit down on a whimper. She shut her eyes against the pain, and the next thing she knew, Cole was brushing his finger across her cheek, intercepting a tear she hadn't realized had spilled over. Mainly because she was trying so hard not to scream.

"I'm going to take you to the ER," he said. "It's already swelling up like a balloon."

"No ER. It's not broken, just sprained." All she wanted was home, an ice pack, and that bottle of wine.

"How do you know?"

"There was no snap," she said stubbornly.

He put his hand just above her knee on her uninjured leg, and she couldn't help noticing the intimate touch, his first since Monday. It almost made up for the amused look on his face. "That means nothing, and you know it."

She shook her head adamantly. "I'm not going to the ER. It's Friday night and it'd take forever. Besides," she said, eyeing her ankle as she gingerly eased her sock down, "it's too swollen for them to tell anything. They'd make me come back on Monday for an X-ray." At least she thought she remembered something like that happening to her brother years ago.

Cole stared at her fat ankle, then trailed a finger halfway down her bare shin, his touch featherlight, pulling away before he got to the injured area. All she could think was, *Thank God I shaved this morning.*

"You're probably right," he said. His gaze moved to something behind her, and she turned to see the rest of her crew, all four of them, rounding the corner of the house, carrying their belongings, talking and joking among themselves with a light, Friday-afternoon air about them.

"Oh," Carlos said when they were a few feet away. He was

young, only twenty-six, but he'd been working for her for almost seven years. "That doesn't look good."

"Better have that checked out," Troy, Dunn & Lowell's master plumber, said.

"See?" Cole said.

"I will," Sierra answered. "Monday." *Maybe*. "Did you guys get everything cleaned up for the weekend?"

"Yes, ma'am," Demetrius said. "Dust vacuumed up, tools put away."

"Thank you. Have a good weekend." Sierra threw a casual wave over her shoulder to all of them, more than ready for them to move on and stop gawking at her ankle, which, admittedly, was getting uglier by the minute.

"You have a way to get home?" Carlos said. "'Cause I don't think you're driving."

"I'll get her home," Cole said, standing and emanating his silent but unmistakable take-charge manner—and maybe a hint of possessiveness? Was she imagining that? "See you guys on Monday."

Her crew got the message and called out their goodbyes as they made their way to their various vehicles.

Cole squatted in front of her again, his focus back on her ankle.

"I'll ice it and stay off it all weekend," she said before he could lobby for the emergency room again. "Promise."

"Let's get you in your truck. I'll take it and you home."

"And do what? Your truck will be stuck here."

"I'll come get it later."

She scanned for his bright blue Ram, found it parked a ways down the residential street. With no other immediate options, she nodded.

"Ready for the hard part?" he asked her, his palms on his thighs as he stood again. Before she could ask what the hard part was, he extended a hand to her.

Yeah. Standing.

She eyed his hand for a moment, mostly trying to gather the nerve to put weight on her bad foot but partly also taking in every detail of Cole's strong, masculine hand. He had his share of callouses, just like her, and…

And she wasn't going to think beyond that.

When he raised his brows in question, she took his hand and snapped back to the challenge of standing. The pain on her right side just from shifting her leg slightly had her biting down on a gasp.

"Can you put any weight on it?" he asked.

"I don't think so. Not until I get a bottle of wine down."

Cole bent over her, and before she could fully register the male scent that filtered to her nose, he grasped her torso under her arms and prepared to hoist her up. His palms were a hairsbreadth away from her breasts and she couldn't think about anything else—until he lifted her to her feet, and though she held her right foot up, balancing on her left, the pain stabbed at her. She let out a sharp exhale and grabbed his arm even though he hadn't yet let go of her.

"I've got you," he said. "We're not moving yet. Just get your balance."

Her balance would be an easier task than her equilibrium, what with him so close, supporting her with such an intimate touch. They were standing a couple of feet away from the tailgate of her truck, and she sized up the distance to the passenger's door. Maybe ten feet, but those were going to be ten excruciating feet.

"I can carry you," Cole said.

"No." Her protest came out quickly. It was broad daylight, they were in the middle of a neighborhood with plenty of people coming and going, including some of her crew who had yet to drive away, and she was not going to have him lugging her around. "If you could just support me and walk by me, I'll make it."

"Your call," he said, his tone saying he thought she was being stupid.

It took forever and a day, but she finally made it to the door, a sheen of sweat breaking out all over her body with the effort. She'd put minimal weight on her bad side with every step, and her eyes were still burning with tears from the ache. Cole had opened the truck door, and it hit her how tall her damn vehicle was. It didn't normally faze her, but this was going to take some doing.

"If you'd like to drop your stubbornness for about five seconds, I'll lift you up there and it'll be over with," Cole said.

One more glance at the truck, the height of the running board, the additional height of the cab…

"Okay," she said. "You win. Please help me."

He scooped her up and set her on the high seat seemingly without effort, shutting her in before she could exhale. She waited for him to open the driver's-side door, and when he didn't, she checked the mirror to see where he'd gone. It took a few seconds, but she finally spotted him at his truck, with the door open as he stretched inside for something. When the door closed, she could see he carried a duffel bag and was still wearing his tool belt.

As he headed back toward her, she turned her attention to her seat belt. He pulled the driver's door open, put his bag and tool belt behind the seat in the extended cab, and climbed up to the driver's seat. When he closed the door, the space shrunk and the air between them seemed to pulse as they looked at each other, neither one speaking. After a few seconds, Cole held his hand out. When she glanced at it, he said, "Keys?"

Keys. Of course.

Sierra dug into one of the baggy pockets in her cargos, pulled out the key ring, and handed it to him.

Her usual country playlist filled the cab with a Maren Morris song, and Sierra turned it up loud enough it wasn't necessary for them to talk. They made most of the twenty-minute drive without conversation, with the exception of Cole asking whether she needed him to stop at the office for anything. She declined and texted Reggie, who'd been working back at the shop behind the office today, making sure he would lock up for the weekend.

Cole turned into the alley behind Sierra's apartment and parked in her spot, turned off the engine. "How's your pain level?"

"My leg hurts up to my ears," she said with a strained smile.

"Stay there." He got out and came around to her side, opened the door, stepped closer.

"I can get down on my own," she said, planning to turn sideways and slide and land on her good foot.

"I'm sure you can, but what are you going to do about the stairs?"

The damn stairs. She hadn't gotten that far in her mind yet. She sagged into the seat, closed her eyes for a moment, then appealed to him with a tired, sheepish smile. "Hope for some hot, muscular guy to take pity on me and carry me up."

"Since you said *hot*..."

With a hint of a grin, he scooped her up again before she was ready, careful not to bang her leg against the truck door, and Sierra wound her arms around his neck.

"My laptop..." she said as he headed toward the exterior steps.

"I'll come back and get it."

As he carried her upstairs, twenty-two steps without breathing hard or breaking a sweat, she relaxed into him gradually. When they reached the outer door, her head rested on his shoulder, and she was lost in the aroma of a man who'd worked his ass off all day—a little natural musk and the slightest hint of shaving cream left over from hours ago. He used her key, and by the time they reached her apartment door inside, she wanted to spend more time with him like this, with their guard down, the stiff, professional boundaries gone.

"Cole?" she said, lifting her head to look him in the eye as he carried her across the threshold into her apartment. He was being so gentle and caring, so different from the hard, seemingly unemotional man she was used to. It made it a challenge for her to think straight, because, while she genuinely liked the nine-to-five version of Cole, this version... He was hard to resist.

She didn't want to resist.

"Yeah?"

"Is your mom waiting for you tonight?"

"No. I'll see her tomorrow. My cousins are entertaining her tonight."

She waited until he set her on the chaise end of her sectional, so there was some space between them, suspecting that would put him more at ease and work in her favor. Then she debated with herself.

She wanted wine, ice, and acetaminophen in the next five minutes. But once she took the edge off the throb in her not-broken ankle, she wanted to get personal with Cole. Work policy be damned. Because she'd been thinking about what Hayden had said all week, and her points were all valid. Maybe Cole *was* special, maybe it was significant that he was the first guy to make her want to break her own rules.

"Stay for dinner," she said, still perched on the edge of the cushion with her bum leg elevated, intent on getting him to agree. "We'll get carryout. My treat. To say thanks." She added that last bit hoping it would sway him.

He exhaled as he straightened, seeming to consider what she'd thrown out there as an order more than a proposal. "Plus you need someone to do the carrying out," he said, the corners of his mouth tugging upward.

"I know people at Clayborne's. I could get it delivered."

He gazed down at her. Whether it was because they were away from work in a private place or because she'd just been hanging on to his neck like a damsel in distress, his uptightness from the past week had disappeared completely. Weekend Cole was back. "I'd planned to get you settled in, make sure you have whatever you need for the night," he said finally. "I'll pick up some food. And I'll stay for dinner."

CHAPTER THIRTEEN

It was becoming a pattern, Cole thought as he walked down the brick sidewalk of Hale Street toward Clayborne's. Once again, he was choosing not to play it smart where a certain brunette was concerned.

He could've said no to dinner, but he'd meant what he said about making sure she had what she needed for the night. Because he couldn't help being concerned for her, caring about her. He'd been attracted to her for years, but those blurred lines were fucking with his head, making him think it was more than physical.

Bottom line, he was staying for dinner because he wasn't ready to go to his quiet apartment. Because he wanted to spend a little more time with Sierra.

While he'd borrowed her shower to get the work dirt off, fighting not to think too hard about her standing in that same space naked every day, afterward changing into clean jeans and a long-sleeved thermal shirt from his duffel, Sierra had called in their order. It still took several minutes once he got to Clayborne's, due, in part, to the Friday after-work crowd that already filled the place. Since there was a band playing later tonight, it would only get worse. He waited by the counter, nodding at Ivy and Violet, who sat at a high-top table halfway across the room.

Thirty minutes later, he climbed the flight of stairs back to

Sierra's apartment. Before he let himself in, he paused outside her door for half a second, thinking how weird it was to let himself in anywhere besides his own place or his mom's house. He'd not gotten that comfortable with anyone before, and he wasn't sure he was comfortable with it now. With a shrug, he reminded himself he didn't want Sierra getting off the couch and hopping across the room to open the door for him.

She looked up when he walked in, and the first thing he noticed was that she'd managed to shower and had a different ice pack on her ankle. Instead of her dusty work clothes, she wore yoga pants and a baggy hooded sweatshirt, nothing but the ice pack on her feet, and her hair was damp and down, falling over her shoulders. She was sitting with her legs stretched out on the sectional, perpendicular to the chaise, her back against the arm of it, facing him and the rest of the room. Her laptop, which he'd brought up before he left, was on her lap, and an almost-empty wineglass sat on a small mosaic table that angled over the cushion of the chaise, a dark, uncorked bottle next to it.

"You showered," he said.

"You're brilliant," she popped right back, sitting up straighter, her eyes lit up like they hadn't been when he'd left.

"Wet hair gave it away." He set the food bag down on the end table next to the couch.

"No. I mean, you're brilliant. This… The Eldridge thing…" She pointed at the laptop screen. "The changes you made… Your writing…" She sputtered like he hadn't heard her sputter before, then shook her head. "We need to talk. There's a story. But food…"

Evidently, she'd been reading the email he'd sent her that morning with his suggested changes to the Eldridge Mansion application. He suspected he knew what she was going to ask about, what story she was going to demand. Maybe she'd forget, be sidetracked by dinner.

As he walked into the kitchen area, he asked, "Where are the plates?"

She directed, "To the left of the sink. There might be a couple of beers in the back of the fridge, or you're welcome to some wine. Or water or soda. Help yourself. I'd get it for you, but—"

"Don't you dare." He took another wineglass from the cabinet. He wasn't a big wine drinker and knew he ran zero risk of overindulging.

He carried the plates, napkins, and the empty glass with him to the living area and sat on the opposite end of the couch from her, a few inches from her feet. As he unpacked the Styrofoam containers and distributed them, poured himself a glass of wine, and settled into the cushions to do some damage on his dinner, Sierra quizzed him on the Clayborne's crowd and the preparations for the band. He learned she saw a lot of live bands at the bar down the block but that she wasn't a big fan of the one playing tonight. He confessed it had been a couple of years since he'd been to any kind of concert.

And that, apparently, was the end of the small talk.

"So," she said after eating her first few pretzel bites dipped in cheese sauce. "Your changes to the Eldridge application, the essays, they're excellent. Huge improvement. Thank you," she gushed.

"Welcome," he said quietly, uncomfortably, turning his attention to his double burger.

"You're a really good writer. Super talented. The way you took what I had and restructured it to make more sense... It's amazing how well it flows now. I had the pertinent stuff kind of spewed out so that it all got on the page, but you made each one read almost like a story. That takes skills. And I see what you mean now about marketing. You were subtle but effective."

His mouth was full, so he didn't respond except for a single nod.

"You can shove that burger in your mouth all you want, but I still want to know some things," she said.

When he'd swallowed the bite, he said, lightly, "Are we on the clock or off right now?"

"Gray area." She took a sip of her wine, emptying the glass, then poured some more. "You've got uncanny math skills, you could do project managing effectively in your sleep, and you write like a freaking *New York Times* best seller. *Why* are you working construction, Cole?"

"Why are you?" he threw back at her even though he knew her reasons.

"It's what I love," she said simply, holding her wineglass up in front of her, seeming to have forgotten her food for now. "It's in my blood. It's my grandpa's legacy. It's what I burn to do. You know that. I'm not quiet about it."

No, she wasn't quiet about it, and her passion for restoring old buildings was part of her charm.

She unwrapped her ham and cheese melt, took a bite, and peered at him, waiting for his answer.

He ate a couple of fries, buying himself some time. Then he said, "Long story. Not very interesting."

"Nice try. Will you tell me?" she said more quietly, less bossily. "Please?"

Maybe he could've kept refusing had she continued to be demanding, but the soft, interested plea... It wouldn't kill him to rehash the past. Maybe it would even throw up an obstacle or two between them. Maybe once she got to know him better, she'd see him differently and back off. Maybe he didn't truly want that, but it sure as shit would be wiser.

He crossed one ankle over the other knee, balanced his plate on his lap, set his burger down, his mind tumbling over the past, his life, a lot of bad stuff, a lot of things he wasn't proud of.

"I chose not to go to college," he finally said, skipping over years of drama. "My high school counselor claimed I could've gotten in anywhere—Ivy League, Berkeley, MIT. I narrowed it down to a handful, filled out the applications, wrote the essays. Never sent a single one in."

When Sierra remained quiet, he glanced at her. She sat there expectantly, head tilted, eyes narrowed, waiting for more. And because he'd always wanted to give her what she wanted, he tipped his head back, sucked in a deep breath, and decided to tell her. What the hell.

"I learned to read early," he said hesitantly, "before preschool.

And math… My mom says I was doing long division when I was four."

"Wow. You're one of those."

"One of what?" he asked, that age-old pit-in-his-stomach feeling ramping up without his permission.

"Smarty-pants." Sierra smiled, angled her head cutely, a long lock of damp hair falling over her cheek, distracting him from the pit feeling somewhat. "Brainiacs. Know-it-alls. Child geniuses."

"I got called all those and more," he said grimly. He'd never let anyone know, back then, how much those names bothered him. Was self-aware enough to understand that letting on that they bugged him would only make it worse, would encourage the names.

"I didn't mean it as an insult," Sierra said quickly. "High IQs are sexy." The dip of her voice as she said that, the flirty sparkle in her eyes—*that* was sexy.

"Not when you're seven," he said, forcing himself to look away. "When you skip first grade and still get pulled out of class to go to 'gifted' sessions, people think you're a freak."

"Kids can be mean."

"They came around pretty fast because they wanted me on their team in baseball during recess."

"You played baseball?"

"My whole family played baseball. When my dad and uncle started North Brothers Sports in the seventies, it was a specialty baseball store. A single location, much smaller, it had nothing but baseball gear. Both of them played in the minors for a couple years. When that fell through for my dad, he had the idea for the store, and within a year, my uncle was cut from his team and they went for it."

"So you've got baseball genes," Sierra said, having finally started eating again but looking wrapped up in his story and only half-aware of her food.

"I guess you could say that. We all played little league, played in high school. Mason and Drake played in college. Gabe had interest from colleges but went a different direction."

"Did you? Have interest from colleges?"

He blew out a breath, that sick feeling doubling back on him. He wanted to scare her off? This was his chance. "From the time I was a freshman in high school, I made varsity. Was one of the starting pitchers."

"Baseball players are hot," she said, her brows rising on her forehead. She said it with a lightness, a playfulness in her voice, but Cole was feeling anything but light and playful.

"I got kicked off the team my junior year," he forced out, and then, maybe to ensure that he erased all the lightness in the room, he added, "That's what my dad and I fought about the day before he died."

CHAPTER FOURTEEN

*S*ierra's features dropped, and she let out a soft sound of sympathy. "I'm so sorry."

Cole shook his head, scowling. "No need to be sorry. My own fault."

"Why did you get kicked off?"

He'd stopped eating a while back, after only getting down half his burger, and now, he set the plate on the end table next to him. "I was an asshole." Still was to this day, matter of fact, but she'd figure that out on her own if she hadn't already.

"I was messed up in the head," he continued. "I stood out in a bad way because I was smart. I knew early that the kids who wanted me on their team were using me. They weren't my friends, not real friends. I didn't really have any real friends. Didn't seem to fit in anywhere." He couldn't help thinking about his mother's comment the other day about him not fitting in with his brothers. Even in his close-knit family, he was different. "I started getting into trouble in grade school. Got in a couple fights on the playground, disrupted class because I was bored and hated being thought of as teacher's pet or the golden boy. In middle school, I argued with teachers, was disrespectful, fought some more." He shook his head, hating the little prick he was describing.

"Defying stereotypes," Sierra said insightfully.

He nodded, not letting himself think too hard about how well she understood, like no one else had. "Still got good grades. The teachers hated that. Here was this little shit who liked to argue in class and disrupt things, and he was a straight-A student. Teacher's dream on the one hand. Worst nightmare on the other." Not for the first time, he felt bad for all the crappy days he must've caused for his teachers over the years.

"In high school, making varsity as a freshman meant I was respected, but it didn't make me any real friends. Maybe it could've, but by that time, I was…" He shook his head again, searching for the right word.

"Jaded?" Sierra tried.

"You could say that. The guys invited me to do stuff, go to parties, hang out, but I knew they only liked me because I was good at baseball."

"You didn't even let them get to know you," she said. "Maybe they would've liked you for you."

Cole shrugged. "Wasn't going to give them the opportunity. I'd spent a lot of years not fitting in."

"And what happened to get you kicked off the team? Junior year, right?"

Cole laughed, but there was no humor in it. More of a scoff. "The varsity coach was a good guy. Always trying to get through to me, make me a better person, but I was so pissed off at the world." He swallowed and looked over at Sierra, found her watching him intently, enthralled, not showing any signs of disgust with him as she should. "I'm not proud of any of this, just so you know." He hated it, all of it, wished he could go back and do it all over. God, how he wished that.

Sierra nodded, obviously waiting for him to finish the story.

"I argued with Coach one too many times. I showed up for practice late—yet again, because I was a shithead—and he'd had enough. Told me they didn't need me at practice that day, that I should sit it out and figure out what was important to me. Like an entitled little bastard, I shot the F bomb at him, and that was it. He booted me for the season."

"Ouch," Sierra said.

"Now you know why I don't tell people any of this."

"We all do stupid stuff when we're growing up."

"I did more than my share. There's no sugarcoating it."

"You needed something that you weren't able to find," she said, and he closed his eyes, a little dumbfounded that anyone could find it in them to be empathetic to his former asshole self.

"I needed a kick in the ass. Which my dad tried to give me that night when I got home. Coach had called him, told him what had happened."

"Oh, no."

He nodded dully, his gut churning so hard he wondered if the half burger might come up. "I'm sure you won't be surprised when I tell you I wasn't open to that kick in the ass."

"Angry teenagers usually aren't."

"It was ugly," Cole said, closing his eyes, remembering some of the horrible things he'd said that night. "All he was doing was trying to get me straightened out, to make me see how my attitude was screwing up my future. I'd blown my chances for a baseball scholarship in a three-minute exchange with my coach."

"Junior year? Just like that?" Sierra asked.

"I might've been able to recoup senior year. Coach told my dad he'd take me back if I got my act together." He shook his head, his jaw rigid, regret so deep he could feel it in his marrow. "I told my dad what he and Coach could do with it—" His voice cracked with emotion and he backed off the story.

"And then the next day…" Sierra set her food and the ice pack aside and awkwardly moved to his end of the couch, putting all her weight on her good leg in the process, her injured foot resting on the floor.

"Don't hurt yourself," he said, glad to have something to break up his memories.

"I'm fine." She sat at his side, only a couple of inches between their legs, shoulders touching. "I can only imagine what hearing about your dad's accident did to you."

Grief rolled through him, heavy and slow, like some kind of insidious mercury spill poisoning him cell by cell. He couldn't have spoken at that moment if he had to. Sierra apparently understood that. She rested her head on his shoulder, and he closed his eyes, breathed in the feminine scent of her shampoo and soap, putting all his attention on identifying the vaguely familiar aroma. Vanilla, he thought, with hints of something sweet and fruity. Citrus or orange. There was another note of something in there but he couldn't figure it out, quit trying, just kept inhaling, letting it, letting *her* level him out.

After some time had passed, a couple of minutes, maybe more, Sierra shifted her arm, laid her hand over his, and wove their fingers together. Their interlocked hands rested on his thigh, and the sight of them together—his large hand covered by her small one, his skin rougher and a darker suntanned hue than hers—afforded him another distraction from the ugly stuff in his head and his heart. Until she spoke again.

"How does working construction fit into all of this?"

He scoffed at himself. "It was expected, mostly unspoken but expected, that we'd all eventually work for the family business. It'd grown into multiple locations plus a corporate office, had expanded into a full spectrum of sports gear and supplies, not just baseball. Mason was already out of college and moving up at corporate. Gabe was about to graduate and join him. I was supposed to follow in their tracks."

She angled her head to look up at him from the side. "No?" she guessed.

"Back then it was a hell no." This, the angry part, was a lot easier to talk about than the accident. "When I look back now, I figure I could've gone one of two ways when my dad died. I could've gotten my act together, changed my ways, gotten back on track, or I could let myself be overcome by the blackest anger. Seventeen-year-old Cole chose anger."

Sierra's only response was to squeeze his fingers.

"They thought I was bad before, but that was nothing," he said. "Senior year was more fights, more visits to the principal's office because of mouthing off. I started skipping classes, stopped doing homework, grades plummeted, but I'd had a high GPA to start with, so I managed to graduate in spite of myself."

"But no college."

"That was my giant fuck-off to the world," he said. "At least that's how I viewed it. I'd show them. Family expectations? Shove 'em. Family business? Hell no. I think I thought, subconsciously anyway, if I didn't go to college, I *couldn't* work for North Brothers. It'd shut them the hell up. To make sure of it, I signed away my rights to my share of the company." He blew out a heavy breath. "I know what a jackass I must sound like." She had to be grasping exactly how giant of one, and even though that was his original intention, it bothered him. "I'm sure you don't understand. Have you ever done anything rebellious in your life?"

Sierra laughed and raised her head from his shoulder. "Have you seen what I do for my career?" She sat up straighter and grimaced when she raised her bad leg. It had to be killing her to rest it on the floor.

"I chose not to go to college too," she said. "I knew what I wanted to do, was already doing it. Couldn't wait to do it full-time. My parents didn't understand. My siblings, I'm sure, thought I was stupid and spoiled. My grandpa was still running the company then, and he supported me. After a couple of years, he encouraged me to get an associate's degree in construction management. I did it online, before online was cool or common or respected. So yeah. I might not have had the anger thing going for me, but I've gone against the grain and done the opposite of what everyone else thought I should."

This time he was the one to squeeze her fingers. He'd not thought about it before, what she must've gone through back then, the battles she'd had to fight herself, whether internal or with her family. She was such a strong leader, so sure of what she was doing now that it was hard to imagine her struggling with the decision back then.

"You are a little rebel," he said with a half grin, attempting to lighten the mood.

She narrowed her eyes at him. "*Little* makes it almost condescending, but I'll let it slide this once."

"You're little." He raised their hands to prove his point. "But fierce," he added, to keep the peace.

It seemed to work, because she said, "So instead of college and the family business, you decided construction?"

"I skipped my graduation ceremony and took a job in road construction because it was available. Found that the hard, manual stuff helped me block out my thoughts, but there was a lot of standing around, waiting, chances for the mind to wander, so I switched to buildings instead of roads."

"Any regrets?" she asked.

Only a planet-sized abyss of them. "I like working at Dunn & Lowell," he said, which was the truth, if only part of it. It was much easier not to get into the rest. And way past time to change the subject and the mood. "Decent boss. If you like bossy."

"Best freaking boss in the industry," she said with exaggerated conviction. "And you guys need bossy. And I need to elevate my ankle." She scooted to the edge of the cushion, stood on her good leg, then, before he knew what her aim was, she climbed on top of him.

CHAPTER FIFTEEN

ole sat there for a couple of seconds, with Sierra's legs draped across his lap, her delectable ass planted on the side next to the end table and her legs pointing in the opposite direction of how she'd started out, letting his brain catch up to his body. His body had already registered that she was on top of him. Need surged through him, centered in his cock, which was alert and pressing against his jeans uncomfortably.

Sierra let out a breath. "That's better. For me," she said and quickly met his gaze. "Is this okay? For you?"

So damn okay. He couldn't stop himself from reaching for her, running his fingers through her nearly dry hair. "Yeah," was all he said.

She averted her eyes, inhaled, which made her chest rise. He'd never had such a front-row view of her tits, and even though they were disguised by a bulky sweatshirt, he was entranced.

"Speaking of boss and work..." she said, and then she lifted her gaze to his, her long, pretty lashes framing doe eyes the color of milk chocolate. "I had good reasons for my rule about not getting involved with employees."

"Smart policy," he managed to get out as he fought the urge to pull her closer.

She nodded. "It was smart. But I've decided that sometimes

you have to adhere to the rules so that you can recognize when they should be broken."

The ache that centered between his legs, approximately point-two inches from her thigh, pulsed harder. "Strangely enough, I follow you."

"I've been doing this job since before puberty, and never once has anyone tempted me until now. It takes a lot to break through my blinders, so I think, now that you have, I shouldn't fight it."

She reached a hand up to the back of his neck, her gaze dipping down to his lips as she pulled his head closer. Cole zeroed in on her rosy lips, the slight bow of the top one, waiting, forcing himself to let her do the advancing. It seemed to take her a year to reach him, to touch her mouth to his, and when she did, he heard a groan escape him, of relief, need, lust. His fingers in her hair tightened, held her to him as every one of his senses was engulfed by her, reacted to her. His body burned for her, and as her tongue swirled into his mouth, the heat of her breath meshing with his, it took everything in him not to roll her under him, strip her down, and bury himself inside of her.

Rein it in, asshole.

One of her hands found its way under his shirt, and her fingers trailed up his chest as she angled her body toward his, her hip pressing into his erection. The friction elicited another groan, had him pressing his body into her, pulling her more firmly against him. It was ecstasy and torture at once, because it wasn't enough, would never be enough until there was nothing between them and he could slide his overheated skin directly against hers.

He trailed his hand to the hem of her sweatshirt, dipped it beneath the thick cotton, expecting to find another layer of material but instead was treated to her baby-soft, taut flesh. Her body was so slender and compact that he could nearly reach halfway around her with one hand, and it awakened some primal, ages-old instinct in him to guard her, protect her, keep her safe.

As their mouths continued to ravish each other, exploring, tongues tangling, Cole let his hand roam upward, searching for the silky fabric of her bra. When he discovered she was completely bare beneath the bulky sweatshirt, his thumb running into the weighty underside of her breast, he let out a growl and managed to hold himself back by a thread. With the tenderness she deserved, he inched his thumb upward until he found the rigid nub of her nipple. He palmed her, molding and squeezing the globe, wondering how it would taste, what kind of sounds he could elicit from her with his tongue. Sierra arched into his hand, pressed closer, then broke the contact of their lips.

"I want…" Her breath was shallow, shaky. "I want to climb on top of you but I can't."

Fuck yes. He wanted that too. "Why can't you?" He brushed his thumb over the tip of her nipple again and she shuddered, her lids fluttering closed.

"My ankle…"

Hell. Her ankle. She was injured and he was so intent on his own needs that he'd momentarily forgotten.

"We need to slow down," he forced out, his voice gritty, as if he'd swallowed sand.

Her eyes popped open, and she leaned forward to kiss him again.

"We don't need to slow down," she said after a few seconds during which his mind got semi-scrambled again. "I want this."

It took an effort to move his hand safely to her back, farther from temptation, but he managed it. "I want this too," he said, and he closed his eyes, thinking it would be easier to get the rest out if he wasn't staring into those gorgeous eyes. "But tonight's not the right time. You're hurt, for one thing."

"You make me forget about the pain," she said, running her fingers over his jaw.

"I need to catch up," he said. "In my head. You decided you're okay with fooling around with the help—"

"You're not the help," she said, flicking him on the chest, grinning.

"But I still need to get my mind around sleeping with the boss," he finished. It wasn't a lie, but it was only part of the truth. The heart of the matter was he needed to figure out if it was possible to hook up the way they both seemed to want to without her hoping for more. It was the "more" he would screw up.

She became serious again, peered into his eyes, as if measuring whether she should persuade him or appease him, which really wasn't the right word for it, because walking out of this apartment tonight was going to be one of the hardest things he'd done in his life. But it was the right thing. He didn't have a long history of doing the right thing, but for Sierra, he would start.

She pressed a light kiss on his lips and then increased the space between their heads. "Okay. I guess that's only fair. The getting-your-mind-around-it part, not the ankle part."

With a halfhearted smile, he said, "Both are legit. Here's what I'm going to do. I'm going to pick you up, and you're going to tell me where you want to be for the rest of the evening. In your bed? Here on the couch? And then I'm going to set you down there and get you whatever else you need. And then I'm going to limp out of here with my jeans threatening my ability to reproduce."

She laughed and lowered a hand to his crotch, but he intercepted. "No, you don't," he bit out, wanting nothing more than her hands all over him.

With another quiet but wicked laugh, she lifted her hand, trailed a finger over his lower lip. "I see I'm not the only one who can be bossy."

He shifted, prepared to stand with her cradled in his arms. "Bed or couch?"

"Couch," she said.

He stood, gently set her back in her corner, refilled her wineglass, took their dinner trash to the kitchen.

"Anything else I can get for you before I leave?" he asked.

She peered up at him with a mischievous sparkle in her eyes, and he thought she might try one more time to get him to stay—and he wasn't sure he could refuse again. After a pause, she shook her head. "I'm good."

Cole bent down and kissed her on the lips, pulling himself

away before he was ready, then straightened, went to the door, and walked out.

Once the door between them was closed, he stood there, eyes shut, and reminded himself that the best way to protect her from being hurt was to stay the hell away from her.

CHAPTER SIXTEEN

As soon as Cole pulled up to his mom's house Sunday evening, he shot out of his truck as if his shirt was on fire. It might as well be, as he'd felt like he was coming out of his skin ever since walking out of Sierra's apartment Friday night. He hadn't talked to her since except to check in with a text message on Saturday to see how her ankle was.

Much better, she'd responded and added an overly happy emoji. *Thanks for being my knight.*

He wasn't a knight and that was a weird-ass thing for her to say. He'd shrugged and simply said, *You're welcome.* He'd started typing a dozen other things then, like *Let me know if you need anything, How about if I bring some carryout?* and *Do you need a ride to the doctor?* but he'd deleted every one of them, acknowledging that he was looking for an excuse to see her, and if he gave himself that, he'd do something ill-advised, something he'd regret, like kiss her some more.

He'd parked along the curb in spite of the double driveway, having learned years ago how likely it was to get blocked in. According to the vehicles in the driveway, he was the last to arrive—Drake's Dugati, Mason's Audi, and Gabe's Tesla were already there. As he went up the wide walkway to the front porch of the traditional two-story, he noticed the yard needed some attention. Though the oak tree was holding on to its yellow leaves, the maple had shed all of its foliage, littering the yard and the usually manicured beds on each side of the walkway. One of them would have to do some raking in the next few days so their mom didn't have to worry about it.

He glanced up at the window of his old bedroom, front and center, above the dining room. The blinds, which his mom normally made a point of opening each day, were closed tight, same as the room Gabe and Mason had shared, to the right of his.

His parents had bought the North family home three years before Cole was born, when his older brothers were early school-age. It'd been a stretch to buy the nearly three-thousand-square-foot home, he'd heard them say many times, and a bit of a gamble, as the single-location North Brothers store was young and not at all a sure thing back then. By the time the twins were in middle school, that had changed significantly, and his parents could've bought something bigger and newer, but his mom liked the idea of giving her family a solid, unchanging home base. In spite of the business's growth and success, Faye and Harry North had stayed humble and wanted their boys to do the same.

Even in the depths of their home, Cole was the odd man out. It was a four-bedroom house—one for his parents, one for the two older boys, one for him, and eventually, one for the twins when they were born. Before they'd come along, the fourth had been used as a playroom. While Cole had liked having his own room, he'd always been aware that he was the only one who wasn't paired off.

The front door was unlocked, and Cole let himself into the two-story foyer.

"Hello?" he called out.

"In here," Drake said from beyond the central staircase that led to the second floor.

Cole passed the stairway and saw the family room was empty, so he headed toward the noise in the guest room on the left, which had originally served as his father's office. It had taken his mom several years after his dad's death to change it.

"What are you doing in here?" Cole asked as he entered the room through the double French doors. It was stuffed full of

Norths, with his mom sitting up in the bed and Mason, Gabe, and Drake spread around the room. "I thought the doctor said stairs were okay."

"Last-minute pivot," Gabe said. "Stairs are okay but not multiple times a day, so we set her up in here for a couple of weeks."

"How are you feeling, Mom?" Cole asked, coming up next to Drake at the foot of the double bed.

"Happy." Her smile was genuine but her eyes showed fatigue, as they had all week. "My own house, no nurses waking me up at all hours, and my boys here with me. I wish Zane could come for a visit, but we're going to FaceTime tomorrow."

"Plus some decent food," Drake said. "I've got three bags full of healthy stuff in the kitchen."

Their mom's shoulders sagged at the mention. "I think I'd like a nap first," she said with a frown. "As ridiculous as it sounds, coming home wore me out."

"That doesn't sound ridiculous at all," Gabe said. "You had open heart surgery a week ago."

"Dr. Beacham said you need to rest a lot," Mason added. "And we're going to see that you do."

Cole had spent a couple of hours that morning in her hospital room, as well as the evening shift the night before. Today had been a waiting game, first to get the news that she would, in fact, be released, and then to get the discharge orders, the paperwork, and all the details checked off before they'd let her go. Mason had been the one who was there for the doctor's blessing and who'd driven her home. They'd all wanted to be here for her first night back. Sundays had always been family dinner night anyway, even if Cole hadn't bothered to show up most of the time.

Gabe closed the blinds on the two windows in the room that looked out onto the darkening backyard. "You get some sleep, Mom. We'll eat when you wake up."

"What time is it?" She checked the red numbers of the digital alarm clock on the nightstand, which said it was 8:14 p.m. "You boys eat now. I know you're starving."

"You know us well," Mason said.

"I'll make sure these thugs save you some food," Drake said.

Gabe snorted good-naturedly. "How dumb do you think we are?"

"When have we ever left you in charge of food?" Mason said to Drake. "*We'll* make sure there's enough saved for your dinner, Mom."

"I don't need much," Faye said. "Cole? Are you doing okay?"

"Good, Mom. Glad you're home." He stepped to her side as she carefully lowered herself to lie flat on her back. "We should've gotten you a hospital bed so you could raise and lower yourself more easily."

"I've had enough of hospital beds for the rest of my life," their mom said emphatically. "I'm more than happy to lie down on my own. Now get out of here. Go eat."

"Don't have to tell me twice," Drake said. He patted her foot, which was buried beneath the blankets. "Sleep well, Mom."

Mason and Gabe followed suit, and Cole bent down and pressed a quick kiss to her forehead. "Get some rest."

"Don't worry about me," she said, already sounding drowsy.

Cole didn't reiterate how much the four of them—and Zane, too, from what Drake said—had worried about her. How could they not? She was the force that kept the North family bonds tight, or as tight as Cole would allow them to be.

When Cole got to the kitchen, on the other side of the family room, Drake was already pulling carryout containers out of bags and popping them open on the counter. "Organic for everyone," he said. "Healthy or bust. Salmon and Brussels salad is for Mom. Burgers for everyone else. Home-baked whole-grain buns, grass-fed beef, local micro greens, smoked bacon, all the condiments on the side."

"Fries?" Gabe asked.

"We're doing healthy," Drake repeated, his tone saying Gabe was a dumb ass. "How would you like to be stuck eating a fish salad while you can smell everyone else's French fries?"

"Burgers and broccoli doesn't have quite the same ring."

Gabe picked up a food box anyway and started dressing his burger.

Cole went over to the cupboard and took down a stack of plates. When they were kids, their mom had started a long-lasting Fiestaware phase and had a set of sixteen place settings of various solid-colored pieces. She still used those today.

"What's the plan for the week as far as having someone here to help out?" Cole asked. They'd discussed it in general over the past few days but, not previously knowing when she'd be released to come home, they hadn't hammered out specifics. She would no doubt insist she'd be fine on her own, but that wasn't going to fly with her sons.

"Aunt Liz and Miranda are splitting tomorrow," Mason said. "Geraldine offered to do Wednesday. We need to cover the rest."

Geraldine Fleming and Liz North were Faye's best friends and had been for decades. Liz, the wife of the brothers' late uncle, Hamilton North, had been the VP of accounting for North Brothers Sports until she retired a couple of years ago. Geraldine had overseen the marketing department and retired three months after Liz. Until her heart attack, Faye had been the holdout of the three—though she'd officially retired as well, she'd been working as some kind of consultant ever since. Miranda North was Liz's youngest, her only daughter, who also worked for the family business. Faye would be in good hands with all of them.

The brothers split up the rest of the week, with Cole grabbing Saturday duty before anyone else could.

"Sounds like business is good at Dunn & Lowell," Gabe said as he carried a bottle of root beer and an aqua plate heaped with a burger, a pile of steamed broccoli, and a heap of roasted red potatoes over to the long, farm-style table that seated eight between the family room and the breakfast bar.

Cole and Drake grabbed drinks from the fridge, then followed him and sat down, Drake at the foot, Cole next to him, while Mason elected to eat standing up, from the kitchen side of the bar, facing them. The guy wouldn't know how to relax if his life depended on it.

"Staying busy," Cole answered as he jabbed a forkful of potato.

"Judging by your boss's reaction to learning you blew off business from us, I'd say maybe not busy enough," Mason said, and Cole straightened, ready to light into him.

"Stop baiting him," Gabe said to Mason.

Mason shrugged. "I would've liked to be able to do business with her. She's building up quite the rep for quality work."

"Easy on the eyes too," Drake threw in.

"Don't go there," Cole warned around a bite of burger.

Gabe eyed Cole from the side, and Cole realized snapping at Drake like a pissed-off Doberman was a bad move. But just the thought of Drake eyeballing Sierra had a jealous fury beating through his blood.

"Seemed like there was some chemistry between you and Sierra at the hospital," Gabe said.

Cole let out an edgy laugh. The phrase *chemistry between you* sounded benign and harmless. He'd been longing so hard for Sierra for the past forty-eight hours that it was a physical ache. There was nothing benign about it, as it was ruling just about every minute of his damn life.

"She's my boss," Cole said through a tense jaw.

"I was in the same room with you for approximately three and a half minutes," Drake said. "Seemed like work positions were a nonissue."

"You can't help who you're attracted to," Gabe said, and he was lucky he was sitting too far away for Cole to reach him without getting up.

"There's no sense in denying the attraction," Mason said matter-of-factly. "It is what it is."

"I'm not denying there's an attraction," Cole said, all of his frustration, both physical and otherwise, exploding out of his voice. He made an effort to level himself before saying more. "What I'm trying to do is have some ethics and not sleep with the boss."

"You could find a new job," Drake suggested as he lifted his feet to one of the empty chairs.

"I don't want a new job." Cole jabbed a potato with too much force, his fork scraping across the plate.

"If you worked at North Brothers, you'd alleviate the problem," Gabe said casually, too casually.

Cole scowled as he dragged another forkful of potato through the olive oil and seasonings that had puddled on his plate. "You two have never wanted me working at North Brothers." He kept his voice casual and matter-of-fact too.

A scoff came from Mason as he set his burger down and then wiped his mouth with a napkin. "We would've taken you in a second if you wanted to work with us. You never wanted to work with us."

Cole expelled a disbelieving snort, then looked at Gabe to see if he was playing along with the farce.

"It's true," Gabe said, his light blue eyes piercing into Cole.

Drake continued to shove food into his mouth, as if nothing was going on around him. As if everything Cole had believed for over a decade had not just been turned on its head in a single sentence.

Mason was watching Cole from the counter, and their eyes met for a second. There was a challenge in Mason's. Cole racked his brain to when he was eighteen years old, searching for a time when either Mason or Gabe might have given him signs they wanted him to join the family business. They'd never said a word.

"I call bullshit," Cole said calmly, quietly, hiding the storm of emotion that was blowing through him.

"Call bullshit all you want," Mason said. "That's your problem."

"You guys barely even talked to me back then, let alone said anything serious about business opportunities." Cole took a bite of burger, not really tasting it but working hard not to show how fucked up he was inside about something that had happened—or hadn't happened—fourteen years ago.

"Oh, we tried. Several times," Gabe said. "Both of us. You never stuck around long enough for us to get into it."

"You had a way of making it hard to talk to you," Mason said, going after his veggies now as if nothing else mattered. "Especially when you signed over your shares. I specifically remember telling you it was a mistake and that you didn't have to do it, even if you weren't ready to work for the company. Let's just say you weren't open to hearing anything we said."

Gabe let out a short laugh. "That's putting it mildly. You were a bear and you know it."

"Bear," Drake repeated. "Son of a bitch. Downright asshole."

There was nothing Cole could argue with in that statement. "That proves my point," he said. "Why would you want your asshole brother who wasn't going to college to work for you or with you?"

"Why wouldn't we?" Gabe said. "You're fucking brilliant. College or no college. Dad wanted all of us to be involved in the company if we wanted, however we wanted."

"Dad's been dead for fifteen years," Cole threw out, in part to cover that he was reeling even more. It was the first time since he was a little kid that he could recall any of his brothers had said anything positive about him, and he recognized, in that moment, maybe he had been dying for it. Mentally, he tamped down on that shit. He'd made it for years without it and he was fine.

"It's not Dad's company anymore," Gabe said, "but he and Uncle Ham started it, and we try not to lose sight of their reasons for doing that. If they hadn't, we'd have different lives, for sure."

Mason, finished with his food, rinsed off his plate, then put it in the dishwasher. "Dad and Uncle Ham always wanted to take care of family, however they could. It doesn't mean we'll put someone who isn't qualified into a position, but it's North Brothers Sports and there's a place for any North brother who's interested."

"Right," Cole blurted, in part because he didn't know what the hell else to say, because his entire perspective was being challenged.

"Try me," Mason said, standing straight at the counter, his palms resting on the surface. "Come work for North Brothers."

Cole felt the attention of everyone in the room on him, and his brain couldn't truly process Mason's words, couldn't entirely take them seriously somehow, though looking at the CEO of North Brothers standing there across the room from him, there was no question he was serious as a funeral service.

His instinct was to snap out a rejection, but he reminded himself he was supposed to be trying to get along, to forge relationships with his family. For his mom's sake if nothing else, though if he shoved down his stubborn pride and was honest with himself, sometimes he could admit it was for his own sake as well.

"I like the job I have," he said finally. "Not looking for a change."

"It'd solve your problem with Boss Sierra," Drake said, leaning back in his chair, holding his root beer bottle.

"Sierra's not a problem to be solved," Cole lied, apparently unable to quit lashing out defensively whenever Drake mentioned her.

"Give it some thought," Mason ordered, and Cole reminded himself that bossiness was a personality quirk that his brother couldn't help. It didn't make it less annoying.

"What would I even do?" Cole asked, to point out the stupidity of his proposition. "I don't have a degree. I'm not planning on getting one."

Mason shrugged. "Whatever you're interested in. I know how you work. If you want to learn something, you will, the ins and outs and then some. If you're serious, let's set up a time to meet and discuss it."

"I'm not. I like what I do," Cole said without thought. He didn't need to think about it. He worked in construction. Sierra depended on him, and he was content in the job. Case closed.

That didn't mean his head wasn't spinning.

He'd harbored a grudge all these years, taken issue with not ever being talked to about the company. At eighteen, he'd specifically not wanted to be involved, had made that clear with the chip he carried around on his shoulder, and maybe it was yet another way he'd been a dumb ass—hating his brothers for not including him when maybe they would have if he'd just lowered his defensiveness. Or maybe they really had tried. He didn't remember it that way. Only now could he start to suspect how his inner rage had affected him so deeply, had dictated his life then and now. The thought didn't sit well, and he tried to shove it out of his head.

It took everything in him to linger after the food was gone, sitting around at the table, acting like he was listening to the banter, the plans for taking care of the day-to-day for their mom, the ins and outs of her care. The discharge papers and home care instructions were on the fridge clipped to a magnet that said *That moment when you realize this IS your circus and those are your monkeys* that had been there for as long as Cole could remember. He could read the instructions when he needed to know what to do.

He caught himself bouncing his leg more than once and forced it to stop each time. Checking the time repeatedly, he made himself stay until 9:15 exactly. Then he made a vague excuse and unceremoniously took off in his truck, heading for anywhere but his apartment.

CHAPTER SEVENTEEN

$\mathcal{S}$ierra set her laptop on the love seat cushion next to her and curled deeper into the thick, fuzzy, oversized throw blanket. It was maybe a little chilly to be working out on her balcony at nearly nine thirty on a late October evening, but with flannel pajama pants, a long-sleeved tee, a lightweight hoodie, and the blanket, she was comfortable and enjoying the peace of Hale Street. Peace and contentment with an underlying buzz of anticipation that stemmed from inside of her.

She'd hit send on Dunn & Lowell's official application for the Eldridge Mansion competition three minutes ago. Thanks to Cole's revisions, she felt more than good about it. Their application was strong and showcased the company's experience and capabilities beautifully. If they didn't make the cut, it was because the competition organizers were looking for something that Dunn & Lowell wasn't.

It turned out she could be grateful to Cole on a professional level while wanting to wring his neck on a personal one.

Apparently Friday night did not sit well with him after all. Not exactly a shocker after he'd practically run out of here, but still a disappointment. He'd said he needed time to wrap his head around their new closeness, and she could give him that, but the one text message since, to see how her ankle was, was short and not really sweet. Cordial but distant. There was no hint of the connection they'd shared Friday night, and her instincts told her he was doing his best to sever that connection, not wrap his head around it. Her shoulders sagged at the physical twinge of disappointment deep in her chest.

She'd meant what she'd told him Friday. She'd decided, after her talk with Hayden, to put her doubts about their work positions to rest. The truth was that she couldn't get Cole out of her mind. She wanted to know him better, wanted to have him in her life after work hours, wanted to be a part of his. After his revelations Friday, she understood him so much better. Knowing some of what he'd been through only made her care more. And her need for him physically…

All it had taken was one evening out of their usual environment—the night of Kennedy's wedding. One evening of her looking past his work façade to see the real Cole, or at least the parts he'd allowed her to see. It was as if she'd had blinders on to the chemistry between them, and once she'd lowered them, shared that intense, charged moment with him in her kitchen that night, the attraction had flooded in, making it impossible for her to go back to seeing him only as the tight-lipped man she worked with. In just over a week, she'd gone from zero to lying in bed at night longing for him.

But it seemed maybe it wasn't as two-sided as she'd imagined on Friday. That or maybe Cole was just that reluctant to let anyone in.

Work could be interesting tomorrow. Interesting or frustrating or, most likely, awkward.

She'd left the balcony door ajar and now a knock at the apartment door startled her. She shoved the blanket aside, grabbed the computer, and went inside, limping only slightly after having iced and babied her ankle all weekend, to the mostly dark living room, illuminated by the faint light over the stove in the kitchen. As she set the laptop on the chaise cushion, another knock sounded, louder, firmer, and, her heart hammering because it was late on a Sunday and that knock sounded like it meant business, she went to the peephole and looked out. What she saw didn't calm her heart for a second.

Cole stood there with one forearm braced on the doorjamb, his head bowed as if he was studying the floor of the hallway. Sierra whipped the door open.

"Hi, Cole. What's wrong?"

He straightened and didn't bother trying to smile, but he did meet her gaze, and she felt herself melting a little into his troubled brown eyes in spite of herself.

"Okay if I come in?" he asked quietly.

"Of course." She stood back to let him pass, closed and locked the door after him. "What's going on?" she tried again.

He glanced around her apartment, which had become cluttered over the weekend. She'd planned on tidying up before bed tonight. "I just…wanted to see you."

Those words sent a thrill through her, and she tried to rein it in. Tried, but damn, just looking at him, dressed in dark blue jeans that were nicer than the old, worn ones he usually wore to work and a faded red thermal shirt that stretched just right over his muscular chest, and standing so close she caught his masculine scent… Losing battle.

"Here's me," she said, throwing her arms out and trying to coax a smile from him, hoping she wasn't what had him upset.

He seemed to try, judging by an upward flutter of one side of his lips, but she wouldn't call it a success. "Pajamas," he said. "I guess it's late."

"I was working out on the balcony. Just sent in the Eldridge app."

"Outside?"

"It's a beautiful evening. Up for it? We could talk—" At his instant frown, she changed direction. "Or not talk. Just sit."

She gestured toward the still-open door to the balcony. She was curious what was up with him and hoped if she got him to relax, he might tell her. When he hesitated, she said, "I have a blanket."

"'Course you have a blanket." He came closer to a smile this time.

"If it's too cold for you though…" she challenged.

"Lead the way."

Sierra stepped out onto the small wrought-iron balcony that held the wicker love seat, a square ottoman, and a dainty side table, as well as a tall potted plant in the corner that she'd need to bring in for the winter soon. She picked up the corners of the blanket from the cushions and motioned for Cole to sit.

Glancing warily around at the surrounding balconies, all deserted and some of them even packed up for the coming winter, he went to the side farther from the door and sat. His tall frame made the furniture seem delicate and less than sturdy. He extended his arm, indicating the spot next to him, and she sat, enveloping them both under the fuzzy throw. He kept his arm around her shoulder, pulling her in closer, and she felt a little more optimistic that he wasn't here to tell her they couldn't be together.

"Ankle's better?" he asked.

"Much. The swelling's mostly gone. I've sat around all weekend, trying to stay off it. I can't afford to miss work this week."

"Have you ever missed work besides the day before Kennedy's wedding?"

"I've taken some days off between projects when we haven't been stacked so tight."

"Not since I've worked there," he said, his voice a quiet, comforting rumble in the night air.

She glanced up at his profile, noting his unshaven jaw in the faint light from the old-fashioned streetlamps below. She wanted to run a finger over his roughened skin but was still treading lightly, unsure about his mood.

"I love my work," she said. "Is everything okay with your mom?"

He breathed out audibly. "We got her home tonight. She's doing okay, I guess. Just really tired."

"She's been through a lot."

He nodded but didn't say more.

They sat in silence for a while, looking out over the neighborhood. The Wentworth Hotel at the left end was lit up as usual, but all the businesses that they could see at street level were closed for the night, Frank's Diner being the last to shut down not long ago. Clayborne's would still be open but wasn't visible from here. A light came on in one of the second-floor apartment windows across the street, and Sierra saw Tilly, Frank Dole's wife, who co-owned the diner, come into view, watched her draw the curtains.

"Peaceful here," Cole said.

Sierra nodded, gratified that he liked it. "What about your place? Peaceful too?" she asked, having realized she didn't know anything about where he lived other than it was an apartment in a not-so-great part of town, according to him.

"Wouldn't say that." He raised his legs to the ottoman, then surprised her by scooping up her legs and draping them over his lap, angling her into him, tightening his arm around her.

"Hi," she said with a smile, burrowing into his chest, feeling more okay about letting her guard down, trusting he was here because he wanted to be.

His response was a contented growl, and as he dipped his chin, she reached up to run her hand over his rough cheek at last. Cole gazed down at her and then breathed in deeply, as if savoring their closeness.

Sierra loved it but couldn't ignore that something was off with him. "Is everything okay?" she asked barely above a whisper.

"Come here," he said, pulling her more fully onto his lap in a straddle. "Okay for your ankle?"

Her knees were alongside his legs, her ankle supported by the cushion. It was more okay than it'd been all weekend as her body forgot that dull ache in favor of the hot ache at her core with their bodies pressed together. She gazed into his eyes and read his raw need there.

Cole ran both his hands up her back, one of them into her hair to the back of her head, pulling her into him until their lips collided. He kissed her hard, seeking out her tongue immediately, as if he'd bided his time and could no longer wait. She welcomed it, drew him in, showed him she was as eager as he was. Though he'd had her worried all weekend that she'd never get another chance to be this close to him, he seemed to be holding nothing back now, letting her see and feel how much he needed her, possibly not just on a physical level. She got a sense that this, their connection, was what he needed to soothe whatever was bothering him.

His lips still locked with hers, he lifted the blanket to their shoulders and secured the edges of it behind his back so it draped over them, covering her. Then his hands were all over her, pulling her into him again, lifting her layers of shirt. He palmed her breasts, kneaded them as he kept kissing her, rolled her nipples between calloused fingers and thumbs. She'd had no idea what a turn-on it was to feel the roughness of a man who worked with his hands on her most sensitive spots. She'd never been with a guy like Cole, tended toward upwardly mobile professionals with smooth, white-collar hands. She'd been missing out.

He was making need shoot from her breasts to her very core, making her grind her body against his erection, and she caught her breath, momentarily breaking their kiss, because...*damn*. He hadn't even taken a single piece of her clothing off and she was about to incinerate.

She sought out the bottom of his shirt and worked her hands under it, running them up to his chest. She lifted the shirt to his shoulders, needing to feel his heated skin directly. Cole let out a moan as she rubbed her nipples over his bare chest. As she returned her mouth to his, he worked his hands between their bodies again, engulfed her breasts with them, molded and massaged and manipulated until she wondered if she was going to come apart from this alone.

Cole guided her body upward and teased the hardened tip of her nipple with his tongue, then sucked her breast into his mouth, coaxing a needy moan from deep inside of her. The blanket fell from their shoulders and pooled around their waists, barely noticed until he switched to her other breast and the cool air hit her damp nipple.

"Cole," she whispered.

"Mm." He didn't stop what he was doing to answer, and the

vibration of his voice on her skin shot another current of aching need to her most female parts.

"Cole," she tried again. "Let's go inside."

He didn't stop, didn't even pause for her words to sink in, and Sierra threw her head back as the sensations overcame her reservations. She pulled his head to her more firmly so he wouldn't stop what he was doing.

The sound of a car door closing in the distance jolted her out of it, and she slid her body down, out of his mouth. She pressed herself back into his chest as she gathered her wits.

"Inside," she tried again, her voice not quite working right. "I don't want to give Frank Dole a heart attack if he looks out his window."

A possessive growl rumbled out of Cole's chest, and she landed a short kiss on his lips, then pulled her shirt and sweatshirt down as she forced herself to stand, taking the weight on her uninjured leg. The blanket fell to the floor of the balcony around her feet. She bent to grab it and held her hand out for Cole's at the same time.

CHAPTER EIGHTEEN

ole had a look on his rugged face as if he was coming back into his senses as he glanced around, from the balcony of the apartment next to Sierra's, which belonged to two of the spa owners and was thankfully still deserted, to the apartments across the way and back to her extended hand. He reached for it and stood, and Sierra led him inside. Once in the door, she shut it and let the blanket drop, then led him to her bedroom. Her messy bedroom, she realized as she stumbled over a shoe.

The room was mostly dark, with the weak stove light barely reaching it and the streetlights filtering in around the blinds. She chose not to hurt their eyes by turning on the lamp on her nightstand, even though she wanted to see every inch of him as soon as she got him naked. "Careful," she whispered. "It's a minefield in here."

As soon as they were next to the bed, she pulled him toward her by the waistband of his jeans and unsnapped them. The rasp of his zipper sounded as she lowered it, and he held himself still and seemingly patient. With his pants unfastened but still in place, she switched her attention to his shirt and lifted it over his head. He finished taking it off and tossed it aside as she went back to his pants. She slid her fingers to his waist, beneath both layers, jeans and underwear, pushing them down his muscled thighs. He helped her, took over ridding himself of them and his shoes as she ran her hands over his sculpted ass. She couldn't see it, but based on feel alone, it had to be the finest ass in the known universe.

Before she finished worshiping his butt with her hands, he was removing her shirt and hoodie at once, requiring her to lift her arms. Next, his fingers were at her waist, dipping into her pajama pants, teasing her, but the drawstring was tight enough he couldn't get his hands very far. She felt the release of the tie, and then her pants slid to the floor and their naked bodies came together, standing there, their flesh making contact from thigh to shoulder. She reveled in the details of him, the strong, muscled back and shoulders, the masculine roughness of hair on his thighs, those irresistible butt cheeks…the thick erection pressing against her abdomen. Insistently.

Sierra grasped him, relishing the feel of the hot, velvet-soft flesh over steel as her fingers explored the length of him and her body responded with an urgent need to have him inside of her. He let out a low, needy rumble that had her stroking him, seeing how far she could push him.

Answer: not far.

With a growl, Cole grabbed her hand and lifted it, entwined her fingers with his as he pressed kisses along her jawline and then rasped into her ear, "On the edge already."

Grinning, Sierra attempted to move her hand back down to tease him some more, but he was having none of it. Before she could blink, she found herself on her back on the mattress with Cole over her, gazing down at her intently in the low light.

"Troublemaker," he muttered, and she let out a quiet laugh as she realized she could no longer touch him the way she wanted to because of the way his body was pressed into hers. This lightness during sex was new to her. Surprising. Especially with Cole, who was usually so serious and reserved when it came to anything personal.

He trailed kisses back down her jawline, her neck, and to her breasts, grazing each nipple with just enough attention from his mouth that she was arching toward him for more when he continued his descent to her stomach. As he circled his tongue around her belly button, his hands toyed with her breasts, molding them, adoring them, rolling the nipples between thumb and forefinger, and again she arched in need. She sought out his erection again, managed to get her fingertips on it before he moved out of her reach, trailing his tongue lower. He swirled it around her center, and Sierra let out a shallow gasp of need.

"You don't play fair," she managed.

The answering low rumble of laughter had his breath fluttering over the parts of her that were screaming out for more. More contact than a whisper of air. Much more. The tease of his tongue was a start, but before he could get serious about what he was doing, Sierra grabbed his shoulders and tried to urge him upward. She ached so deep inside that only one thing would quench her need.

"Want you inside," she said.

"Busy here," he said offhandedly, as if he couldn't be bothered by her demands, then lowered his mouth to her again. He grasped her thighs and opened her more to him, then focused every bit of his attention on her center, and she couldn't have argued if she'd wanted to.

She so didn't want to.

It seemed like milliseconds later when the orgasm shot through her, had her clamping his head to her as waves of ecstasy took over, turning her inside out.

When she came back to herself, she lay there for a few seconds, getting air into her lungs, thoughts into her head.

"You're stubborn," she finally said when she could speak.

"Complaining?"

Her eyes were closed as she recovered, but there was both smugness and laughter in his question, and she found herself falling for this side of Cole. This unexpected playful, open side.

"Not complaining," she gave him as she reached for his still-rock-hard cock and this time got her hand wrapped around it.

Instead of fighting it, Cole moaned. "Need a condom. There's one in my wallet."

"Some in my nightstand," she said.

"How old?"

The question made her stop stroking him abruptly as she tried to think straight. She didn't sleep with many guys and it had been a while. How long did condoms last? "Not last week," she said vaguely, thinking it was probably closer to a year than a week.

Cole rolled over and sat up, picked up his jeans, dug through his wallet, and apparently found what he was looking for, because he threw the jeans back down. "This one's okay," he said as he ripped it open, then sheathed himself.

Dates and lovers from the past disappeared from her mind as he crawled back over her and kissed her thoroughly, more deliberately now than earlier, as if he was fighting to control himself. She couldn't resist trying to break that control again and sought out his chest with her fingers until she could run a thumb over his nipple. He groaned and kept kissing her. As the ache in her own body built up again, her goal became less about teasing him and more about directing him to impale her and put her out of her ever-loving misery.

She took hold of him, squeezed him gently, then arched her body as she guided him to her entrance.

"So impatient," he rasped out in a gravelly voice, his amusement audible along with his own need.

"Yes," she said, fully owning it, and then he pressed inside of her, and she held her breath as he stretched her. "God yes."

Once he was fully seated, he paused, held his head up, and gazed into her eyes in the near dark. The intensity in them twisted something in a different part of her body—in her chest— and there was the vague thought that she was in trouble, but then he started moving, out and then in, and all thoughts escaped her.

She wrapped her legs around his waist, held on to his upper body as well, gave herself over to him completely, and it didn't take long for another orgasm to build in her. They came at nearly the same time, with her riding the euphoria as he thrust a final time, stiffened, and rasped out an impassioned swear word before collapsing on her chest. Several heartbeats went by as she relished the weight of him on her, the pulses of him in her, the scent of sex and Cole enveloping her, the sound of his labored exhales.

"Was that a good swear?" she asked eventually, unable to keep from smiling.

Without lifting his head, apparently too wiped out, he said, "Was a good swear."

Then, a few seconds later, he rolled to the side and pulled her with him. He pressed a kiss to her forehead, her nose, then her lips, lingering there. The tenderness in his kiss made something in her chest dip, but she chose not to think about it. Focused her attention instead on every detail of Cole—the intensity in his eyes each time he looked at her between kisses, the light sheen of sweat on his skin that tasted salty when she touched her tongue to it, the heat of his body pressed along hers, their legs tangling together. He was so unguarded in that moment, so unlike the man she worked side by side with every day, the strong, capable, confident but contained man. The work version of Cole was appealing, sexy, but this private Cole… He had the power to turn her inside out.

He burrowed his nose along the side of her neck and mumbled, "Oranges. Never going to think of them quite the same way again."

It took her a second to realize he referred to the citrus scent of her shampoo. "I like to think of it as Creamsicle. Oranges and vanilla and sugar."

"Definitely sweet." He nibbled on her earlobe, sending a shiver through her. "Also sexy." After another kiss to her lips, he untangled himself from her. "Be right back."

As he walked away from the bed toward the hallway and, she assumed, the bathroom, she mourned the fact that it wasn't light enough to check out the view. Later, she promised herself. Whether later tonight or another time, she would get the chance to roam her eyes over his naked backside at leisure. She hoped.

She registered the chill in the air on her still-sweaty skin. The bed was unmade, the covers half on, half off, partially lumped beneath her. She crawled underneath them, pulled them over her. At the sounds of the toilet flushing, the water running in the sink, the bathroom door opening, she moved closer to the side she rarely inhabited, to make room for him.

As he rolled into bed and pulled her in close again, she said, "Welcome back."

"Good to be back." He ran his hand up her side, over the curve of her waist, down her butt, back again, as if he couldn't get enough. As he nuzzled up against her neck, he let out a playful, contented growl.

"You seem to be in a better mood than when you got here," she said, loving the attention as much as the easiness between them.

"How could I not be with this?" He gave her butt a playful squeeze, coaxing a laugh from her.

"My butt is amazing," she said facetiously.

"Whole package is amazing."

"You're not so bad yourself." In the dark, she rubbed her knuckles gently over his stubble-roughened jaw. "Where were you before you came over?" she asked, still curious about what had upset him.

"My mom's. Drake got carryout."

"Family dinner?" she guessed.

"Sort of. Mom was sleeping."

So just the brothers, which could explain the mood. "Why were you upset when you got here?"

He blew out a breath. "You really want to hear about that?"

"I'm guessing one of your brothers did something?" She was still trying to figure out the North brothers' dynamics and Cole's relationships with them. They'd seemed like nice guys at the hospital, in spite of the situation with their mom, but the tension between Cole and them had been palpable, especially Mason.

He rolled onto his back and she watched his profile in the dark as he gazed up at the ceiling. Moving closer, so there was no space between them, she rested her hand on his chest, rubbed it in light little circles, wishing to soothe him somehow. She shouldn't have brought it up, she realized. She didn't want to ruin the evening, only make him feel better.

"It's okay—" she started.

"Mason offered me a job," he said at the same time, and Sierra felt herself tense involuntarily at the thought of losing Cole on a professional level. Reminding herself this wasn't about her, she forced herself to relax.

"Wow," she said. "Doing what?"

"Whatever I want, in theory."

They were both quiet for several seconds as Sierra processed, tried to imagine him leaving Dunn & Lowell, him working in a corporate office. Her working without him.

"Are you going to?"

He shifted on his side toward her again, pressed a kiss to her forehead. "Nah."

Okay. She couldn't deny her relief, though she told herself again this was about Cole and not her.

"It made you mad that he offered? Or what?" She was still trying to understand his mood earlier. She didn't see how a well-meaning job offer could piss him off.

Cole again put space between them, then sat up, propping the pillow against the headboard and leaning against it, letting out an aggravated sigh. He ran his hands over his face, and though Sierra knew she should forget the whole conversation, she didn't take back her questions. Waited for him to answer.

"It's fucked up," he said.

She sat up next to him, pulling the blankets with her. "What is?"

"You ever wonder how your life might be different if you'd made one different decision at some point in the past?"

She cradled her knees to her chest, rested her head on them, her face turned toward him. "Sure. Like, what if I'd gone to a four-year college, or what if I'd sold the business and gone to work for my brother's company instead?"

"You ever get any good answers?"

She thought for a moment, then said, "No. I don't think too hard about it because I believe every little thing gets us to the place we are, makes us the person we are." At his silence, she said, "Do you?"

"Do I what?"

"Get any good answers?"

"I mostly try not to think about it too hard because I've fucked up a lot."

She didn't see that, but she was still getting to really know him. Starting to sense that he was hard on himself, judged himself harshly. "But tonight you're thinking about it?"

"Mason and Gabe told me some stuff that got me started."

"What kind of stuff?"

"They said they wanted me to work for North Brothers when I graduated from high school."

"Which you didn't want to do," she said, remembering what he'd told her before.

She could see him narrow his eyes in the dimness. "I don't know. That's what I wanted everyone to think, because"—he laughed, but there was no humor in it—"I didn't figure they wanted me."

"I get it. You went on the offensive. Thinking they didn't want you, you made sure they knew you didn't care because you weren't interested in the first place."

"Pretty much."

"Seems human."

"Seems immature."

"You were eighteen and grieving."

"And stubborn and stupid and pissed at the world."

"And eighteen and grieving," she repeated.

He didn't answer, just reclined his head against the headboard, his gaze pointing toward the ceiling. She could feel his emotions pouring off him, negative ones.

"So you're thinking what if you hadn't been grieving and had gone to work with your brothers at eighteen?"

"Maybe."

"What if you had? You'd be doing something way different. Not construction. Brain stuff, which you're good at. Do you think you'd like that?"

"I like what I do," he said. He turned his gaze to her. "I like working for you, and I'm not saying that because I'm in bed with you."

She tried to fight off a grin. "Let's keep those separate. Working together and sleeping together."

"I'm good with that." He reached out and grasped her arm, tugged her toward him. "Come here. Let's focus on the sleeping together. Or the not sleeping part, more accurately."

She scooted closer, and he guided her onto his lap, straddling him. "This is how you handle a serious conversation?" she asked, her breath coming out unevenly as she felt his hardness rubbing against her naked body.

"Not much else to say. No answers, only questions, and I'm questioned out." He palmed her breasts and leaned in to kiss her. There was no question in his kiss, only demands. And she was only too happy to meet those demands.

CHAPTER NINETEEN

*B*efore he even opened his eyes, Cole felt the weight on his chest, as if Tito and a dozen other cats were sitting on top of him. He popped his eyes open, knowing on some level it wasn't Tito, wasn't anything tangible, but taking a moment to figure out where and when he was.

Sierra's apartment.

She was curled up against him, facing him, one leg resting on top of his, her hand on his upper arm. Her hair was everywhere, and he might've taken a few seconds to run his fingers through the silkiness, breathe in the orange-vanilla scent—if he didn't feel like he was coming out of his skin.

He wasn't supposed to fall asleep. Wasn't supposed to stay. That crossed a line, took things from a physical *let's quench our mutual needs* to…something else. Something more. It was the "more" that he was guaranteed to screw up, whether he wanted to or not.

His phone was likely on the floor, either still in his jeans or next to them. In the near dark, he could barely see his watch, which was still on his wrist, but holding it a couple of inches from his face at a particular angle to the light from around the window let him just make it out—3:26 a.m. Middle of the night, and he had to get out of here before it was morning.

On one level, he fully recognized the dick move for what it

was. That didn't stop the gut reaction that he needed space, needed to breathe. Needed to make sure he didn't let Sierra think there could be something deeper.

Managing to keep from bolting on the spot, he did take the opportunity to inhale the scent of her hair now, fainter but still distinctly vanilla-laced orange. For the rest of his existence, the smell of Creamsicles would equate to sex. The best sex of his life, a little voice in his head insisted—or maybe that was coming directly from his dick, which was awake and starting to throb.

The temptation to lose himself in Sierra jabbed at him, but the need to make a clean escape was stronger. It was only a couple of hours till the time he'd wake up on Monday morning, and the thought of waking up together, going to work together was not a comfortable one.

Lucky thing he'd fallen asleep on the side of the bed closer to the door, but getting out without waking her up was going to take some effort. His conscience surging again, he tried to tell himself he didn't want to disturb her sleep, wanted to allow her the best rest possible because they had a labor-heavy day planned at the Draper site, but that was only part of the truth, and not the part driving his actions.

He was an asshole who didn't know how to do more than casual sex. *That* was the truth. He'd never been motivated enough to try, had never had what he'd call a real relationship with a woman he'd cared about.

Moving his body a couple of inches to the right, he managed to slide out from under her hand. Her leg was more of an issue, but he went with the yank-the-bandage-off-quickly philosophy and turned on his right side, away from her, pausing for a few seconds to see if she stirred.

His heart pounded as he lay there, listening for a change in her breathing, knowing he was going to follow through with his escape one way or another. A leopard couldn't change its spots.

Sierra was still, continued her even, barely audible breaths, so he sat up and bent down, feeling for his clothes, locating his phone and wallet, gathering everything in his arms. He'd dress in the bathroom. Less chance of bothering her.

Less chance of getting caught, asshole.

"Cole?"

He froze, bent over with his bare ass pointed to her, his hand outstretched toward his shirt.

"What are you doing?"

He straightened, searched for the right thing to say, or the right*est* in the situation.

"Gotta feed Tito," he said, and went ahead and picked up his shirt.

"Who's Tito?"

"My cat." He stood, having secured all his clothing and belongings and leaving Sierra's shirts and leggings in a pile next to the nightstand.

She raised her upper body and supported herself on one elbow, the sheet staying where it'd been, giving him a shadowed view of her tits. His mind filled in the blanks for the parts he couldn't see, and even in the dim night, they were fucking first-class.

"I didn't know you have a cat," she said.

"He's a son-of-a-bitch tom cat who goes asshole if he doesn't get his dinner." That wasn't a lie. Tito had been known to knock things off counters or shelves or claw the crap out of the area rug when he went too long without being fed. What made it a stretch was that it took longer than a few hours for Destructo Tito to strike. Cole had fed him later than usual Sunday morning, and the cat's evening meal was only three or four hours delayed so far.

She didn't respond, and the silence made him antsy. Since the cat was out of the bag, so to speak, he set his clothes on the mattress, dug out his boxer briefs, and put them on.

"You're freaking out," she said, not really as a question, as he pulled his jeans up.

He felt even more busted than he had when she'd woken up, but there was only so much dishonesty he could allow himself. Because it *was* Sierra, and dammit, he couldn't help caring more than he wanted to.

As he sat on the edge of the mattress, he allowed himself to touch her hair, running his fingers through the ends, pushing a chunk of it back over her shoulder. "I'm not good with sleep-overs, morning afters," he admitted. "I've never stayed the night."

Her surprise at that was tangible, as she moved her head minutely and he could just barely make out the wrinkle in her forehead.

"Never?"

He shook his head.

"You take women to your place," she said matter-of-factly.

"Never."

She sat up, losing the sheet completely, moving her legs criss-cross style, and he was sidetracked by the parts of her that were hidden in the dark well between her legs.

"You sleep with women a lot though, right? I mean, just asking. It's fine, part of your history. I'm just curious."

"I sleep with women some. Wouldn't call it a lot. That'd be Drake. The man-whore North."

"Okay…" She was obviously struggling to grasp what he was saying, as if she wasn't fully awake yet. "Staying till morning doesn't mean you're locked in. To us, I mean." Her husky-from-sleep voice dipped lower and tugged at something in him, something besides the insistent member jutting uncomfortably into his jean zipper. "We don't have to do strings."

"Yeah," he said. He didn't do strings, general rule, but he couldn't say this night with Sierra was a one-off, no matter how much smarter that would be. Couldn't imagine not having another few chances to be with her. But strings… No. "Tonight, last night, whatever you want to call it—*this*—was good, better than good. A thousand times better than good. But I'm not a strings guy."

She reached out and ran a finger over his bare chest, sending a shiver through him.

Could he stay? Would it suck to crawl back under the warm blankets, sweep her hot body into his arms, sink inside of her, sleep for a few hours, then start his day with yet another dose of sex with Sierra?

Maybe he could try it once. Maybe he could start to blur the edges of his leopard spots after all. Sex with this woman, okay, sex and more with this woman… If anyone could change a man, change him and his fucked-up selfish ways, it would be her.

He leaned down and kissed her, in part to buy himself time, in part because how could he not kiss her? As their lips met and her fingers closed around his biceps, a vision of them heading out to their trucks together in the morning to go to work popped into his mind, and the domesticity of it snapped him out of the temptation to stay. He ended the kiss, sat up, shook his head.

"Tito needs his tuna," he said as he pulled his shirt over his head. "I'm sorry, but I can't stay tonight."

He was sorry, all right. Sorry-ass bastard. But he was what he was, and he'd have to keep that in mind before he tangled with Sierra again, because she deserved so much more than he could give her.

CHAPTER TWENTY

"Something's going on with you," Hayden said as Sierra slid into the red-vinyl booth across from her at Frank's Diner bright and early Monday morning. Just hours after Cole had retreated, as a matter of fact. Sierra had texted her friend first thing to set up the impromptu breakfast date.

"Just because you've known me since second grade and have been right there with me in my best and worst moments ever doesn't mean you can tell something's up before I even sit down," Sierra said, unable to keep a grin off her face. "Maybe I just need coffee."

"You undoubtedly need coffee. You also need to tell me why you forgot to wear your coat and why your eyes are lit up this early in the morning."

"I forgot my coat because I was running late, and unlike you, I don't set my stuff out the night before, nor do I wake up before the roosters or the sun." Sierra looked around at the buzzing diner and waved at her friend and neighbor Roxie Giardini and her guy, Will, who were several tables down.

"Morning, girls." Tilly scurried up to their table with a pot of coffee and efficiently filled both their mugs. "Where's your coat, Sierra?"

"I don't need one today," she said. "It's not that cold."

Tilly eyed her briefly, then nodded at the customers who'd just walked in the door. "The usual for you girls today?"

"Plus a plate of hash browns," Sierra said, adding to her blueberry pancakes and bacon order. At Hayden's raised brows, she said, "Starving. And I need calories to get through my day. I don't get to fluff pillows for the next ten hours."

"Your loss. It's much better than hammering nails." Hayden poured multiple single-serve containers of fat-free creamer into her coffee, then watched Sierra expectantly.

Sierra folded easily, mostly because she was dying to pick apart her situation with Cole and figure out what to do next. "I slept with him."

Hayden had been about to take a sip of coffee but set her mug down hard. "Cole?"

She said it loudly enough that Sierra glanced around to see if anyone had picked up on it.

"Who else would it be?"

"Weren't you just, less than a week ago, debating whether you should ever look at him again because he worked for you and things would be awkward and it's against your personal policy?"

"Well..." Sierra dumped in a packet of real sugar and stirred her coffee. "Yeah. Then you told me to go for it."

"And you went for it." Hayden's smile was smug.

"Hole in one, baby," Sierra said, making Hayden roll her eyes and shake her head as she allowed a short laugh.

"It was unquestionably good," Hayden said. "It's written all over your face."

"It didn't suck."

"But did you?"

"Stop," Sierra said, laughing.

"How did this happen? Last I knew you were limping around after he rescued you from your clumsy self."

"No limp left. Only a little soreness." Sierra leaned forward and told her how he'd showed up last night, quiet and withdrawn and all too willing to get physical. "And then he ran."

"Midnight bolt?"

"Three a.m. He slept for a while," Sierra said, "and I think it freaked him out. Which I mentioned to him."

"And he said?"

"He had to feed his cat."

"Liar," Hayden said.

"Hundred percent, and I told him that. He then admitted he doesn't do sleepovers or mornings after."

Tilly appeared with their plates and set them in front of them. "Frank said to tell you the hash browns are even better with cheese."

"Frank doesn't have girl hips," Sierra said. "Tell him thanks for the best pancakes in the world."

"You can butter him up yourself," Tilly said. "He's acting like a grizzly today. Can I get you two anything else?"

They both shook their heads as they dug into their food. Tilly hurried off to another table.

"So what's next?" Hayden said once she'd swallowed down a syrup-drenched forkful.

"With Cole? I'm thinking about cornering him in the conference room at work."

"Naked?"

Sierra grinned and shook her head. "In my mind, maybe. I'll be a little more subtle. At work."

Hayden drew in a long breath and shook her head.

"What?" Sierra forked some potatoes and had a fleeting thought that cheese *would* make them even more amazing.

"How much of this is good sex and how much is you wanting more than just sex with him?"

"It was good," Sierra said with feeling. "So much better than good."

"Yeah?" Hayden's eyes twinkled conspiratorially. "Can I live vicariously through you?"

"You need to find a guy. A North brother."

Hayden shook her head, which was a lot more positive than her usual reaction to Sierra's suggestion that someone of the male persuasion would make her world temporarily better. "So he was unselfish and hung like a horse?"

"Five orgasms, less than two hours."

"Who had the extra one?"

"Five for me. Two for him."

"Jeez. You need to not screw this up."

"Hey. Who says I'm the one who'll screw it up? He's a guy."

"A scared guy. A guy who sounds like he's way into you and not ready to be way into anyone."

"What makes you say he's into me?" Sierra checked her phone for the time, saw she had a few more minutes, and stuffed a large bite of bacon in her mouth.

"He fell asleep next to you, for one."

"Maybe," Sierra said after swallowing her food.

"He came to you when he was upset about something."

"Maybe."

"He admitted he doesn't do mornings after. A guy doesn't just say that, he makes up an excuse."

"Like feeding his cat?" Sierra asked.

"See? He even tried to lie but couldn't keep it up."

"Oh, he could keep it up."

"I don't want to hear any more," Hayden said as she pushed her half-eaten pancakes to the side and moved the bacon front and center. "I'm at hating you level now."

"You love me. You want what's best for me."

"Is that Cole? Like, long term?"

Sierra set her fork down, thinking about that question, as she had been for the past several hours. "I like him a lot," she admitted. "He's different from any guy I've gone out with. Rough around the edges, not so white-collar—"

"Not at all, right?"

She nodded. "He's so reserved normally. Keeps his feelings to himself. But he's opened up to me about his family. The things that are bothering him."

"I told you he's into you."

"And while he's normally so serious, sex was…fun. Like, we laughed together."

"Weird."

"And good," Sierra said. "I want more. More sex and more him in general. A lot more."

Hayden picked up her coffee cup and held it in both hands as she studied her. "You're going to have to rein it in then," she said after a few seconds.

"Rein what in?" Sierra frowned.

"Rein your Sierra in. Turn your overzealousness off."

"I'm not overzealous."

"You're not patient, and this one's going to require patience."

Sierra's scowl deepened. "I can be patient."

"You're excited to see him, right?"

Of course she couldn't wait to lay her eyes on him, but she wasn't stupid. "I'm not going to jump him."

"And no flirting," Hayden said authoritatively. "No anything out of the ordinary if you don't want your whole crew figuring it out. That was one of the issues, right?"

Sierra set her mug down and exhaled. "You're no fun."

"If you're cool with everybody knowing, then—"

"I won't flirt. I won't give him special attention. I'll try not to look at him." She knew she would look at him, probably a lot. But she also recognized Hayden was right. Work today would be challenging enough as they painted the interior and prepped for the floors. Acting like there was nothing between her and Cole… She was sleep-deprived, had only drunk a single cup of coffee, and her hormones were stuck in the on position. And yet she couldn't help wondering what the chances were for a redo with Cole tonight.

"If you don't want to scare him away, you need to play it cool, even in private," Hayden dictated.

Sierra wanted to growl at her, wanted to argue, wanted to do anything but play it cool with Cole…but she suspected her friend's advice was legit. Problem was, she wasn't sure if she *could* play it cool.

CHAPTER TWENTY-ONE

*A*fter an extra-long day at work, Cole needed two things —a shower and a drink, in that order.

Tito greeted him at the door of his apartment and trailed him into the bedroom, raising hell the whole way. Cole shed his clothes and tossed them in the laundry basket in his closet, then went into the attached bathroom, the cat zipping in in front of him.

"Rough day at the office?" Cole asked Tito, who jumped up onto the bathroom vanity and sat pear-shaped on the corner. He rubbed the cat's ears, noted he was purring.

A few minutes later, Cole was clean, his hair was mostly dry thanks to its shortness, Tito was tearing into some beef paté, and an overpowering need to go see Sierra jabbed at Cole. He refused to give in. If he showed up at her place tonight, it'd set a precedent. If he couldn't stay away for one goddamn night, he was screwed.

He would stay away. It was just going to take some distractions.

While Tito was still absorbed in his food bowl, Cole walked out the door and back down the stairs to Sunshine's.

All day, he'd been taunted by thoughts of last night, from the way she'd so willingly come to him on the balcony to the sounds she'd made when she came apart to the feel of her hair cascading over his chest, his arms, everywhere. All of it was imprinted in his brain, the memories visceral, unrelenting.

Work had been a mind fuck. While the rest of the crew had painted, he and Sierra had prepped for laying the floors, which would be a multi-day project. On the outside, it would've looked like any other day between them, with them working as a team, problem solving, ensuring that the appropriate materials were in each room, the tile saw ready to go in the garage. But beneath the surface, it was anything but usual. His mind had played an all-day game of what-if. *What if I guided her into that closet and kissed her till she couldn't remember her name? What if I lowered her onto that waist-high pallet of boxed ceramic tile and made her come with my fingers? What if I propped her up on that oversized bathroom vanity and unleashed my tongue on her?*

All the while, they'd kept their discussion professional and work-related. He was grateful for that and yet he hated it. The only hint that he hadn't dreamed up the night before was a single moment when, after they'd carried the last of the wood floor planks to the living room, she'd touched him, given his biceps a seemingly nonchalant squeeze as she peered up at him with a flash of heat in her eyes. There was technically nothing sexual about the gesture, and some people wouldn't even have registered it as being out of character, but Sierra didn't touch her crew, ever. And the look in her eyes, as if she wanted him to do all the things he'd been fantasizing about the entire damn day... He'd had to lie and tell her he had to take a break to call his mom, just to give him an excuse to go sit in his truck, away from her, and get his mental shit together.

"Hi, handsome," Winona said as he sat on his usual stool, second from the right end, in the dingy, dim tavern. "How's your mom doing?" She asked it every time he saw her, like a mother figure herself.

"We got her home last night. It wore her out but she's happy to be home."

"Good." Winona slid a tall mug of cold beer to him. "Food?"

"Usual."

"Got it." She disappeared into her kitchen, and Cole noted the place was fuller than normal, which meant close to two dozen patrons needing to drown the Monday blues. Across the way, at a table near the wall, was a trio of women, good-looking, dressed for an evening out, and blatantly eyeing him. For about two seconds, he pondered the possibility of taking one of them to bed to get Sierra out of his head, but if he was honest, he had zero interest in any of them. He wanted to be interested. Wanted to think about anything but his brown-eyed beauty…

Not *his*.

Hell. If it was tough to keep his mind off of her at work, it was nearly impossible now, with nothing to occupy him but a mug of beer.

His phone vibrated in his pocket, and he pulled it out to find a group text message from Gabe to him, Mason, and Drake.

Aunt Liz says Mom did well today, did some walking around the house, ate well, was in a good mood. Miranda is there now, playing Scrabble with her.

Drake replied, *Don't know who I'm more afraid for, Miranda or Mom.*

Both their cousin and their mom were cut-throat Scrabble players. Cole and his brothers had stopped playing the game with their mom years ago because no one could beat her. Miranda could and did frequently.

Mom should be able to sleep well post word battle, Mason texted.

Though Cole didn't have anything to add—he wasn't one for extraneous conversation—the distraction was welcome, and it got him thinking. ·

He opened a new message window on his phone, this one going only to Mason.

You busy? he typed.

Trying to finish at the office. What's up?

Cole paused before sending the next message, debating with himself. He hadn't planned any of this, had mostly written off the mention of working for North Brothers. Mostly. But he wasn't sure how he could continue to work side by side with Sierra when he wanted her so badly he walked around with a semi all day. Wasn't sure if that need would ever go away.

You eat yet? Cole asked.

Planning to grab something on my way home.

You familiar with Sunshine's?

Never heard of it.

Of course he hadn't heard of it. It wasn't the type of place his designer-suit-wearing, R8-driving CEO brother would ever step foot in. As Cole had never invited Mason to his apartment, his brother had no familiarity with Cole's part of town.

Cole grinned to himself, getting a twisted sort of pleasure from the thought of Mason walking into this place he absolutely didn't belong.

Little place on Galveston Avenue, Cole typed. *Stop by for a drink or a sandwich, my treat. Got some questions for you.*

There was a pause for a minute or two, probably as Mason reeled in his shock at Cole's invitation. First time for everything, Cole figured. He really didn't want to sit here alone all evening, thinking about the woman he shouldn't have. And his questions were legit.

Twenty-two-hundred block? Mason finally texted, and Cole imagined him searching on his phone for the Sunshine's address.

Yep.

Be there in twenty, Mason texted.

When Mason walked in the door, Cole had finished his beef and cheddar and was on his second beer. When Gabe followed directly behind Mason, Cole did a double take. Of course, they were both wearing suits, which made Cole glance at the stools next to him to make sure they were clean.

"Sweet mother of God," Winona muttered to herself when she saw them. "Do not pick a fight with them," she instructed Cole.

Cole hid a grin, realizing she had no idea who they were. "I could take 'em both at once." He hadn't done it for more than a decade, but he knew his pretty-boy brothers honed their muscles in the gym for a couple of hours a week, not as part of a forty-plus-hour job.

"Don't you dare."

His brothers spotted him, and as they made their way toward

him, he downed several gulps of beer. This conversation wasn't going to be comfortable, but as he'd sat here for twenty-some minutes thinking things through as he waited, he knew he needed to gather info.

"Hey, Cole," Mason said, unbuttoning his jacket and sitting on the stool to the left.

Gabe gave Cole a friendly smack on the back as he took the stool to Cole's right.

Cole looked pointedly at his Timex. "Four minutes late," he said to Mason, trying to keep the corner of his lips from lifting. "Losing your touch."

"I had to park a block away," Mason said dismissively, but Cole suspected, deep inside, he was pissed at the blemish on his early-to-on-time record.

When Cole turned his gaze to Winona, he caught her with her mouth literally hanging open and her eyes narrowed, and that brought out an honest-to-God laugh from him.

"Winona," he said formally, "meet Mason, my oldest brother, and Gabe, second oldest. This is Winona James, owner of Sunshine's and my apartment upstairs."

She shook both their offered hands, and Cole swore he'd never, ever seen her unable to speak as she was now. He knew his brothers, tall and, he supposed, good-looking, made an impression in their monkey suits, especially in contrast to the Sunshine's clientele, but he was starting to wonder if she was having a stroke or some other medical emergency.

"You okay?" he asked her, knowing that, as long as she didn't actually keel over, he was going to give her shit about this for years to come.

"These are your brothers," she stated stupidly. "The North brothers." She tilted her head suddenly, the crinkles at the corners of her eyes and in her forehead deepening, as if a realization had hit her. "North brothers," she repeated, eyeing them, then Cole, then them again.

If Cole were nicer, he'd help her out, but nice was something he'd never been accused of.

"You don't have anything to do with North Brothers Sports, do you?" she asked suspiciously.

"Guilty as charged," Mason said with a charming smile he must practice in front of the mirror.

"Our dad is one of the original North Brothers," Gabe added, and Cole had to work not to roll his eyes out of habit. He needed to break that habit.

Winona glared at Cole, accusation in her eyes. "This one never mentioned it."

"Now you know," Cole said unapologetically. "Maybe they're thirsty?"

After a last second of pronounced glare, Winona asked his brothers for their drink orders and handed them the single-sided, nonlaminated paper menu of sandwich fixings. As soon as she'd slid bottles of beer to each of them, she disappeared into the back to make their requested sandwiches.

"You spend a lot of time here," Gabe said, not in question form.

"It's like having a personal chef," Cole said.

"So you said you have questions," Mason said, ever the down-to-business guy. "What's up?"

Cole finished off his beer and shoved the mug toward Winona's side of the counter so she could refill it when she came back in. That she hadn't already replaced it proved that his brothers had her off her game.

He reminded himself he was only collecting info, not giving in. Keeping his gaze straight ahead at the wall of liquor behind the bar, he tapped his fingers on the counter, wishing he had his mug back to fidget with. "*If* I were interested in working for the family biz, what would you have me do?"

"It's like I told you the other day—whatever you want," Mason said.

Cole frowned, shook his head. "That sounds good and all, but let's be real. You can't just hire me to make nice. It needs to make financial sense. Am I wrong?"

"You're not wrong," Gabe said, "but I think what Mason's

trying to say is that we can find something that will make you happy while benefitting the company."

"Like what?" Cole persisted. He was far from being convinced that there was even anything for him to consider.

"You have an analytical mind," Mason said, and Cole couldn't argue. "You like what you're doing now? I mean, beyond working for Sierra?"

"I do. I like being active, working with my hands. Can't imagine being stuck in a suit or at a desk all day, so I'm not sure there's anything at North for me."

"It wouldn't have to be in the corporate office necessarily," Gabe said.

"I'm not going to work retail like Drake." No fucking way.

"It wouldn't have to be retail," Mason said, his cool blue eyes narrowed in thought.

Gabe leaned forward and addressed Mason. "What do you have in mind? I can tell something's brewing," he asked as Winona reappeared, plates heaped full with double-decker sandwiches and chips in hand.

Cole nodded at Winona when she raised her penciled-in brows to ask if he wanted another beer.

"We're looking at expansion," Mason said once Winona headed out to the tables to wipe off some recently vacated ones. His voice was quiet but firm, telling Cole this might not be common knowledge yet. "*Major* expansion," he said. "It's an aggressive undertaking, with new stores throughout the region, not just in state."

That was the first Cole had heard of plans to expand beyond Tennessee, not that they'd have reason to tell him. He took it to mean the company was doing well.

"We're working on the first few locations, securing properties. If things work out, there's going to be remodeling involved. Branding of each location from the ground up is vital, from layout to building materials. That's something the CEO oversaw in the past, but that was one store at a time, and it was before the company was so large."

"Cole would be a perfect fit," Gabe said, nodding thoughtfully as he shoved a chip in his mouth and chewed.

"Would this position call for a suit or a tool belt?" Cole asked, intrigued but cautious.

"Not a suit," Mason said. "Maybe not a tool belt either. I envision you working closely with the contractors at each site to ensure they do things our way, overseeing quality, branding, and budgeting."

"And timeline," Gabe added.

"Definitely timeline." Mason nodded pensively as he paused with his beer raised halfway to his mouth. "We'll need to hammer out the details—"

"Don't get overeager," Cole said. "I was only asking about possibilities. I'm not ready to change jobs." If he didn't put the brakes on, Mason would have him hired before walking out of the bar tonight.

That wasn't what he wanted. He wasn't sure what he wanted professionally. He needed time to consider, needed his brothers to give it more thought as well, because leaving Dunn & Lowell... He couldn't do that on a whim. Couldn't do that to Sierra without good reason.

As he imagined not being with her for eight to ten hours a day... Hell, he wasn't sure if he could do it at all.

He steered the conversation to baseball and the World Series fallout, effectively ending talk of a job change for now.

CHAPTER TWENTY-TWO

*W*ednesday evening, Sierra triple-checked the reflective black address numbers above the solid-looking wood door right next to Sunshine's, a bar she'd never in her life heard of that looked anything but bright and cheery. More like dark and eerie and potentially a bad decision.

Her misgivings started before she even climbed out of her truck. Maybe she shouldn't have come. Maybe she should've done what a normal person would do and texted Cole the news. Or even asked him to her place. He'd never given her his address, not on a social basis, and she'd had to look it up in his personnel records. It was a bad idea, and maybe he'd see it as crossing yet another ill-advised line. But she couldn't deny a burning curiosity about where he lived.

It'd been three days since their night together. Three long, torturous workdays of acting professional, keeping her hands to herself, catching him looking at her like he wanted to devour her. The sexual energy between them was tangible, and if none of her other employees had caught on, it was act-of-God miracle level. But she'd managed to keep herself in check and "play it cool."

Playing it cool sucked, and there was no question in her mind she was using her good news from the Eldridge contest as an excuse to see Cole somewhere besides the office or jobsite. Did she mention she'd made it three full days?

"I'm going in," she said out loud to no one. She got out of the truck and went to the wooden door. Inside, she found a barren concrete stairway going up and not much else, so she climbed. The single door at the top wasn't marked. Without giving herself more time to doubt her actions, she knocked.

She heard footsteps and felt someone peering through the peephole at her, and then the knob turned and her heart pounded as the door seemed to open in slow motion. And then there he was, the man she'd had on her mind nonstop, standing in all his glory. Half-naked glory, as the only thing he had on was a pair of faded jeans. She'd run her hands over the stacks of muscles and the valleys between in the near dark the other night, but that had nothing on seeing his sculpted body in the cozy, warm light of his apartment.

"Hi," she said, tearing her gaze from his torso to take in the upward quirk of one side of his mouth, the five-o'clock shadow on his jaw, the glint of heat in his eyes that told her maybe he was happy to see her too.

"What are you doing here?" he said, tilting his head and seeming to fight a full-out smile.

"I just—"

"How'd you know where I live?"

"I have my ways—"

"Never mind," he said with a little shake of his head. "Get in here." Peering down at her with a lingering half grin, he took her hand and pulled her in, and Sierra didn't fight it one bit. He closed the door and locked it, two locks, and then turned to face her again.

Sierra's attention was drawn to the apartment, and she took in her surroundings, trying to be subtle at first, but then it was no use. "This is not what I expected."

The living room, where they stood, was connected to a compact kitchen with a charcoal-and-white-swirled granite-topped breakfast bar in between that appeared to serve as his dining area. The kitchen was stunningly updated and masculine, with stainless appliances, dark gray cabinets, and a simple white tile backsplash.

She pivoted back toward the living room to take in the details —a slate-gray couch along the wall, floor-to-ceiling shelves on either side of the TV filled with scores of books, and the element that took a comfortable room and made it cozy, a lived-in saddle-brown leather chair with a matching ottoman angled in front of the only window in the room. On the end table next to it was a pile of three books, a beer bottle, and a remote for the TV. A solid cream-colored rug nearly filled the area, covering what looked to be old but well-maintained wide-planked wood floors.

"What did you expect?" Cole asked, crossing his arms as he leaned his back against the door.

"It's not in a new part of town," she said with only a slight hesitation. "On the outside, it looks a little sketchy. That bar downstairs…"

He laughed. "Not your kind of place."

"I'm not sure I'd go there alone," she acknowledged. "But this…" She gestured around them. "Your home is really nice."

It was an understatement. His apartment was like a view into the side of him he didn't let anyone see. Maybe a glimpse of the true Cole. It felt familiar, comfortable in a way she couldn't really explain to herself. It felt right. Which made no sense.

"How did you get your landlord to let you do this?" she asked. Because it was unquestionably his work, his taste. She'd worked with him long enough to recognize that.

"I've lived here for so long she'll let me do just about whatever I want."

"Why? Why do you live here?" Sierra asked, catching a glimpse of his bedroom through the doorway on the left side of the kitchen. "Why not buy a house if you were going to do all this work making it the way you want it?"

Cole pushed away from the door and shrugged. "Didn't want the hassle, I guess. This is comfortable. Winona—my landlady— doesn't want to find a new renter, so she lets me fix the place up. I don't want to hunt for a house and start over. Plus she makes me dinner whenever I want it."

"Your landlady cooks for you?"

"*Cooks* is a stretch. She serves sandwiches at Sunshine's."

"You read a lot," Sierra said, somehow surprised and yet not surprised at the same time. She took two steps to the nearest shelf and ran her finger down the spines of some of the books at shoulder level. "Smarty-pants."

"Why are you here, Sierra?"

Oops. The smarty-pants thing might've hit a raw nerve again, because an edge sounded in his voice.

She angled away from the custom-made bookshelf to face him fully, a smile bubbling out as she remembered the news she'd come to share. "We," she said dramatically, stepping closer to him, "did it. We made it to the next round of the Eldridge contest. One of ten companies."

"Yeah?" A smile inched up the corners of his mouth and sincerity shone in his eyes. "That's great news. You deserve it."

"*We.* I know you're behind the scenes, but you're part of it. A big part of it, as I'm pretty sure it was your excellent writing that did it."

He blew out a lighthearted scoff as if to disagree. "Come here."

Before the words were all the way out of his mouth, he'd pulled her into his arms, and this...this was exactly where she ached to be, enveloped by his strong biceps, pressed up against his hard chest, breathing in his masculine scent.

It took about half an instant for the tone of the hug to switch from celebratory to charged, the awareness between them jumping straight to sexual. Because...three eternal days...

As one, they pulled their heads apart enough to look at each other, and Cole nudged her chin up with his finger. At once, they met in a kiss, with him leaning down, her stretching up, and the sensual sound that came from Cole's throat was earthy and raw and affected the most female parts of her.

Cole had her against the door in no time, and there was no mistaking his hardness pressing into her lower abdomen. On the one hand, she wanted to get him the rest of the way naked before she took in her next breath. On the other, the way he was suddenly kissing her, as if he'd thrown the brakes on to slow down and milk the goodness out of every second, with a thoroughness, a gentleness that made her feel cherished… She could stand here and kiss him for days.

She was lost in the way he was making love to her mouth when something brushed up against her calf, startling her, causing her to pull away with a loud gasp as she looked down.

The cat, she realized.

When Cole saw what she was looking at, he let out a low laugh and shook his head. "Such a jealous bastard. Can't be bothered to come out of his nest in the dirty clothes basket until he figures out someone else is getting the attention he thinks he's entitled to."

Still holding on to Cole, she watched the black-and-white-speckled cat, almost like a feline version of a Dalmatian, saunter into the center of the living room and hop up on the ottoman. "Tito?" she asked, drawing the name from her memory of the other night.

"One and only."

Before she could say more, Cole's lips were back on hers and she forgot about the animal in the room. She ran her hands over his bare chest, around to his strong back, down over his ass outside his jeans, thrilling in the feel of it even through the thick denim. She gave his butt a playful squeeze and pulled him more firmly against her body. In a heartbeat, he lifted her off the floor, his hands on the backs of her thighs, lining up their bodies perfectly, eliciting a breathy sound from her. She wrapped her legs around his waist as he trailed his lips and tongue over her jawline to a spot beneath her ear that sent shivers through her.

"Question," he said, his voice low and gravelly, his breath wisping over her ear. "Did you really come all the way over here just to tell me about the contest?"

A smile broke out over her lips, and she tried to hold it in even though he couldn't see it as he was focusing his attention on her neck. "Of course," she lied. "Why else would I?" She nearly laughed as she said it, because with the things he was doing with his tongue, she could barely remember there was a contest.

He pulled his head away from her, met her gaze directly. "I

should stop then?" There was a spark in his eyes and a hint of a grin that said he was teasing.

"I mean, if you really want to," she bluffed back, knowing if he so much as tried to pull away, she would hold on for all she was worth, with both arms and legs.

He peered down at her, brows raised. "All you gotta do is admit it."

"Admit what?"

"You came over for more than conversation."

With a low laugh that sounded nothing like her, she said, "Not at all. I thought, after all your work on the application, you deserved an in-person message."

"Then you're probably ready to get going now, huh?" He put his hands up as if in surrender, and the only things keeping her from falling were her grip on him and the way he had her pressed between him and the door.

"Okay, okay," she said, laughing again. "Maybe a part of me wanted to see you half-naked."

"Just half-naked?"

She reached between them and unsnapped his jeans. "I'm up for full-on naked anytime you want to stop the games." To show she was serious, she dipped her fingers under the waist of his jeans in back, skimming them over the skin of his ass.

His arms came back around her. "Thank God," he said on an exhale, now fully letting a smile out. Then he went serious in an instant. "It's been killing me not to see you outside of work. Not to touch you at work."

"Thank God," she mimicked, completely serious as well. As he had a hold of her again, she was able to ease away just enough to lower his zipper.

With a grunt, he stopped her and carried her to the bedroom, then lowered her to the floor. "Get naked," he said, his voice a sexy rumble.

"Bossy," she said, not minding at all as she took off her slip-on sneakers and let her oversized cardigan fall off her shoulders. The lamp by the side of the bed was on a low setting, casting a warmth over the room, which wasn't big enough to hold more than the queen-sized bed, a nightstand, and another wall full of shelves and books.

Cole disappeared into the bathroom on the far side of the room and she heard a drawer opening and him rustling around as if searching inside of it as she whipped off her long-sleeved tee and slid her leggings down and off her legs. She was down to her bra and underwear, a matched set in coral, when he emerged from the bathroom carrying a box of condoms.

"Not naked yet," he said as he tossed the box near the pillows on the bed, which was neatly made. "But I like those." He indicated her lingerie.

"You're not naked yet either."

In a single quick move, he shoved his jeans and underwear down his legs and stepped out of them, and God's truth, his body was even more spectacular than she'd imagined the other night and a thousand times since. She stepped back enough to look him up and down, appreciating every inch of taut skin over muscle on his chest, abs, thighs…

She moved forward again and reached for his erection, barely sliding her fingers over it before he backed up.

"Naked," he repeated. "Need help?"

So that was how he wanted to play it. With a smug grin, Sierra walked a few steps to the end of the bed and faced him, out of his reach. Cole cocked his head sideways, no doubt wondering what she was up to, and then she unhooked her bra, pulled the straps down her arms, and let it fall to the floor. An appreciative growl came from Cole.

"Is this what you were after?" she said as she playfully grasped her breasts.

He took a step toward her and she held out a hand. "Nope. Stay there till I say."

She was a little surprised when he stopped as she'd ordered. Her body was on fire from the way he gazed at her, lust and approval burning in his eyes. Her eyes on his angled face, she hooked her fingers in the sides of her bikinis and pushed them slowly down her thighs, calves, ankles, then stood. Before Cole could move, she went to the opposite side of the bed from him, pulled the bedding down, and positioned herself on her back in the center, propped up on pillows, one leg straight, one knee bent up in invitation. It wasn't a move she would normally make, so bold and confident, but the look in his eyes drove her.

"Is this what you wanted?" she asked coyly.

Without answering, he was on her in a millisecond, kissing her lips, his hands all over her body as if making up for the few seconds she'd made him stand back and watch from a distance. She responded in kind, running her hands over that magnificent ass as she'd been dying to, pulling him into her body, beyond ready for him to be inside of her.

Taking one hand away momentarily, she felt around the mattress for the box of protection, pulled out a foil packet, opened it, and sheathed him. In the next second, she welcomed him into her body, closing her eyes as that feeling of rightness once again washed through her.

CHAPTER TWENTY-THREE

Sierra lay next to Cole in his bed, face-to-face, her body still tingling from the aftereffects of off-the-charts amazing sex and her mind only beginning to come back online. His arm was around her, and he nuzzled his nose along her forehead and then trailed lazy, sated kisses over her cheek, down to her lips.

That was the thing about him, she was learning. He wasn't just considerate and attentive working up to the main event. He was just as focused on her afterward, showering tenderness on her like no other guy she'd been with. He didn't seem to be the type to roll over and fall asleep as soon as he got his needs taken care of.

The more she learned about Cole, the more he surprised her, in delicious, heart-melting ways. He was unselfish and certainly skilled at the sex part, but it was the moments afterward and in between that had the potential to make her fall for him. Minus the whole escape-in-the-middle-of-the-night thing.

"Don't think for a second you're going to kick me out," she said lightly, her voice husky and lower than usual.

She felt the low rumble of a laugh in his chest more than heard it. "Who said anything about kicking you out?"

"Not now and not after round two or round three or however many times you ravish me."

"Ravish? It's a good word but maybe not the right one."

She laughed quietly at the thought of debating vocabulary post-sex. That was a new one for her, and she sort of loved it. "You just ravished the hell out of me."

"Maybe, but only after you showed up and seduced the hell out of me," he echoed. "And then the semi-striptease and the way you threw yourself on my bed in invitation—"

"Did you not like it?" she said, fully confident he had.

"The image of you in my sheets will be with me till the day I die. But *ravish* conveys that I was the only aggressive one. You came over here with a mission, and while I wholeheartedly approve, we shouldn't mislabel anything."

"I've never slept with a word nerd before. It's kind of sexy. But"—she ran a finger along his jawline—"you're still not making me creep out of here in the middle of the night."

"I have no intention of that," he said, and he seemed to mean it. At least at this moment.

"What happens when you get that panicked feeling like you did the other night?"

Bull's-eye.

Cole pulled away and rolled onto his back with a heavy exhale. "I won't," he said after some time had ticked by. "But we should probably get some things straight."

Her gut tightened, but she'd never been the type to shy away from the tough things. "Such as?"

"I don't want to give you the wrong idea. About us. I'm not the relationship type."

Though his words didn't entirely shock her, she still felt a sinking in her gut. She rallied quickly, not allowing the sting to sink in. "Staying all night doesn't have to mean relationship. I mean, if you want to get technical, we've had a relationship since the day I hired you."

"Yeah. I'm not good at them. The man-woman kind or anything else. I screw them up."

He'd never, for as long as she'd known him, spoken of a girl-friend before, but then he didn't tend to talk about anything personal at work. She hadn't known he had brothers until the night of his mom's heart attack. "When's the last time you were in a serious relationship?" she asked.

He reached over to the lamp on the nightstand and flipped it off, plummeting the room into darkness. If that made it easier for him to talk, she was okay with it. For now. As long as he talked.

"I've never had a serious relationship," he said quietly into the dark.

"Never?" She was surprised and yet not surprised at the same time.

She felt him shake his head.

"How about sorta serious?" she asked.

He shook his head again. "I'm not good with people, Sierra. I like facts and logical, practical things. Those are easy to get right."

Easy for a literal genius, she thought with a private grin. She sobered up instantly, glad he couldn't see her, because he was revealing parts of himself that she suspected he didn't show to most. "You could be good with people. If you wanted to."

"I want to. I mean, now I want to. I used to not want to, and I ruined nearly every relationship I had—with my dad and every one of my brothers, coaches, teachers, bosses, coworkers."

"What about your mom?" Sierra had yet to meet her, and she longed to because, just like seeing where he lived had done, she suspected meeting his mom would help her understand more about Cole.

"She's always understood me better than most." He scoffed. "Better than I realized she did. I wouldn't say we've been close over the years, but we've never been on bad terms, in spite of me being a jackass in general."

She rolled toward him, so that she was perched over his chest. Though the darkness was close to one hundred percent in the windowless room and she couldn't see him, she hoped to get her point across to him. "You're not a jackass, Cole. I don't like when you talk like that about yourself."

"You don't know me that well," he said in a challenge.

"I might not know your history or your family, but I've worked with you for more than three years. I know the kind of man you are. You're hardworking, dedicated, smart as hell, a good leader, respected by the rest of the crew—"

"I get in fights, I've been a shit to my family for years, I push people away before they can try to get close, I've never in my life had a close friend—" He cut himself off, blowing out another hard breath. She could feel him shaking his head, but even more telling were his words.

He'd never had friends because he'd felt out of place from the time he was a little boy. He was different. He was amazing, in her eyes, but he'd always been *different* from everyone else. She had a little experience with that herself, having been absorbed by her passion for renovating houses even as a kid. That wasn't normal, and she'd taken shit for it, but thankfully she'd still had some really good friends along the way. Hayden from almost the beginning, and others here and there, some of whom she still kept in touch with.

Cole hadn't had that. He hadn't trusted anyone enough to let them really get to know him and his differences. Ever, she realized now. Not the kids at school, not his brothers, not his coworkers, not any women along the way.

Her heart ached for him, for the loneliness he must feel. And the fear, still today, he apparently felt about letting someone know him.

That he had opened up this much to her made her breath catch. She instinctively knew it was more than he'd let anyone else in, and that was likely what caused him to panic at her place the other night.

"Have you ever spent an entire night with a woman?" she asked, remembering their conversation from the other night and suspecting his answer before he said it.

He blew out a humorless laugh. "No."

"But you think you can do it tonight?" she asked gently, all hints of her earlier refusal to leave gone.

"I want to, but..." He went silent and she waited for the but.

"Cole?"

"I don't want to mislead you."

"You don't want me to think we're in a relationship. Because you don't do relationships. Because they're confusing."

He laughed a little. "You definitely get full credit for listening. But where do we draw the line? I like being with you. I love the hell out of ravishing you. But I'm not capable of anything more."

"Maybe I'm not asking for anything more."

Yet.

She wanted more. It was suddenly clear how much she wanted more, but also evident was that she'd have to give him time to ease into it. The smallest bit of pressure and he'd shut her out. She was beginning to understand how right Hayden was about playing it cool.

"Maybe you should tell me exactly what you're asking for then," he said, and it felt like a victory that he was even asking. If she could lay it out as facts, not feelings, maybe he would feel okay about this. About them.

"Well," she said, trailing her finger over his chest, back and forth, reveling in the textures of muscle and masculine hair, "sex is good."

"I can't argue with that. I could have sex with you every night, but then it starts to seem like a relationship."

"And we can't have that," she said, making her tone light. "So sex but not every night. And maybe dinner sometimes so we don't start feeling cheap."

Another quiet laugh rumbled out of him. "Maybe I should write this down. Put a list on my phone."

She flicked his chest. "Don't you dare. The whole point is it's casual. It's no-obligation. All we have to do is communicate. If you don't feel like spending time with me, tell me. If you do, tell me. Let's just take it one day at a time."

"One day at a time and communicate," he repeated, seeming to consider. "I think I can do that."

"You're pretty smart," she said, grinning, relaxing a little for now, though she wasn't under any illusion that getting what she wanted, more of Cole, was going to be easy. She herself wasn't all about jumping into something serious, but she liked him a lot. Wanted more of him. A lot more. If she really thought about how much she wanted him in her life, it could get scary fast, so she didn't think about it.

One day at a time.

"Today is yes to sex," he said, the lightheartedness creeping back into his voice.

"Definite yes." She moved her hand down his abdomen to his man parts and found the main attraction stirring, already semi-hard. "And if you can make it through the whole night without kicking me out, tomorrow morning is looking pretty good too."

He groaned as she grasped him, a sexy, drawn-out sound that checked in directly with her hormones. "That's a pretty good incentive."

"Pretty good?" She took her hand away.

"The best," he rumbled, his smile evident.

A girl couldn't ask for much more than that. For now.

CHAPTER TWENTY-FOUR

There was nothing Cole liked to watch more than Sierra in her element, and she was full-on in her element right now. In her element and flying high, as she should be after yesterday's news that she, or *they* as she insisted, had been selected as one of three finalists in the Eldridge competition after the second round, the interview stage.

Sierra had shined, charmed, and impressed with her knowledge and experience during the recorded interview—Cole had been on-site for moral support and watched on a monitor. He could fully cop to being biased, but obviously the unbiased production people and probably Eldridge himself agreed with him that she could carry any show they wanted to give her—as well as any renovation project.

Today, they'd been granted entry into the Eldridge Mansion, along with the other finalists, in order to survey, measure, research, and plan for the final stage of the competition—full business proposals.

"Cole!" Sierra grasped his arm as they walked from the rear hall on the main floor into what appeared to be a den. "Look at the two-sided fireplace. That must be the living room on the other side."

He followed her to the fireplace and ran his hand over the drywall. "I wonder if there are bricks under here."

"There has to be. My grandpa nearly stroked out whenever someone put drywall over bricks. He always said bricks are like glimpses of the building's soul."

He couldn't help a grin at the drama in her voice. No one was as animated as Sierra when it came to her favorite subject.

It'd been nearly three weeks since they'd started sleeping together, nearly twenty-one days of one-day-at-a-timing it. It made him sweat a little to think about how many of those nights had been a yes, some at his place, some at hers. Probably too many to be considered casual or a non-relationship. So he made a point of not thinking about the big picture and instead focusing on the moments. Because the moments with Sierra were so damn good.

He'd taken her to Sunshine's to meet Winona, who'd of course loved her. And contrary to what he'd feared, Sierra had embraced both Winona and her dim, outdated bar with its rough patrons.

Work-wise, they'd been swamped and spread thin. The Draper project, thanks to every kind of unforeseen challenge you could think of, had run a week and a half longer than planned. Sierra felt strongly about starting the next project, a full renovation of a historical bank building, on time, so they'd divided the crew between the two, with Cole overseeing the Draper site and Sierra at the bank. In general, he and Sierra didn't make a habit of splitting up—in fact, they generally only scheduled one project at a time—but because the Draper shit show had eaten up the contingency days and then some, they'd done what was necessary to try to keep everyone happy. The result was that he saw her less during the day, and though he missed her, he suspected it was just as well. It was getting harder to keep things strictly professional when they woke up together several mornings each week.

Cole was inspecting the window trim in the den—it had suffered water damage and would need to be replaced, along with the window—when he felt Sierra's arms wrap around him from behind. He twisted to face her, glancing around to verify that no one could see them. Though Carlos and Troy weren't due to show up for another half hour or so, the only two they could spare from the bank site today, teams from the other two finalists were here, taking notes and measuring as well.

He pressed a quick kiss to Sierra's forehead and nonchalantly slipped out of her arms. "Nine-foot ceilings make it seem bigger, especially with the tall windows. The crown molding will need to be replaced."

"I agree," she said from behind him, a hint of confusion in her voice, which had to be because he'd walked away. She was rarely confused about a renovation project. "Colonial revival molding, for sure."

She pulled out her measuring tape, as she'd done in every room so far, and together they measured everything—twice—from the windows to the fireplace to the room size.

"What do you think about some built-in shelves on this wall?" Cole said, imagining the room with a little less space and thinking it would only add to the coziness of it.

Sierra came over to him, so close he caught her Creamsicle scent and, in spite of himself, imagined pressing her up against the wall and devouring her with his mouth. He wouldn't, not here, but he thought about it in graphic detail for the seconds Sierra took to consider his shelf idea.

"I think," she said slowly, her eyes starting on the wall behind him and then veering up to his face, a flirtatious sparkle in them, "that a man who likes to read is super hot." She ran her hands up his chest, went up on her tiptoes, and planted a kiss on his lips.

He was drawn in for a few seconds, unable to pull himself away from her tempting body, her sexy onslaught. Footsteps on the creaky floor above them pulled him back to the reality of where they were and what they needed to be doing. It wasn't kissing, but they could make time for that later.

Again, Cole ended the kiss. "As much as it pains me, this isn't the place. Carlos and Troy are due any minute.

"So?" Sierra smiled up at him, her cheeks rosy, stray strands of her hair around her face shifting with every movement.

"It's not a good idea for the rest of the crew to find out about us."

Her smile faded as she seemed to really think about it. She blew out a breath. "You're no fun," she said in a pout.

"I'm lots of fun when I'm off the clock."

With a flirty grin, she said, "Yes, you are." The grin faded again. "And you're probably right about keeping it private."

He leaned his back against the wall, increasing the space between them, because no matter how much he believed they shouldn't be all over each other here, there was always a pull, anytime she was nearby. "Of course I'm right," he said lightly. "We don't want to make any of the crew feel uncomfortable."

"We don't." She took a half step back herself, obviously disappointed, and he hated that, but he knew she'd regret it if their sleeping together affected her business.

Beyond that, there was also a faint voice in his head that said if the guys he worked with every day found out, then there'd be expectations. Whatever he and Sierra had going on between them would then become a thing, a defined thing, a more-than-one-day-at-a-time thing, and Cole wasn't ready for that. Wasn't sure when or if he would be. He fully recognized his asshole was showing with that, wasn't proud of it, but he'd never misled Sierra about what he was up for.

He straightened, and she still had her gaze glued on him. "I guess your smarts are part of what I like about you," she said begrudgingly, but her lips were once again flirting with a smile.

"It doesn't mean it's easy for me to keep my hands off you," he said honestly, his fingers itching to brush back a stray strand of hair that had fallen over her cheek.

He stepped away from her, breathing through the urge and pulling out his phone to check the app where he was recording all the data. They had what they needed in this room.

"Ready for the living room?" he asked her.

"Yes, Mr. Foreman. Let's get this done so we can go home and I can ravish you."

No way in hell Cole could argue with that as he led her into the next room and ignored the faint pulse of discomfort deep inside his screwed-up brain.

CHAPTER TWENTY-FIVE

ole hadn't been to the corporate office of North Brothers Sports since he was a kid. Nothing had changed, at least on the outside. Same nondescript building, same suite on the second floor. Well, the suite had expanded to take up the entire second floor, but beyond that, even the faint old-office-building odor was familiar if not welcome.

He exited the elevator and paused outside the door of the main reception area, which also hadn't evolved. The logo on the door had been updated, probably more than once, though Cole didn't keep up with it, but beyond that, the sameness took him back to the time when he'd been young enough to get excited about visiting his parents' workplace. He'd been ten or eleven the last time and had shadowed his dad for an entire day—a take-your-kid-to-work day—and back then, Cole had thrived on it. Welcomed the time away from school, where he didn't fit in, welcomed the special treatment at his dad's company, where he was the boss's son.

Shit. Nostalgia blindsided him, rolled through him like an undertow that could either take him where he needed to be or pull him under and drown him. Swallowing, he shoved the emotion aside as he opened the door.

It was after six p.m., so the receptionist's desk was deserted. He hesitated, unsure where to go, annoyed with Mason for not being more specific when he'd called earlier today and asked Cole to meet tonight, saying he had something urgent to discuss. Cole and Sierra had stayed at the mansion until they and the other finalists were kicked out at five, then he'd rushed home for a quick shower before heading here—instead of the ravishing they'd discussed earlier.

With no idea whether the CEO's suite was in the same spot as two decades ago—back corner on the left—Cole meandered that way through a nondescript hallway formed on one side by high cubicle walls. He could sense there were a few employees still at their desks on the other side of the wall, but he didn't come into contact with anyone directly, which suited him. Though he'd cleaned up, put on non-work jeans and a long-sleeved T-shirt, he felt like an interloper.

He reached the corner office that had once belonged to his dad, and there was his oldest brother, still wearing his suit, jacket and all, sitting at the polished mahogany desk that had been their father's, chair swiveled around to face the bank of windows as he spoke on the phone. Cole knocked lightly on the doorjamb to let Mason know he was there, feeling vaguely like he had countless times in his adolescence when he'd been sent to the principal's office. Mason spun around and nodded him in as he ended his call.

"Hey," Cole said as he sat in one of the visitor chairs opposite Mason. "What's up?"

"Thanks for coming in, Cole," Mason said, sounding businesslike and formal and yet as if he truly appreciated it.

"It's been a while. A couple of decades since I've been here. Kind of a mind fuck."

Mason looked around briefly, as if trying to see it through Cole's eyes. "Things have changed, huh?"

"And yet they haven't." Cole shook his head, again trying to escape the unexpected emotions that swept through him—surprisingly, not all of them bad. "You said you had something urgent."

Mason grinned. "Straight to business. I like that."

"Have to admit I'm curious."

Mason straightened in his chair, pulled up closer to the desk. "I told you we're working on expanding outside of the state. It's happening even faster than I expected. Today we finalized a deal for four new stores, two in Florida and one each in Alabama and Kentucky."

"Congrats," Cole said, not surprised at all. When Mason set his mind to something, he did it. Always had.

"Thanks. All four locations are existing buildings, and they need various amounts of work. We'd like to get at least two of them open before the holidays."

"Christmas is only six weeks away. Are you talking you just need to clean things up and put up signage or—"

"The insides need to be gutted on two and partially renovated on the other two. We've already been working with architects and the plans are close to finalized."

"No way it could happen before Christmas if they weren't," Cole said.

"We took a gamble and proceeded before the deals were finalized. Happy to say everything worked out. Now we need someone to oversee all four renovations, and that's why I called you."

Cole raised his eyebrows, intrigued in spite of himself.

"I don't have the time to do it, and neither does anyone else. Besides that, I don't have the expertise that will come in handy to get these turned around so quickly. You do."

Cole nodded, waiting for Mason to say more.

Mason grabbed a manila folder from the side of his desk, opened it, slid a couple of sheets of paper across to Cole's side. It was an offer of employment for the position of special projects manager. Cole skimmed over the first page, noting it was a permanent position, that the person who took it would be based at the corporate office but would travel to sites as necessary, and that the salary was almost double what he was currently making. The money was good but not something that would make him drop everything and take it. He made a comfortable living working for Sierra, as his rent was dirt cheap—Winona had barely raised it over the years he'd lived there—and he wasn't a big spender. But he couldn't deny his interest was sparked anyway.

"So I'd be the foreman at each project?" he asked, trying to wrap his head around exactly what Mason was looking for. There was a description of duties, he realized, on the second page, and he'd pore over that later.

"More like the supervisor of the foremen. You'll hire a contractor for each project, and you'll be the liaison. You won't be able to be four places at once, but I want you to be in constant contact with all of them and riding them as hard as necessary to make sure everything is done to our specifications on our timeline."

"And when the four projects are complete?"

"There will be more," Mason said. "We have a corporate remodel in the plans, and our expansion plan for the next five years is aggressive. You might even need to hire an assistant down the road."

Cole sat back, holding the offer, flipping between the two pages even though he wasn't really paying attention to the words on the paper as his thoughts spun.

"I'd report directly to you?" he said as that part of the offer came into focus.

"That's how we have it structured right now. It could change." Mason sat back in his chair, studied Cole. "Is that a problem?"

"I don't know," Cole said honestly. "I don't think so, as long as you're not going to micromanage me and make me wonder why the hell you bothered to hire me."

Mason chuckled at that. "Don't hold back."

"You like to control things," Cole said.

"I do. But I've been at the helm for several years now, and I've learned I can't do everything myself. Not even close. That's why I hire good people."

"And you think I'm good people."

Mason leaned forward, all but getting in Cole's face. "This is my livelihood, Cole. Our family's livelihood. And more than that, Dad and Uncle Ham's legacy. This company means everything to me," he said passionately. "The last thing I would do is make a mercy hire to a family member."

"Okay," Cole said, suitably convinced. He hadn't seen Mason get so worked up about anything for a while.

"You're a literal genius," Mason continued, "with more than a decade of experience in construction, including as a foreman. You know your shit, and if you come across something you don't know, I know you. You'll research the life out of it. If you need or want any kind of classes or certifications along the way, we'll cover it. We give our employees the tools they need to better themselves. It benefits them and it benefits the company. Cole, everyone in the family knows you'd be damn good for the company. Everyone but you. So if you can work through all the stuff from your past, you can do pretty much do whatever you want to at North Brothers."

The bit about his past put Cole on the defensive, and he reined in his reaction, knowing on some level it was irrational. "You done?"

Mason sized him up. "No. I have one more thing to say. Dad loved you and he would want you to be a part of his company. That's not why I'm offering. I'm offering because, frankly, we need you."

"How soon?" Cole asked, ignoring the part about their dad. Maybe he would pick that apart later, when he was alone.

"I need you in Florida on Monday."

"This coming Monday?"

"I know you can't screw Sierra over. I'm willing to share you for as long as you need to give notice, but we have meetings set up with the architect and two potential contractors."

Cole blew out a breath as he imagined giving notice at Dunn & Lowell. Imagined not working with Sierra anymore. More emotion than he would cop to rolled through him, and he worked to keep his face neutral. "It's a lot to think about. How long can you give me?"

"How long do you need?" Mason asked, and Cole sensed it was causing his brother physical pain to put the ball in Cole's court.

"I'll let you know something tomorrow."

For the first time in ever, he needed to talk through a major life decision with someone. Unfortunately, it couldn't be Sierra, since the outcome would affect her directly. He hated the thought of that. He couldn't talk to his brothers, because they had their own agendas.

Winona it was then. He hoped she was in the mood to advise.

And he sure as shit wouldn't be sleeping tonight.

CHAPTER TWENTY-SIX

The day after the Eldridge Mansion exploration, at 6:22 a.m., Sierra's mind was already back on overdrive, spinning with ideas for the proposal for the competition, when Cole had texted. He'd asked if she was planning to hit the office this morning before heading to the worksite, and when she'd said no, he'd asked if he could stop by her apartment before work to talk.

To talk. Crap.

Having agreed, she'd rushed through the rest of her morning routine, her nerves in a knot. A talk at this hour couldn't be good, and she couldn't help but think he was going to put an end to their non-relationship—the personal one. She tried not to dwell on that thought and the gutting disappointment it brought with it, but even cranking up Maren Morris in her earbuds didn't help. By the time he knocked on the door, she was busy lining up in her mind all the reasons they were good together.

"Hey," she said with a shaky smile when she opened the door to him. "Come in."

Absently, she took the teal bakery box from him, vaguely noticed he also carried two coffees, and peered into his eyes, trying to read…anything.

First thought, he was exhausted. Shadows under his eyes

spoke of a sleepless night, and that didn't do anything to convince her everything would be okay.

As soon as he closed the door behind him, though, he leaned down and pressed a brief but intense kiss to her lips. It didn't feel like goodbye, but it didn't feel like *I'm going to lead you into your bedroom for a morning quickie* either.

She wouldn't be opposed to a morning quickie.

"What's up, Cole?"

That he had yet to say a word hadn't escaped her, and she followed him over to the kitchen island, where he set down the coffees.

"Sorry to barge in so early," he said, taking the lid off one, seeing it had whipped cream on top, and sliding it across to her.

"You're not barging."

He gestured to the bakery box, which she'd set on the island as well. "Muffins from Sugar Babies."

Normally she would kill for breakfast from Sugar Babies, but right now she didn't care about muffins.

"Thank you." She watched him, noted that he had shaved, that he was wearing his usual sweatshirt, old jeans, and worn work boots, and the only sign of anything different was his eyes. Besides showing his fatigue, they didn't meet hers. "What did you want to talk about?" she prompted, because though she didn't want to hear what she thought she was about to hear, the not knowing was worse.

"I told you last night I was with Mason," he said, still not looking directly at her.

It was his reason for them not being together last night, not that he really needed one, and she definitely hadn't asked, because she'd spent the previous night with him, and she was trying hard not to suffocate him—with the exception of the impulsive moment in the Eldridge den yesterday.

"He made an official offer of employment and I'm going to accept," Cole said, finally making eye contact, allowing her to see, at last, a world of emotion. Emotion that looked an awful lot like anguish.

It took a moment for the words to register, for her mental whiplash to take hold. "A job?"

"Special projects manager, he's calling it. They signed deals for four new stores, all of which need to be renovated. I'll be overseeing them."

"Cole, that's fantastic," she said, meaning it, and not just because he wasn't breaking up with her. "You're finally going to work for North Brothers."

"One thing has driven me since the day you hired me—I never wanted to let you down. And now I am, and I'm sorry—"

"Are you kidding me? Don't you dare apologize. You're going to work with your family. You need to work with your brothers." She was genuinely happy for him, knew what a big thing this was, how many years it'd taken for him to be able to do it. And she couldn't discount her relief that he wasn't dumping her. His new job would certainly solve the issue of whether or not they were open about their involvement at work.

"I'm leaving you in the lurch," he said. "I can give you two weeks, but I'll need to take a day off here and there because Mason has me jumping in right away out of necessity. I'll put in extra hours when I'm here, whatever I can do to help."

"It's okay, Cole. We'll figure it out. Whatever you need to do for your new job, do it." She went around the island to him and put an arm around him from the side, since he made a point of not facing her. "I'm so stoked for you. This was such a long time coming."

He exhaled noisily and shook his head. "I feel like shit for leaving you. You're in the middle of the bank job, in the last stage, the most crucial one, of the Eldridge thing, and now you have to hire too. Maybe I can help with that."

"I'd take your help, but I don't think you're going to have time, Mr. Manager. I'll be fine." Working long hours, but fine, and that was the truth. She'd brought the contest on herself, and she didn't regret it a bit, with or without Cole. The bank renovation was going well and, so far, on time. The only thing she'd be adding was a hire, since she knew without much thought that none of her guys were ready to take on foreman responsibilities yet, and she'd figure that out as soon as she had a few minutes to breathe.

"I wouldn't have taken it right now if it didn't seem like the exact right opportunity. In fact, I'd told him and Gabe multiple times I liked where I was working."

Sierra allowed herself a minute to imagine going to work every day without Cole at her side. They'd only been sleeping together for a month. It hadn't been much longer since that fateful evening when he'd volunteered to take her to Kennedy and Hunter's wedding. It would be an adjustment for sure, on both a personal and professional basis. He'd be tough to replace —he really was that good—but that was her problem, not his.

"Tell me about the four stores. Here in town?" she asked.

Since he was still facing the island, as if he needed to shut her out, she pulled the bakery box to her, opened it, held it out to him. He shook his head, so she went for the double chocolate muffin.

"North Brothers is expanding outside of the state for the first time. Two locations in Florida, one in Alabama, one in Kentucky. I have to be in Tallahassee on Monday."

"Whoa. They're not messing around," she said, smiling, and not just because the muffin was decadent and to die for. Though Cole had not exactly said how much a part of him wanted to be involved with North Brothers Sports, she could tell he did. Knew he'd been trying hard with his family ever since his mom's heart attack. How could she be anything but thrilled for him?

"Birmingham a week from tomorrow. They want to have those two stores open before the holidays."

"Do you know how big the reno projects are?"

"I haven't even told my brothers yes yet," he said, finally angling partially toward her. "I wanted to talk to you first."

"Well, thank you. And quit worrying about me. I'm really happy for you. You're exactly what they need. Mr. Manager," she added with a raise of her brows.

"You're not going to let that one go, are you?" he said with the first hints of a smile.

"Not anytime soon. Come here." She yanked on his arm,

pulled him around to fully face her, and threw her arms around him—finally. "Congratulations, Cole. You deserve it."

She heard him inhale deeply, as if taking in the smell of her shampoo, the way she was breathing in his masculine, clean scent. She closed her eyes and allowed herself a second of gratitude that she still had him in her life, like this. Yes, things were about to get batshit crazy in her schedule, but that was okay. She'd make it through just fine.

And maybe tonight she would have this man back in her bed.

CHAPTER TWENTY-SEVEN

"You absolutely nailed that," Kennedy said to Sierra a week later—an intense, overpacked week of doing triple duty as she kept the bank project on schedule, interviewed candidates for the foreman position, and put together a formal half-hour presentation for the Eldridge contest.

Kennedy gave her a supportive one-armed squeeze as they made their way from the room where the three Eldridge finalists had presented their proposals—on camera—down the hall toward the informal reception. The event was being held at the corporate office and studio of one of Eldridge's networks, Country365. Thankfully, they'd scheduled it in the evening, so Sierra hadn't had to miss time from the jobsite, but now that she was done with the hard part, she was counting the minutes till she could take off her heels.

Sierra exhaled for what felt like the first time in the thirty minutes she'd been in the hot seat. "It felt about two steps away from a disaster," she said under her breath, glancing around to make sure no one else heard her.

"Are you kidding me? You handled that"—Kennedy, too, checked to make sure no one was listening—"*pig* like a pro. He's the ass, and everyone who was in that room knows it now."

The pig happened to be one of the four panelists she'd presented to, the producer of *Historical Homes*, the show that would feature the Eldridge project, from initial applications to the final selection and then the renovation itself. Roger Crum had missed the previous interview round, and that was, Sierra suspected, one of the reasons she'd made it through to this final round. It was clear as fricking day the guy didn't think a woman should own a remodeling company.

That fact made her stomach hurt, even though he was only one of four panelists and William Eldridge himself, who she'd never met, would make the final decision on the winner based on the recorded presentations.

They entered the reception room, where a couple dozen people were milling around, munching on cookies, and drinking what appeared to be champagne, which seemed premature to Sierra. This might be the final hurrah in the search for the winning remodeling company, but she was far from being ready to celebrate.

"How long do we need to stay?" Kennedy asked, leading the way to the dessert table. Sierra's sister was not generally a people person, which made it interesting that, in addition to being part owner of Sugar Babies Sweet Shop, she had a flourishing marketing consulting company.

This time, though, Sierra was on the same page as her sister. "I'm thinking twenty minutes max. Long enough to be seen by the panelists and meet the other two finalists—and devour a few of these cookies."

"Not as good as Ivy's," Kennedy said after taking a bite of a chocolate chip one.

"Nothing's as good as Ivy's." Sierra limited herself to two cookies to start with, though she was now famished. She'd been too nervous to eat dinner beforehand. "Thanks again for coming with me," she told her sister. "I didn't think I'd be so nervous, but my hands were shaking for the first fifteen minutes."

"It didn't show," Kennedy said. "Champagne?"

Sierra shook her head. "It goes straight to my head, and who has time for a buzz? I've got a seven-a.m. interview with a potential foreman."

"Maybe this one will be the one and you can hire him and inform the panelists it's taken care of."

"I can't decide which fact hurt me more—that I'm a female or that I don't currently have a foreman."

"Foreman. The assistant guy—Adam?—was really concerned about that, and he's the one who works closest to Eldridge if I understand right."

"You do," Sierra said with a nervous exhale.

"You addressed it perfectly by detailing your low turnover rates. I think it could even work in your favor after your answer about searching for the right candidate and not just promoting someone on your crew who isn't ready for the responsibility because you're in a hurry."

"Yeah? That came out okay?" Sierra had prepared comprehensively, had even had Hayden role-play with her and throw questions at her, but the foreman question had blindsided her.

"It was a genius answer," Kennedy told her as she smiled at a couple of the camera guys who'd just come into the room. "What happened to Cole, anyway? I mean, I know he took another job, working for his family's company, but why now? Did the wedding and reception date scare him off?"

Sierra smiled as she thought back on that night that had been the start of so much. "He did pretty well with that, all things considered. We, um…" She wasn't sure what to call it, but her sister didn't know they were involved. "We're sort of together."

Kennedy's hand landed on Sierra's arm as she steered her over toward the end of the cookie table, giving the appearance that they were deep in discussion and shouldn't be disturbed right now. "You told everyone he was a fake date!"

"He was, I promise."

"But now you're together? And you didn't tell me?"

"You were honeymooning and then newlywedding," Sierra said. "And I wouldn't really say it's official. Cole is convinced he's not the relationship type, so we don't talk about it much. I'm trying not to spook him."

"Is it serious for you?"

Nonchalantly grabbing another cookie, Sierra thought about

her sister's question, felt the warmth settle in her chest, and nodded as she smiled at one of the servers behind the cookie table.

Turning to face the room again and ensure no one was approaching, she confided, "I think it is. I think I might be falling for him."

Kennedy wasn't one to show a lot of emotion, but she let loose a girly excited sound and leaned her head against Sierra's briefly. "Bring him to Thanksgiving."

"Are you listening? Talk about spooking a guy."

"We're not that bad," Kennedy said, laughing.

They dropped the conversation as one of the other finalists introduced himself, an older gentleman based in Boulder, and his wife, who ran his office for him. It wasn't long before the third finalist joined them, the owner of a Memphis remodeling company. He was maybe forty and definitely hot enough for TV, looks-wise, though he'd been unpolished and rough around the edges during his presentation.

They exchanged pleasantries and complimented each other's proposals before splitting up as a couple of the panelists—Crum and Preston Morris, who was the host of *Historical Homes* and becoming a celebrity because of it—wandered in together. They stopped to talk to the Boulder guy.

"Back to Cole while we have a minute," Kennedy said.

Sierra felt her phone vibrate in the pocket of her wine-colored blazer, and she pulled it out to see that Cole had texted three times, wondering how the presentation had gone. "Speak of the devil. Let me tell him I'll talk to him when we're done here."

She typed in a quick message that it had gone well, she was still at the reception, and she'd call him as soon as she got home.

"What about Cole?" she asked Kennedy as she slid her phone back out of sight.

"If you're involved, I'm surprised he didn't make a point of being here. His trip couldn't be postponed?"

"He hated that he had to miss tonight, but his brother needed him." She explained briefly about the new North Brothers Sports acquisitions, Cole's position, and how it was such a long time in coming for him to join the family business.

"The North Brothers? North Brothers Sports? And you didn't tell me?" Kennedy said.

"I only found out the night of your wedding."

Kennedy's mouth was still hanging open when Adam Riccio, who was William Eldridge's assistant, blond, close to Sierra's age, clearly ambitious and organized, and had been the main contact throughout the process so far, entered the room and made a beeline for Sierra.

He shook her hand and said, "You did a fantastic job tonight."

"Thank you." Sierra smiled and hid all of her doubts. She introduced Kennedy and then said, "It sounds like the mansion will be beautiful regardless of who wins. But I hope it's my company."

Adam laughed, then got serious. "I'm sorry about the inappropriate questions from other panelists," he said, his voice dropping in volume so that said panelists didn't hear. "I assure you Mr. Eldridge is not concerned about the winner's gender."

"That's reassuring," Sierra said, feeling gratitude down to her toes that he'd clarified that.

"I'll be honest," Adam said with a conspiratorial tone, "if anything, your answers to those questions knocked it out of the ballpark and helped your cause rather than hurt it."

Kennedy gave Sierra's wrist a subtle squeeze, as if to say *I told you so*, and then Adam was off in a flurry to grab a flute of champagne and congratulate the other finalists.

Exhausted now that the adrenaline of presenting was wearing off, Sierra forced herself to thank each of the other panelists, Crum included, and then she and Kennedy took their leave, walking out to her truck in silence.

"How do you feel?" Kennedy asked once they were inside the cab.

Sierra exhaled and thought about the question, the keys still in her hand. "I feel pretty damn good. It's been a hellaciously crazy week of prepping, but I stand behind every last bit of my proposal. I did my best."

"You rocked it. I'm so proud of you."

It was almost embarrassing how much those words meant to Sierra, but she'd spent her life wishing her older siblings took her more seriously, respected her. Maybe they had all along and she hadn't seen it. She didn't know, but she believed her sister now, and she leaned across the cab to pull her close in an awkward, one-armed hug. "Thank you. Love you."

"Love you back. Now let's go home. My sexy husband is waiting for me, and you need to call your sexy guy."

"Not mine," Sierra qualified. "Yet. At least not that he'll admit." With a smug grin, she started the truck and backed out.

CHAPTER TWENTY-EIGHT

"You sure you're ready for this?" Cole asked Sierra as he parked his truck in front of his mom's house Saturday evening.

For the dozenth time since he'd shown up at her apartment half an hour ago, he shoved down the guilt that was dogging his ass, determined to not let it ruin their time together. He'd been in Birmingham since Thursday, putting everything into place for construction to start on the remodel Monday morning. Of the four new properties, Birmingham was the simplest and also the most urgent. But because of it, he'd let Sierra down on her big presentation, and he was still trying to forgive himself for that. At least she'd been able to hire a new foreman yesterday, though it would take time and extra work for her to get him up to speed once he started.

"Are you kidding? I can't wait to meet your mom and get to know the rest of your family."

Shaking his head as he smiled—he couldn't seem to get the smile off his damn face since he'd laid eyes on her, in spite of his underlying self-recriminations—Cole opened his door, hopped down, and hurried around to help her out. She was already climbing down when he got there, but he took her hand anyway, not because she needed it but because he wanted to touch her.

"You look good," he said into her ear, then pressed a light kiss along her jawline as they walked up the driveway.

Good was an understatement, even though this was a casual family get-together, a laid-back gathering to celebrate his job with North Brothers Sports. It was late November, the Saturday before Thanksgiving, and winter was flirting hard with Nashville, but Sierra had skipped wearing a coat. He'd inventoried every piece she wore when he showed up at her apartment, imagining taking each one off of her later tonight—a button-down shirt with the ends tied at her waist under a long, soft gray cardigan, jeans that hugged her slender legs, and ankle boots with a slight heel that made her legs look all the longer. Around her neck was a necklace with multiple strands and charms, and a silver bracelet jangled at her wrist, both of which he might or might not remove later, because a guy only had so much patience. Her hair cascaded in soft waves over her shoulders, and he ached to run his fingers through it as it draped over his pillow…

With a little laugh, she leaned into him. "You look good too."

He laughed with her. "In my jeans and thermal shirt."

"Your good jeans and thermal shirt."

When they got to the front door, he opened it, as usual not stopping to ring the bell, and guided her in with his hand at her waist. He kept it there as they headed through the two-story entryway toward the noise that was his family, hanging out in the open family room, dining, and kitchen area.

"There he is," his aunt Liz said as they came around the corner into her view. She stood near the dining table, well-dressed as always in dark jeans and a cowl-neck sweater, her chocolate-brown hair with lighter highlights making her look younger than her sixty-three years. "Man of the hour."

The rest of the family called out greetings as he and Sierra approached.

"What do you mean? I only get an hour?" Cole said.

He went to the head of the table, where his mom sat, looking happy and content, even though Cole suspected she detested being parked at the table instead of in the kitchen, busy and in charge. Her color was good, her cheeks the slightest pink, and her eyes sparkled with the joy of having her family around her. He put his hand on her shoulder and said, "Hi, Mom."

"Hey, cousin." Miranda, the only female of all the North siblings and cousins, came up to him and bumped him with her hip before putting one arm around him and giving him a side hug. "Congratulations. We're happy to finally have you in the family biz."

"Thanks," Cole said, kissing the side of her head, hoping to hide his discomfort with being the center of attention.

"Took you long enough," Connor, the oldest North cousin, said, reaching up from one of the dining chairs to give Cole a fist bump.

"Everyone, this is Sierra Lowell. This is the North family," he told Sierra, "plus a couple of wannabes."

"I'm their third mother," Geraldine Fleming called out as she removed a pan from the oven.

"That's about the truth," Liz said of her and his mother's best friend.

Cole went around and introduced everyone. "Geraldine Fleming, a.k.a. Third Mother, and Logan North, tech geek extraordinaire in the kitchen with Gabe, who you met. Liz North, my aunt—"

"And second mother," Liz said as she poured red wine into a glass and handed it to Miranda.

"It's a good sign that these ladies claim you all," Sierra said, garnering a collective laugh and a couple of smart-ass remarks directed toward the two women.

"You've met Mason, and next to him is Gabe's lifelong friend Lexie Gallagher, who we've pretty much adopted as a sister, Miranda, Connor, and this," he said, squeezing his mom's shoulder, "is the leader of our people, my mom, Faye."

"Only because she's oldest," Liz said.

His mom pushed up from her seat, and Sierra graciously said, "You don't have to stand, Mrs. North."

His mom straightened the rest of the way, turned toward Sierra, smiled at her, and pulled her into a hug. "It's Faye, and it's so nice to meet you, dear." When the hug ended, she said,

"I've been sitting so much I think my butt size has increased by two inches on each side, just in the last hour. These people are bossy. Every last one of them."

"Everybody likes to boss the boss," Mason said.

With a laugh, Sierra said, "It's nice to meet you. Cole's told me a lot about you."

Faye put her arm around Cole and pulled her middle child to her side. Craning her neck to look up at him, she said, "I can assure you only the good stuff is true."

"It's all good stuff," Cole said, elated that she was in such good spirits. She usually was, was an optimist at heart, but there'd been a couple of days lately when frustration and impatience with the slow healing process had gotten her down. "All the bad stuff was me." He kept his tone light, even though truer words had never been spoken. "Where's Drake?" he asked to the room in general.

"Who ever knows?" Mason said.

"He said he'd be here," Gabe said as he pulled down a tall stack of plates and set them on the edge of the counter. It appeared dinner was buffet-style tonight, catered in, which made sense and smelled damn good—and was no doubt making his mom twitchy.

Within a few minutes, Geraldine, Gabe, Liz, and Logan had everything ready, and all twelve of them—including Drake, who'd sauntered in, unhurried, claiming his afternoon shift at the gym had run late—filled their plates and squeezed around the table and at the breakfast bar to enjoy a typical loud North family dinner. Except it wasn't quite typical because, for once, Cole realized he was starting to feel like he belonged here. And that, in turn, made him wonder when the other shoe would drop.

CHAPTER TWENTY-NINE

A couple of hours later, the food was devoured, the few leftovers stored in the fridge. Liz kept the beverages coming, whether refilling wineglasses or distributing bottles of beer or brewing a pot of decaf coffee.

Most of the group had migrated to the connected family room, though Sierra was still camped out at the breakfast bar with Lexie and Miranda, deep into a conversation about Keith Urban's music. Cole sat across the living room in an oversized armchair, one of two that flanked the fireplace, half listening to Logan, who was the VP of technology at North Brothers, go on to him and Gabe about the virtual reality rig he'd recently bought and keeping an eye on Sierra, wishing she were closer, near enough to touch.

That was a new experience for him, the wanting her close even while they were in the middle of a group of people. He wasn't going to think too hard about the significance; in fact, he told himself it was just the result of being out of town for a few nights, being away from her, anticipating taking her to bed later.

"Cake time," Geraldine called from the kitchen. "Cole, get your butt in here and look at this thing."

He narrowed his eyes at his brother and cousin closest to him.

"You know this family doesn't celebrate without cake," Gabe said.

He did know that, but from here, it looked like someone had gone all out and ordered a professional one, because he could see layers. Tall layers. Multiple layers. Like a damn wedding cake.

"One layer of snickerdoodle caramel, one layer of chocolate, and one layer of white," his mom said from the couch.

Snickerdoodles and caramel were two of his favorite things. "Guess I better eat some cake then," he said, standing.

"We want to get your picture," Geraldine said as he and everyone else headed back toward the breakfast bar, where, indeed, a miniature wedding-type cake towered. It had white icing with royal-blue ribbon, the North Brothers Sports colors. Scattered around it and on it were sports decorations—edible, it appeared— from footballs and baseballs and soccer balls to ice skates, lacrosse sticks, and hockey pucks. Sticking out of the top was a 3D sign, scoreboard-style, that said *Congrats, Cole! Welcome to NBS!*

"You guys outdid yourselves," he said, his mouth watering at the smell of the sugary frosting. "No photos."

"Have to," Geraldine said. "A North brother comes home to the family business—that's PR gold, honey."

"Spoken like a true marketing maven," Mason said.

"Aren't you retired?" Cole asked, knowing full well she'd ended her career as the North Brothers Sports VP of marketing.

"Happily, yes I am, but after thirty-two years, it's in my blood." Geraldine cleared the counter of crumbs from dinner and then slid a champagne flute, two-thirds filled with bubbly pale gold liquid, in front of the cake, and fanned some custom-printed North Brothers napkins—there was always a stash somewhere— on the opposite side to make a picture-perfect scene.

"Just an impromptu idea," Cole said dryly.

"Come around here. Mason, where's your phone? You take the photo," Geraldine barked, and they followed her orders. Cole knew it was easier to just get it done than to argue.

Once the shots were taken, Cole glanced around for Sierra while Geraldine and Liz disassembled the layers and cut into each of them so that all three flavors were up for grabs. Sierra was standing back, out of the way, next to Lexie, as if they didn't want to intrude on the North family. He went over to her, because he'd rather be with her than anyone else in the room, even if he was coming around to not minding his family.

"Want some cake?" he asked her, unable to resist sliding his hand down her back and to the side of her waist.

"My sister has a saying…" Sierra said.

"Yeah?"

"Is a duck's butt wet?"

"Only if the duck is in the water," Cole pointed out.

"The duck is always in the water."

Grinning, Cole asked, "Which flavor would you like? Or maybe you'd like one of each?"

"Then the duck's wet butt would get too big. Just chocolate please."

"Lexie?" Cole asked.

"Still trying to decide. I'll get my own in a minute."

"Guest of honor, get your ass over here and get your cake," Drake said from the counter.

Cole grabbed the oversized piece of snickerdoodle caramel his aunt shoved at him and waited for Sierra's chocolate, then got out of the overcrowded dining area, heading straight for the prettiest girl in the room. Hell, in the whole city.

Sierra led him to the couch and sat on the middle cushion, next to his mother, and something about her choosing to sit by his mom got him. "You need cake," Sierra said to Faye, her tone sounding scandalized.

"Miranda's bringing me some," his mom answered.

"Which kind did you choose?" Sierra asked, setting her fork on her plate, as if waiting for Faye to be served.

With a sparkle in her eye, his mom answered, "I didn't. I asked for a sample of all three."

"You are a smart woman," Sierra told her, grinning. "But then, I already knew that, even before I met you, because you have some great sons."

"They're pretty good boys, most days."

Sierra laughed at the word *boys* to describe her sons, all of whom were well over six feet tall, good-looking, and dripping with testosterone.

Miranda delivered Faye's cake, thin slices of all three flavors, and then walked to Cole's other side and shoved at his legs. "Scoot over, Colester. I'm sitting by you."

Sierra moved closer to Cole's mom, and Cole squeezed right up next to Sierra, breathing in the scent of her hair and liking it even more than the cake smell.

Connor and Drake took up the love seat, and Gabe delivered a slice of cake to Lexie, who waited in the corner armchair, and then he parked himself on the arm of it next to her.

Sierra leaned toward Cole's ear and asked, quietly, "Are Gabe and Lexie a thing?"

"No," Cole answered, tossing a glance their way, understanding how she might think that, as the two were sharing a private conversation, with Lexie gazing up at his brother with a grin. "They've been best friends since kindergarten."

"Are you sure that's all?" Sierra asked, glancing over at them again.

"She's got a serious boyfriend, last I knew." Raleigh or Ryder or Roman or something like that. Cole couldn't remember because he'd never met the guy, which was kind of odd, especially as much as Cole had been around the family lately. He wasn't even sure his mother had met Lexie's boyfriend.

"Okay then," Sierra said, sounding like she still wasn't sure she could believe him.

It didn't take them long to demolish their cake, even Faye with her three flavors—declaring the white cake was the best—and then Gabe made his way around the room distributing champagne, thoughtfully handing his mother a flute of sparkling white grape juice.

"Wait for the toast," Gabe said to the room in general. "See if you can make it all of ten minutes before you imbibe."

"I thought the champagne was just for the PR pics," Cole said, setting his flute on the coffee table.

"As if," Miranda said. "If there's champagne and an event worth celebrating, this family's going to drink."

"Amen," Liz said, dragging a dining chair next to the couch. "We raised these children right."

"Good thing I didn't have my own, so I could help you," Geraldine said, settling into another chair that Mason brought in for her. "These eight were a handful."

"Has anyone talked to Zane lately?" Logan asked about the only one who was absent.

"Last week," Drake said. "He's still somewhere in the world doing something we can't know about."

"I still miss that boy like crazy," Cole's mom said, as she always did, ever since he'd left home years ago.

While everyone else had taken a spot in the armchairs or the love seat or the dining chairs or on the floor, Mason and Gabe sauntered over to stand in front of the gas fireplace, which wasn't on today, as if they had something to say. Uneasiness bubbled up in Cole's gut because chances were good they were going to make a big deal out of him joining North Brothers. Bigger than an obnoxious—but damn good—cake. He wasn't a fan of being the center of attention and had told his family, when they'd initiated the celebration, that it better be casual and chill. He waited till Mason met his eyes and then mouthed *fucker* to him.

His brother laughed and said, "Long time coming, Cole."

"Is this where they haze you?" Sierra asked.

"Not if they're smart." Cole took her empty plate, stacked it with his, and passed them to Liz, who'd gestured for them. She took them, along with several others, to the kitchen counter, then retook her seat.

"Hey," Mason said over all the other voices. "Gabe and I have a couple things to say."

"What he means to say is shut the hell up," Gabe said, his voice raised, aiming his grin at Miranda and Geraldine, who were still going on about who knew what.

Miranda's eyes widened when she noticed everyone was staring at them, and she made a smart-ass motion as if she were zipping her lips, her brows raised as if to say, *Happy now?*

"As you all know," Mason said in his serious CEO voice,

which was pretty much his everyday voice, "we're here today to celebrate our black sheep brother coming back to the flock."

"Mason," their mother scolded, the only person in the world who could get away with that to him.

"Said with brotherly love—and honesty," he replied. "And it's nicer than what he called me under his breath two minutes ago."

"That's a fact," Cole said as everyone laughed.

"First of all," Mason said, "I want to thank you, Sierra, for being understanding and a good sport as Cole, at my insistence, basically screwed you over."

Again, a round of laughter, Sierra's included, though inside, Cole cringed. He put his hand on her thigh, wishing he could soothe away the inconveniences he'd caused her in the past week plus.

Sobering, Mason continued, still addressing Sierra, "Sincerely, though, we found ourselves in a tricky situation, and Cole was the answer to our needs, but unfortunately, that put a burden on you, and for that I apologize. I know he's been out more than in work for his last two weeks, and if it were me in your position, I'd be ready to lose my shit."

What he said was a hundred percent true. Cole had missed days, had squeezed in some half days, and had been there for maybe two full days since giving his notice. He hated it, even though Sierra insisted it was okay.

"I lost it long ago," Sierra said with a good-natured laugh. "I know what an opportunity this is for you," she said directly to Cole, sincerity in her eyes. "It's all good."

"We owe you," Gabe said to Sierra, "so we got you a little something as a token of North Brothers Sports' appreciation." He stepped to the couch and handed Sierra one of two envelopes he was holding. "That's a gift card to Selma's, enough for two people and then some to get some high-end grub. Whether you choose to take this guy or not is your problem." He gestured to Cole and garnered another laugh.

"Wow. This is completely unnecessary, but thank you," Sierra said. "We'll see if he can work me in for a date night." She gazed up at him with a flirty look, and hell yes, he'd work her in for a date night and more.

"It's worth noting," Mason said, "that our middle brother has never—not once—brought a girl home, for dinner or anything else, before tonight. So it seems he's turning over a new leaf or two."

"I've turned over so many damn leaves I think I have a different tree altogether," Cole said, shoving down the uneasiness that truth stirred up, entwining his fingers with Sierra's without thought, and then, belatedly, realizing what he'd done—and liking it.

"We're happy about that," Mason said, "because I'm not sure when I've been so impressed by a new hire. We've always known you're brilliant and suspected you could do whatever you decided you wanted to do." Mason shared a knowing big-brother look with Gabe. "We were right. I don't think we could've found anyone else who could step in the way you did, last minute, learning the company details on the fly, and handling some crucial projects for our business. The company's future depends on these undertakings going smoothly, and the way you came in and took control, using your renovation experience and knowledge... So far, you're killing it. Just like we knew you would."

"It's like you were born for this position," Gabe said. "Just took a few decades to realize it."

Everyone else laughed, but Cole was overcome by the praise, because for years, he'd thought his brothers, especially hard-ass Mason, considered him nothing but a fuckup.

If you took Sierra out of the mix, Cole could admit he was glad he'd taken the job. Though he'd been thrown directly into the fire, it turned out he knew what he was doing, could handle the challenges hurled at him from day one. A lot of that was thanks to Sierra, who'd included him in almost every aspect of her business, from codes and permits to architects and planning.

The intensity of the North Brothers projects—all damn four of them—was tenfold, in part because of the scope of each and in part because there were four at a time, but Cole was handling that too so far.

Mason had accompanied him to the first meetings in Tallahassee, Cole's getting-his-feet-wet treat, Mason had called it, and though it was said as a joke, Cole found that having the CEO of the company there at his side gave him an appreciation for the clout the company carried. It gave him confidence going forward, knowing his family's company was respected and revered. And Mason's confidence in him turned out to be genuine and not something he'd spouted just to get Cole to take the job. Though the oldest North brother had been at his side for those first meetings, Mason had told him numerous times, *That's your call, You decide,* or *You're the renovation expert.*

"You're my hero, Colester," Miranda said, grinning, smacking his knee. "But really, so happy you're with us now."

"Hear, hear!" Logan raised his champagne flute as if ready for a toast, but Mason waved him off.

"One more thing," Mason said, then gestured to Gabe, his eyes on the remaining envelope.

"Yeah." Gabe took a half step forward and cleared his throat, as if he had a ball of emotion stuck there. He'd always been the soft-ass North brother, Cole thought in an effort to shove aside his own emotions. "So…as most of you know, back when we were kids, all eight of us, when North Brothers Sports began taking off and expanding, becoming successful, Dad and Uncle Ham agreed that they wanted the company to belong to the whole family. As you also probably know, they had it set up so that the profits each year are divided among us, their children and spouses."

None of this was news to Cole, but he waited to see where Gabe was going with it, a kernel of unease lodging in his gut.

"What you may or may not know is that Cole, during what we'll call his rebel period, decided he wanted nothing to do with earnings from the company, and shortly after he graduated from high school, he insisted on signing away his rights to his share."

"What?" Miranda gasped, and had it been any other topic, Cole would've laughed at her scandalized tone. "Is that true?"

Cole merely nodded, his uneasiness blossoming.

"I advised against it," Gabe continued.

"As did I," Mason said, "but one thing Cole wasn't good at back then was taking advice."

Cole couldn't deny that, so he merely shrugged, hating that everyone was looking at him.

"Anyway, we had the appropriate paperwork drawn up back then, and he signed it and gave up his right to the share that Dad and Uncle Ham had intended him to have."

"Dummy," Miranda breathed.

Again, Cole shrugged. He still stood behind it. He hadn't done a thing to help the company, so why should he reap the benefits from it?

"What he didn't know," Gabe said, "is that Mason and I, with the help of the company lawyers, had it set up so that his share still exists and still earns every year, along with the rest of ours. He just didn't have access to it."

"You're shitting me," Cole said, unsure how to feel about it. In essence, they'd blown off his wishes all those years ago. "Why the hell did you do that? I told you then it should go to the people who contributed to the business. The rest of you." He indicated the whole group.

"We've all been well taken care of by the company," Connor, sitting on the far end of the love seat, assured him.

"Dad and Uncle Ham didn't set these up to reward us for being employees," Mason said. "That's what paychecks are for. They set these up to take care of their families, to provide for the people they loved. And that's why we'd like to present you with the paperwork to put the share back in your name, along with all the proceeds from all the years, including from investments that Aunt Liz, our finance wizard, has ensured increased the value several times over."

"No arguments. It's rightfully yours," Gabe said.

Cole swallowed, overcome and unable to speak as a shit storm of emotions thundered through him. He felt Sierra squeezing his fingers, felt the entire room gazing at him, then realized Gabe was still holding the business-sized envelope out in front of him. Like a robot, Cole took it, gauging from the weight of it there were two or three pages inside spelling out the details.

"Take it home, read it over, sign it, bring it in on Monday," Gabe said. "It's pretty straightforward."

Cole nodded, or he was pretty sure he did anyway, but he was so overwhelmed he couldn't swear to it. "That's…" Shit. He worked at keeping his cool, tried not to let on that this was fucking with him big-time. Swallowing hard, still holding on to Sierra's hand, he said, "Thank you." He nodded. "I'll look it over." When he saw that Gabe was about to argue, he said, again, "Thanks."

The room burst out into cheers and clapping and congratulations, then Mason interrupted by clinking his cake fork on his glass.

"Toast time!" Liz called out, and Cole realized Sierra was holding his flute out to him.

When everyone mostly shut up, eyes on Mason, he held up his glass. "To our brother Cole. It's been a long journey, and I strongly believe that journey has forged you into the more-than-capable special projects manager you are today—"

"Badass special projects manager," Miranda added.

With a grin, Mason amended, "Badass special projects manager. From all of us, welcome to North Brothers Sports, Cole. Here's to a fulfilling, successful future."

Various calls of *hear, hear* and *cheers* rang out around the room.

"To Cole," Sierra said at his side, and he met her gaze briefly, reminded himself to smile as he clinked glasses with her.

As everyone drank to the toast, Cole tried his best to savor the moment, to look forward to a rewarding future, and to block out the little voice inside that said he didn't deserve any of this.

CHAPTER THIRTY

wo days after Cole's family party, on Monday evening, Sierra stretched out on the couch in his apartment, her feet next to his lap as he sat upright on the end near his easy chair. She would've had her head in his lap, but they were entrenched in game three of a best-of-three Words with Friends battle, and she didn't want him to see her letters. God's truth, he had a big enough advantage with that brain of his as it was, and the stakes were high—loser had to clean out Tito's litter box.

Cole had slaughtered her in game one, she'd won by two points in game two, and now she was determined to somehow overcome a sixty-point deficit in game three, in spite of having nothing but one-point letters in her hand.

Once she finished her turn, she popped off the couch and picked up their dirty plates from dinner, which they'd set on the coffee table. Cole could hold his own in the kitchen and had made them chicken enchiladas and Mexican rice. After spending Saturday night and yesterday together at her apartment, they'd arranged to meet here at his today after work—he'd worked the morning with her and her crew for the very last time, as they'd agreed, and spent the afternoon in meetings at North Brothers.

Yesterday, Tito had managed to get the cabinet under the kitchen sink open at some point while Cole was at her place, knocking over the cleaning supplies stored there and then chewing through the bag of cat crunchies—even though his bowls were still half-full—scattering the pellets all over the kitchen floor in the process. A cry for attention, Cole had explained, then called the cranky cat a home wrecker at the same time he rubbed the beast's jowls. Tito was stretched out on the easy chair now, taking up far more room than any twelve-pound cat should need, and Sierra had to admit it was hard to resist his fuzzy cuteness.

As she rinsed off their plates and put them in the dishwasher, she couldn't help thinking about Cole and her, as a couple, and how close they'd become in a short amount of time. Close and domestic, she thought with a private grin. She'd figured out that the less they talked about *them*, the more Cole let her in. And his frequent traveling made him even more apt to spend the nights he was in town with her. Playing it cool was okay for now, but it wasn't a long-term option as far as she was concerned.

Though they'd spent a chunk of Sunday naked, they'd also watched a movie, hit the bookstore on Hale Street, and gone to Clayborne's for dinner. In a way, it felt like they'd been together for years—natural, comfortable, companionable, with a healthy dose, or probably an above-average dose, of the most incredible sex of her life.

Tonight, however, Cole seemed a little distant. Preoccupied.

With the kitchen semi-tidied up, Sierra headed back toward the couch, noticing the envelope lying on the breakfast bar on her way.

"Is that the document Gabe gave you Saturday night?" she asked.

Cole looked up distractedly, then mumbled an *mm-hmm* when he saw what she pointed at.

"Have you signed it yet?" she asked, pretty sure Gabe had said something about bringing it into the North Brothers office today.

"Nah," he said, apparently sending his play, as her phone dinged to notify her it was her turn.

As she opened the game, she eyed him. He'd told her the story of giving up his share of North Brothers Sports back when he was eighteen. It'd been seven figures at the time, but he hadn't wanted a thing to do with it. She had no idea how much it was worth now, but she got the impression the amount would be staggering to her.

She made a comfortable living with Dunn & Lowell, basically had everything she needed, and she couldn't fathom what a person would do with so much money. Especially a guy like Cole, who was humble, didn't spend a lot, didn't seem to need a lot beyond the basics. But even as an outsider to the North family, she could appreciate the significance of the gesture, the love and respect for his brothers to have kept his share separate and well-tended all these years, waiting for the right moment to return it to him. Now that he was working with them, getting along with them, it seemed like signing and accepting was a no-brainer. She bit down on any questions, as it wasn't her business.

"Only twenty-seven points?" she scoffed as she saw his play and sidled up next to him on the couch. "You're slipping. You must have terrible letters."

"Accurate assessment. Just waiting for you to play something decent that I can play on."

That wasn't going to happen anytime soon. Her letters were mostly vowels and fully uninspiring. The man beside her, however…

Inspired, Sierra tossed her phone to the couch cushion next to her and executed a quick move that had her straddling Cole, her face inches from his. Hoping to distract him from his distractedness, she kissed him, slowly, thoroughly, feeling the usual heat spark between them, pulsing from her core outward. She could swear Cole felt it too, based on the low, sexy groan that rumbled out of him, but then he pulled away slightly, let out a dazed laugh, and said, "Conceding already? Litter box is in the bathroom."

She straightened, her competitive spirit fueled by his cockiness—and she really did hate litter boxes. Besides, she'd seen the ten-point *J* in her hand, and Cole had left one of the Triple Word spaces vulnerable. Hopping off him, she went to work, determined to make a large dent in his lead.

A few minutes later, Sierra had managed to come within two points of him. They'd trash-talked with each turn, and it might seem ridiculous to trash-talk about a word game, especially a phone version, but this was them, and she loved it. When Cole saw the updated score and that she was closing in, he made a show of intensifying his efforts. She rolled her eyes and laughed, then opened her email to check it, recognizing that he was going to take his sweet time and likely come back with a big play.

She hadn't checked her email since leaving work and saw that there were forty-two new messages. Skimming over the list of senders, she paused and her heart skipped a beat when she saw Adam Riccio about halfway down, with the subject line *Eldridge Mansion Renovation Contest*. She sat up on the edge of the couch and hesitated before clicking on it, gauging her gut feeling. She still felt good about it, she discovered. She'd given it her best effort, and her proposal for the project was damn good. Disregarding the half thought that a phone call would be a more dramatic way to impart good news, she clicked, skimmed the first paragraph, and felt her heart sink in her chest at the words *unfortunately* and *not selected*.

Her body seemed to forget to breathe as the words sank in.

"Damn," she said on a shallow exhale, closing her eyes. *Damn, damn, damn.*

Thinking maybe there was a chance she'd read that wrong, she held her phone up and double-checked. Read each word this time instead of skimming. Nope, still the worst news. It was short and not so sweet, and it didn't make her feel better to learn she was first runner-up. The winner was the good-looking guy from Memphis, who'd, in Sierra's opinion, had the least appealing presentation of all of them. But her opinion didn't matter.

Her phone sounded with the notification that Cole had played, but she didn't really register it.

There'd be no TV show for her, no opportunity to reap the publicity, expand her business, add a second crew, tie in her episodes with a YouTube channel and blog. Though she'd made peace with her interview answers, even to the tricky questions about her lack of a foreman at the time and her gender, she hadn't realized quite how strongly she'd believed she was going to win. Like a fool, she'd believed if she didn't allow herself to consider a negative result, she wouldn't get one.

All I can do is give people my best ideas. If they can't see the value in them, that's their problem. She heard the words her grandpa had spoken countless times, probably every single time he didn't win a bid. She'd always believed they were true, but this one was tough. This one wasn't just another remodeling project.

"I'm such an idiot," she said to herself.

"Still sixteen letters left. You can—" Cole cut himself off, apparently finally realizing that she wasn't talking about the game. "Hey, what's wrong?"

Sierra sucked in a shaky breath, because saying it out loud was going to hurt so much. "I didn't win. The Eldridge contest. Dunn & Lowell is first runner-up."

"What?" Disbelief and outrage collided in his tone. "How do you know?"

She held her phone up. "Email."

He extended his hand, palm up, a silent request to read it, and she handed it to him. A few seconds later, he handed it back and shot up off the couch. "Son of a bitch."

"Yeah," she said, her shoulders drooping and every muscle in her body suddenly feeling so bone-tired she could collapse into a puddle. She propped her elbows on her thighs and buried her face in her hands.

Kennedy had been texting her every day since the presentation to ask if she'd heard any news. Now she'd have to tell her sister she hadn't won…as well as the rest of the family. For about two seconds, Sierra felt herself slipping into thought patterns from the past, of not being good enough, of having to repeatedly prove her skills to both her older siblings and the world in general… No. She refused to go there. The proposal she'd presented was damn good—unique, practical, emphasizing historical details while incorporating top-notch technology and convenience. That was what she did, who she was, and that's what had been at the heart of her proposal. She still stood behind it to the smallest detail.

Which made her feel exactly zero percent better about losing.

She curled back into the couch cushion as she breathed out a sigh, her heart hurting. Twelve hours. That's what she'd give herself to mope and be sad about it, but when she got to work tomorrow, it was time to move on.

Cole, who'd been over near the kitchen, smacked his palm into the breakfast bar, rattling the whole kitchen, startling her. He had a scowl on his face, his forehead creased with anger.

"You seem mad," she said dumbly, trying to understand what she'd missed.

"Pissed at myself," he said, straightening to his full height, his expression thunderous, alarmingly so.

"What? Why?" She racked her brain for what she'd missed between his Words turn and now.

"Dammit," he said with so much remorse her eyes widened. "I let you down."

Her mouth fell open and she tried to catch up to what he was thinking. "You… What?" He was not trying to take the blame for the contest, was he?

"The most important two weeks of your life and I. Let. You. Down."

"Oh, my God, no you didn't, Cole."

He let out a laugh that held no amusement and a whole lot of self-recrimination. "Let's see…I flaked on helping you research and write the proposal itself—and while I don't for a minute think you needed my input, you could've used the manpower. I know you spent hours and hours after work on it. On top of that, I left you with the task of hiring a new foreman in the midst of it —something that might've affected the results—"

"It didn't," she said emphatically. "You saw the recording of the presentations. You said yourself I handled those objections well and turned it around to a way to show my strengths."

"And in case that wasn't enough, I also screwed you over on the day-to-day by splitting my time with my new job. Not even splitting," he said with a shake of his head. "I've spent the majority of my time since giving you notice trying to get up to speed with my family's business, which left you with twice as much to do on the bank project and everything else."

Sierra forced herself to her feet, walked the short distance to him. "Cole. Stop it. It's not about you. It's not that I presented a subpar proposal. It's not about anything except what I presented wasn't what they wanted. It's okay—"

"It's not okay," he said through a clenched jaw, and something snapped in her.

"Dammit, Cole. You're making it worse," she said, her voice raised.

"It's what I do," he muttered with so much self-loathing she wanted to shake him. The urge startled her and she turned around, paced over to the chair where the cat was sprawled, nearly unbothered, save for one ear that was twitching in discontent.

"It's not what you do. Not normally." Why couldn't he see that?

With unshed tears brimming in her eyes, her chest rising and falling with emotion, she watched him, waited for him to snap out of it, to realize all she needed right now was his arms around her, his lips pressing to her temple in comfort and understanding. He was a bright guy…

But not when it came to himself.

This was about more than her contest loss for him—she recognized that on some level, but right now, she didn't have it in her to care. Right now, she needed to be reassured, cared for. She was exhausted, she was reeling, and she didn't have the energy to convince him he was a good person.

Her heart heavy, so very sad and heavy, she picked up her phone from the couch and stuffed it in the back pocket of her jeans. She trudged to the stool at the breakfast bar, picked up her overnight bag, and stuffed her feet into her sneakers.

"What are you doing?" Cole asked as she grabbed her coat from the back of the couch.

"I'm leaving."

"I thought you were staying tonight." There was a thread of

anger in his voice, and that did it. The reins she'd been holding on to by a thread broke loose.

"I thought I was too, but I don't have it in me to do this."

"Do what? Us?" he said.

That wasn't what she'd meant but… He didn't get it. He so didn't get it. "I'm going home so I can nurse my wounds, make peace with losing the biggest opportunity of my life. *My life*, Cole! All I needed was a hug, an *I'm sorry you didn't win*, not because you feel responsible but because you understand I'm hurting. Somehow you've made my loss all about you because you have issues that you need to figure out." Her volume increased the longer she went on, but she was nowhere near stopping now that she'd started.

"You're an amazing man, with so much to offer, so many good qualities, but you've sold yourself some line of bullshit that you're no good, that you don't deserve good things, that you don't deserve to be happy. It's like you're punishing yourself— still. You won't listen to anyone who tells you differently. God knows you won't listen to me, but you're hurting yourself, and now you're hurting me too. I love you, Cole—yes, I said it and I mean it," she added when his eyes jumped to hers, "but I can't seem to make you see the man I see, the man I know, the man I love, because you're too set on believing you're still that angry teenager who made some mistakes. We all make mistakes, and we have to get over them, let them go, move on, but you can't. You're stuck, and I can't help you!"

She stood there for a good five seconds, catching her breath, watching him, willing him to ask her to stay, to apologize, to… anything. But all he did was rub the back of his neck while an angry tic pulsed in his temple. He didn't even look at her.

And there was her answer.

She closed the distance to the door, wasting no time now, anger, disappointment, and sadness warring within her, blurring her vision with tears that she refused to let fall. With the door open, her hand on the knob, she paused, looked over her shoulder at him. "I hope you can figure your shit out, Cole. If you do, let me know. Otherwise"—she swallowed the lump in her throat—"I can't be with you anymore."

———

C**OLE STOOD** next to the breakfast bar as she closed the door somewhere between quietly and an all-out slam.

There it was then, what he'd been expecting all along. The other shoe had dropped. Sierra had left him.

There was no satisfaction in having been right though.

She'd said she loved him. She wasn't the type to throw those words around for impact, so he was pretty sure she meant it.

As that sunk in, he battled with himself. He hadn't wanted her to love him. Hadn't wanted her to care enough to be hurt, because there was no question in his mind she was hurting. And yet, when she'd said those three words, her voice raised in anger and frustration with him, there was no denying…a part of him wanted nothing more than her love, wanted to be the man who deserved her love.

Too bad he didn't know how to be that guy.

He slammed his fist down on the countertop again, punctuating it with a "Dammit!"

His chest hurt with loss, and regret bubbled up like acid in his throat, and he didn't know what to do with any of it. Didn't know how to fix it.

What he did know was that he couldn't take another minute of his empty apartment, couldn't stand to spend another second alone with himself.

He grabbed his keys and wallet off the counter, shoved them in his jeans pockets, and headed downstairs to Sunshine's, slamming the door on the way.

CHAPTER THIRTY-ONE

*T*oday was about gratitude.

Sierra had reminded herself of that when she'd woken up that morning with an ache of loneliness in her chest. She'd reminded herself of it numerous times since arriving at Kennedy and Hunter's house for Thanksgiving dinner—every time she found herself envying her siblings' relationships with their significant others and every time she noticed Hunter's dad's devotion to Loretta, his wife who'd suffered from a stroke a couple of years ago and recovered nearly fully, though she still sometimes got dizzy. Sierra's parents, though far away in Arizona, had called earlier on video chat to say they missed them all and would see them for Christmas.

She had so much to be grateful for—a family who loved her, a successful, in-demand business, a kick-ass apartment on Hale Street, and some wonderful people for friends. There was Hayden, of course, who was spending the day with her own family, and also Asia, Jackson's fiancée, who was here for the holiday, along with her sister, Vegas. Sierra had gotten to know Vegas through the Hale Street book club that Vegas started a few months ago, along with a multitude of women who worked or lived in the neighborhood, all of whom had also become Sierra's friends.

Today, Vegas and Asia had brought their mother along, a

220

quiet, kind woman who had recently completed rehab for alcoholism. Because of that, Kennedy and Hunter had decided not to serve alcohol today, and Sierra fully understood and definitely supported that—except she could really use a drink. It was getting harder to keep her smile pasted on, her upbeat attitude in place.

They'd finished the midafternoon meal a couple of hours ago, and now Hunter, his dad, and Vegas were in the family room watching football. Asia, Jackson, Hunter's mom, and Hunter's brother, Miles, were at the dining table playing a game of Scattergories, and Sierra was helping Kennedy cut the pies—pumpkin, cherry, and chocolate pecan—and serve them. The whole main floor of the house was a big, open area, so the noise level was high, between the sports fans yelling and cheering and the jibes that went along with the board game.

Once Sierra had distributed dessert to everyone, she went back to the kitchen counter to grab her own slice, intent on drowning the extra-large piece of chocolate pecan with an extra-large dollop of homemade whipped cream. As she was about to grab her plate, though, Kennedy picked it up, along with her own plate, and headed to the back door.

"Grab forks and napkins," Kennedy said as she slipped out onto the three-season porch.

Sierra stared after her for a second, then glanced at the rest of the group. No one was paying them any attention. With a shrug, she did as her sister ordered.

"Isn't it considered rude to ditch your guests?" she asked after easing the door shut.

"Sit," Kennedy bossed. She'd set their plates on the high-top cafe table that overlooked what was usually a lush, green backyard but was now showing the last signs of any color before the winter freeze. She flipped the power on a space heater nearby.

With a glance toward the inside of the house, Sierra slid onto the stool, because there was her pie, and she was going to eat it no matter where her sister led her. "Why are we out here?" she asked.

Kennedy went over to the wet bar, selected a bottle of red

wine from a countertop rack, and busied herself opening it. "We all have our needs. Mrs. Knowles needs an alcohol-free environment, and my sister needs a glass of wine."

Sierra thought she might weep in gratitude. "I was managing without," she said stoically.

Kennedy got the cork out, took down two stemless goblets from a hanging rack, and poured the deep garnet liquid into each. She brought them over to the table, handed Sierra one, and sat on the other stool. "Your smile is too wide today."

That one sentence had the charade screeching to a halt. Sierra's throat thickened with all the emotion she'd been trying to block out for the whole day, and she couldn't respond.

"I admire the effort, and I think you fooled everyone else, but I'm your sister," Kennedy said. "And I know not winning the Eldridge thing was crushing."

Sierra set her fork down before she could take a single bite. Tears popped into her eyes as if they'd been right there under the surface waiting for the first moment she was alone, or almost alone. "Dammit," she said, and the first tear rolled over the rim of her eye and down her cheek. She'd texted the contest results to Kennedy on Tuesday when her sister had asked, had given her the few details she knew, and then changed the subject. Her sister had let her get away with it then, but clearly that wasn't to be now.

Kennedy slid off her stool, closed the space between them, and pulled Sierra in for a hug. She held her for a minute while Sierra silently let a few tears fall. She didn't want to give in to a full cry, because she knew, if she did, it would be an ugly one. *Another* ugly one.

She clung to her sister, breathing, squeezing her eyes shut, trying to force out all the thoughts, but then Kennedy ruined everything.

"And then there's Cole," her sister said.

The sobs came then, though she kept them silent. Just giant heaves of her shoulders and periodic gasps for air, and Kennedy held on.

"You can let it out," Kennedy said. She had never been the

nurturing type, and that made her gentle care now all the more meaningful to Sierra. Which only made her cry harder.

Sierra grasped on to her and couldn't have stopped letting it out if she'd wanted to. When the sobs finally calmed a few minutes later, she pulled away enough to look around for the napkins she'd brought out. She used them to dab at her eyes, knowing her mascara had to be a mess, and then she blew her nose. When she could get words out, she said, "How did you know?"

She hadn't told her sister about splitting up with Cole, had never really committed verbally to bringing him for Thanksgiving dinner even though Kennedy had told her to invite him. Yesterday Kennedy had texted to see if he was going to be there, and Sierra had merely replied that he was spending it with his own family.

"Not born yesterday," Kennedy answered. "You guys were spending a lot of time together. Every time we texted, Cole was either around or out of town. Then, the last couple of days, he was neither. What happened?"

Sierra took a shaky breath as Kennedy moved her stool closer and climbed back up. She launched into what had happened Monday night between her and Cole, told her enough about Cole's background that she could understand his issues without giving away the most private stuff he'd told her. Kennedy caressed her arm with one hand and held on to her wineglass with the other, sipping quietly as Sierra got everything out.

"You did the right thing," Kennedy said when she finished.

With that pronouncement, Sierra's tears came back with a vengeance, when she'd thought she had cried them all out. "I miss him, K."

"I know you do. But he's got to figure out his shit. You can't do that for him."

Sierra merely nodded, swallowing down another round of crying, because damn, she was exhausted. Instead, she took a swig of wine, closed her eyes, savored the subtle spice of it, and took another few swallows. To hell with sipping politely.

"I admire what you did," Kennedy said sincerely, picking up

her fork and shoveling a bite of pecan pie onto it. Their desserts had been sadly ignored until now, and Sierra followed suit. Pie was easier than feelings.

"Part of me feels bad for not hanging around to help him through it," she admitted, her heart hurting when she thought of the internal things Cole struggled with.

"He has to get through it. He has to want to get through it."

Sierra nodded slowly, thinking about that so hard that she barely tasted the creamy sweetness of the chocolate in her mouth. "I don't know. He's been wrangling with a lot of things from his past, making peace with his family. Going to work for them was monumental for him. But I just don't know if he can get past some things he needs to get past."

"You were smart to end it now then," Kennedy said. "I think back to my ex and wish I'd done that. Walked away when he couldn't be what I needed. It would've saved a lot of pain in the end."

"It seems like I missed out on saving myself a lot of pain," Sierra said.

Kennedy shook her head. "It hurts now, but it would hurt worse later."

Sierra knew she spoke from experience. A bad experience. But it didn't really make her feel better now.

"Damn, that doesn't help a bit, does it?" Kennedy asked.

All Sierra could do was shake her head, sniffle, and shove another bite of pie in her mouth. As she did, another round of tears ran down her face.

"Sometimes you just have to cry over pie," her sister said with a sad half smile, reaching out again for her hand. "But I'm right here with you."

Sierra nodded and sniffed again. With a pathetic laugh, she said, "You're just here for the pie."

"The pie doesn't suck," Kennedy said.

Sierra had told herself Monday night she could be sad for twelve hours, but that was before Cole had been added to the mix. She was on day three and tired of crying, tired of hurting, just plain tired.

"You're going to get through this tough part," Kennedy said. "It's super hard, I know. But you're going to be okay."

Sierra nodded automatically.

"You'll go back to work on Monday and get involved in your current project and lose yourself in the job that you love." Kennedy said it without any kind of judgment, because she knew Sierra, knew how she was, how much she thrived on her work.

Sierra set her fork down and picked up her wineglass, held it in both hands, swirling the liquid around and watching it. Her sister was spot on in some ways, but Sierra was no longer sure that loving her job was enough.

Unfortunately, her job was the only thing she had now, so she'd have to figure out how to be happy with that.

CHAPTER THIRTY-TWO

hanksgiving had never been Cole's favorite holiday, but it turned out it was even worse when you couldn't spend it with the person you loved. Oh, he'd put in his time with his family, and yes, he loved them, every single one of them, brothers, cousins, and all, with all their foibles and irritating tendencies. But as content as he was to be at peace with his family, he would've happily skipped out on time with them today if he could've spent it with Sierra.

Because, yes, he was pretty damn sure he loved her.

"Didn't expect to see you tonight," Winona called out as he sat on a stool in roughly the center of the counter at Sunshine's for a change. "Thought you'd be spending it with your family."

"I did. Stayed as long as I could stand it," he said.

Winona narrowed her eyes at him in the middle of drawing his usual beer. She finished it off, slid it over to him, then knowingly went for the Johnnie Walker Double Black.

"Thanks," he said when she set a full glass of the whiskey in front of him. "Guess you know me."

"Going on eight years now," she said. "I'm no dummy."

"Did you get some time off earlier?"

"Don took me to Cadence for their Thanksgiving buffet. We ate way too much. Pretty much the perfect holiday." Don was her longtime beau who she refused to marry. He helped her out at the bar sometimes on the weekends, filled in for her when she was under the weather, generally seemed to take good care of Winona.

"Want food?" she asked, and Cole shook his head.

The place wasn't busy so far, only two tables full, but it would fill up later, Cole knew from experience, when people hit their limits with family time and relatives and gathered at the watering holes that made a point of opening on the holiday. Winona headed around the counter to check in on the customers.

Dinner for the North family had been at Liz's this year, because they all recognized if they'd allowed his mother to host the holiday, there'd be no getting her to relax and let others do all the work. She was weeks post heart attack now and so much stronger, but she still tired easily and would've exhausted herself before the turkey was even in the oven.

Everyone had been there—Drake, Mason, Gabe, Miranda, Connor, Logan, Cole's mom, his aunt, and of course, Geraldine— all but Zane, but they were hopeful he could make it home for a couple of days over Christmas. They'd had enough food for four armies and had gone through at least half of it at the early-after-noon meal. When they'd started pulling out the leftovers for round two this evening, though, Cole had slipped out. He'd had enough of the togetherness, the happy family, the warmth. He was lucky to have them, glad they were happy, but he himself was miserable inside, and hiding that was a lot of work.

He had no one to blame but himself for the miserableness, and that made it all the worse. He'd let Sierra down, no two ways about it. After going over everything she'd said the other night, sixty or seventy times or maybe a thousand, he couldn't argue with any of it. He'd taken her bad news and made it about him instead of being the support she needed. Deserved. If he could punch himself in the face for that, he would.

Having gulped down half of the Johnnie already, he set down the glass, propped his elbows on the counter, and absently cracked the knuckles of each hand as he beat himself up mentally.

Winona appeared out of nowhere, reached across the bar, and

grasped his hands in hers, stopping his knuckle cracking. "It's been a while since you got in a fight. Maybe a record for you. Think you could keep it going a little longer?"

"I'm not gonna fight tonight," he said, knowing full well it *was* a record and that he hadn't fought since he'd gone to Kennedy's wedding with Sierra. Knowing full well, also, that it wasn't a coincidence. The truth was, he'd been walking around without the ongoing haze of anger that he hadn't truly realized had been clinging to him for, shit, years. "Fact is, I'm tired of fighting."

She released his hands, and he took another deep swallow of whiskey, thinking about how true that statement was, how encompassing.

He felt like he'd been fighting his whole life. Fighting being different when he was a kid. Fighting the need to belong. Fighting the need for friends. Fighting his family and his dad and his brothers and the family business. Fighting his feelings for Sierra.

Fighting the bad stuff as well as the good.

"Sometimes it feels like I've wasted most of my life fighting," he said as Winona, more relaxed than usual tonight, leaned her elbows on her side of the counter and stopped tidying, pouring, stocking, fixing, and serving for once.

"Sounds like it's time to stop fighting then."

Cole laughed, a sound lacking any real mirth. "I think I'd like to do that. I'm not sure I know how." He ran his hands over his face, feeling like he'd sprinted a marathon but found himself at the same place he'd started.

Winona's gaze was locked to him; he could feel it. He made a point of not meeting it.

"Not just the fistfights," she said. "Maybe it's time to stop fighting what you feel for Sierra."

He lowered his hands and blew out a breath. "It's not that simple. I screwed up."

"I know you did."

There was so much matter-of-factness in her tone that Cole finally looked at her. "Did you talk to her?"

"Didn't need to. I saw her speed-walk by the windows the other night early in the evening, the way a girl does when she wants to get to the car before she starts bawling her eyes out."

"She was walking fast so you assumed she was going to cry?"

Winona nodded. "And then I peeked out the door and verified it. She was parked right down there"—she pointed to the left —"and when she pulled out of the parking spot, I could see tears running down her face. A few minutes later, you stormed in here in some kind of mood."

The knowledge that Sierra had been crying hit him like a punch in the gut. He knew he'd hurt her, but the thought of Sierra in tears… That it was because of his dumb-assery made it worse.

"Well," she said, straightening, eyeing something over his shoulder, "it looks like you've been found. I trust you won't fight with this guy."

Cole looked behind him to see Mason approaching and clamped his jaw down. No matter how much peace he and Mason had made, he wasn't in the mood. There was a reason Cole had escaped the family gathering, or more like nine reasons, one per happy family member.

He frowned as Mason tossed his jacket on an empty stool, then sat on the one next to him. "What are you doing here?"

"I figured I'd find you here," Mason said. "Hello, Winona. Nice to see you."

"You too, handsome. Can I get you a drink? Sandwich?"

Mason checked out what Cole was drinking, saw both the beer and the whiskey, and pointed at the beer glass. "Just a draft."

She pulled out a mug, filled it, slid it across the counter. Another group had come in, and she headed out to their table to help them.

"Did Aunt Liz run out of booze or something?" Cole asked.

"No, but the pie is just about gone, and that might be worse."

"I don't think Winona has any pie."

"Mom's worried about you. You didn't say goodbye."

"I'll text her," Cole said. "She could've texted me."

"She did."

Cole pulled out his phone, not surprised to find he had it silenced, and saw three messages from his mom, four from Gabe, and one from Miranda. "You drew the short straw?"

His brother shrugged and took a swallow of beer. "What happened with Sierra?" he asked, and Cole supposed cutting to the chase was part of the reason Mason was successful at business.

Cole thought about denying it, playing dumb, diverting the conversation, but all that took energy, and he was running low on it. "She got smart."

Mason, still wearing khaki pants and a denim button-down shirt, still tucked in, said, "It seemed to me like you made her happy."

The image of Sierra laughing, happy, filled Cole's head and made his pulse pound in his throat. "Until I didn't."

Mason looked over at him, as if to check if he was serious. "Sorry to hear that. I thought you two might have something worth fighting for."

There was that word again. All these years of fighting, probably for the wrong things and the wrong reasons, and now that there was something—someone—worthwhile, he didn't know what to do. Because he wasn't convinced, deep down, that *he* was worth fighting for.

If Mason had tried to pry then, insisted on knowing what had happened, Cole probably would've downed the rest of his whiskey and walked away. Gone out the door, up the stairs, and into his apartment where he'd… Hell. Stare at the walls? Throw shit around? Drive himself batshit with questions he couldn't answer? Being alone had been his MO for most of his life, but if he chilled the fuck out, he had to admit that it wasn't terrible to sit with his brother at his side. Especially when Mason didn't talk.

Ten or fifteen minutes passed with them sitting there, watching as more people wandered in and Winona got busier but remained unbothered. She told them Don was coming in after-while to help, then scurried off with a full tray of drinks.

Maybe it was his third glass of whiskey that loosened his lips. Maybe it was because the growing noise around them felt like it insulated them. Maybe it was the thought of facing his empty apartment and Tito's accusing eyes that seemed to say he'd ruined the best thing either of them had ever had. Cole wasn't sure which, exactly, but he found words popping out of his mouth. "She said I need to let go of the past."

"Sierra?" Mason asked, eyeing him from the side.

Cole didn't answer, because who else would he be talking about? "I guess I don't know how to do that. How the hell do you let past fuckups go?" Then he let out a half-assed laugh. "How would you know? You've never fucked up."

"That's bullshit and you know it."

Cole didn't know any such thing, but he didn't have a chance to say so before Mason said, "How do you *not* let things go? They eat away at you if you don't."

Shit. Cole realized he'd picked the wrong guy to try to talk to. Talking was stupid anyway. It wasn't going to fix anything, as much as he was dying to fix things, fix himself. "You wouldn't understand," he said, resigned to getting another glass of Johnnie the next time Winona had a second.

"You talking about your fight with Dad the night before he died?" Mason asked, and Cole felt like the oxygen had been sucked right out of his lungs and all the blood froze in his veins.

"How do you know about that?" Nobody knew about it, except Sierra, of course. He'd never spoken a word of it to anyone else.

"I was there. I overheard it."

The whole family had been out that night. Their mom had been somewhere with Zane and Drake, who were still in middle school, and Gabe and Mason had already moved out. When Cole had stormed out, he hadn't run into anyone, had no idea Mason was close.

Cole eyed the whiskey bottle on the shelf, glanced around for Winona. She probably wouldn't be mad at him for too long if he went behind the counter—

"Don't you dare," Winona said as she appeared in front of him. She reached up, took the bottle down, refilled his glass.

Cole, still shell-shocked as fuck, simply nodded his thanks and then took a healthy gulp as she disappeared into the kitchen.

"That's it, isn't it? You regret it?" Mason said. "Have regretted it for all these years?"

"It was ugly," Cole admitted. "But then you know that if you heard it all."

"You were a teenager, Cole. Teenagers fight with their parents. They say bad shit to their parents. Dad knew that."

"When did you ever say anything contrary to Dad?" Cole distinctly remembered all the poison that had come out of his own mouth that night. Hateful words, things he wouldn't allow himself to admit out loud today.

"I fought with Dad plenty. Gabe fought with Dad. I guarantee you if Dad had been alive when the twins hit high school, they would've fought with him too, probably an exponential amount, knowing those two."

Cole tried to imagine the golden brother being cross with their dad. "What'd you argue about? Did you get a B on your report card?"

"Don't be an ass. It's not important what I did. Just know that Dad and I butted heads plenty of times. We all did."

Cole could remember, back when he was in grade school and Mason and Gabe, seven and five years older than him, were in high school, hearing raised voices a time or two. He hadn't thought much of it at the time, probably so caught up in his own angst. He didn't, for a minute, believe Mason could be as awful as he himself had been to their dad.

"We were shits, as kids are," Mason continued. "And every single time, he forgave us for being shits. The thing is, he just wasn't around long enough after your big fight for you to understand he forgave you."

Somehow Mason might've just homed in on the heart of something significant. For all these years, Cole had been hung up on his dad dying while he was mad at Cole, disappointed in Cole.

Before he'd been able to forgive Cole. But maybe he would have eventually. Cole had fucked up pretty majorly, more than his brothers ever had, and then been a big shithead about it, but their dad did eventually get over whatever he and his brothers pulled.

"Dad told me after one of your battles," Mason said, "when I was home from college for a break, that you, out of all of us kids, were the most like him. He hated that and loved it at the same time."

Cole frowned, trying to make sense of that. "How was I anything like him?"

"There were the obvious things you had in common, like pitching and reading and being wicked smart, but I think what he was really talking about was that Dad had some rebel in him just like you. He gave his parents hell growing up. So he understood you and thought that should've made it easier to get you through the hard stuff."

Cole shook his head, knowing there'd been nothing easy for Harry North. Not where Cole was concerned.

"He loved you," Mason said. "He knew you loved him. There's not a doubt in my mind about that."

The din around them disappeared from Cole's awareness as he took in what his brother told him, pondered whether it could be true. Wondered if it could make a difference in his damn head. He remembered Sierra had said something similar all those weeks ago in the hospital.

Several more minutes passed with the brothers sitting there in silence, Cole lost in his thoughts and barely registering that Don had arrived and jumped right in to help Winona, who had a nearly full house. Mason's beer was empty, his mug pushed to the serving side of the counter, and when Don, who was doing behind-the-bar duty while Winona hit the tables, asked if he wanted more, Mason waved him off.

Eventually Mason asked, "Have you ever grieved for Dad?"

The question hit Cole like a broadside from a semi. He stared into his glass, turning the question over in his mind. "You mean, like, cried?"

Mason shrugged. "I don't know. Cried, punched a wall, yelled, anything."

Cole felt his brother's eyes on him now, but he himself kept staring into the amber liquid in his glass.

"I'm no psychologist, so what the hell do I know, but maybe if you tried to get past your fight…let it go…"

"I don't know how to do that," Cole said, his voice sounding raw, making him thankful for all the background noise.

"What do you think about when you think of Dad?" Mason asked.

"I try not to think of Dad."

That that was a grave problem didn't need to be spoken between them. It hung in the air like a neon sign.

"When you do, what do you think about?"

"That last argument." Which was why he did his best not to think about him at all.

"Maybe try remembering some of the good stuff. There was a lot of good stuff. Dad loved you. He loved all of us. He was a good father…"

Harry North *was* a good father. Those words registered as true now. Their dad had been a damn good father. He loved all of his sons. According to Mason, he'd loved Cole, had known Cole loved him, had understood Cole. That would take some time to absorb, especially the part about them being alike, and Cole intended to give it some thought, see if it would sink in.

"I don't know how to tell you to get past it," Mason said, "but I suspect it might have something to do with what Sierra was talking about. If you could get past that fight with Dad, maybe quite punishing yourself with a crappy apartment in a crappy part of town, let yourself accept what's rightfully yours from the company, from Dad…maybe you could give yourself permission to be happy."

Cole jerked his head toward his brother, met his eyes for the first time tonight, because what he said, that last bit…something about it resonated. Penetrated his thick skull. Rang fucking true.

Mason stood, tossed some bills on the counter, and grabbed his coat, then slapped Cole on the back. "It seems like Sierra could make the right guy pretty damn happy," he said, then, "Don't forget to text Mom," and he turned and walked out the door.

There was no doubt in Cole's mind that Sierra was the one woman who could make him *pretty damn happy*. He wanted to be the guy who could make her happy too, and he was starting to think maybe it was possible. Maybe it was time get past all his shit, enough to be the man she needed. Deserved.

Maybe, thanks to his brother, he could finally think his way through to that.

CHAPTER THIRTY-THREE

Four twenty-seven in the morning on Thanksgiving, or technically the day after, and Cole had yet to get a wink of sleep.

After Mason had left Sunshine's, the crowd noise had become annoying instead of reassuring, and Cole had headed up to his apartment and his grumpy feline, who'd stalked Cole until he'd lain down in bed. The night was cold, with snow in the forecast, and Tito seemed to believe he was entitled to a share of Cole's body heat.

The conversation with Mason had Cole drowning in thoughts, his mind spinning on topics he usually blocked out, hard topics. His dad, Sierra, his past, his fuckups, his future…

Four o'clock had been his tipping point. He'd been thinking about what Mason had said about their dad, about remembering the good stuff. Because Cole hadn't ever done that, in the fifteen years since Harry North had died. And there was definitely good stuff. He'd felt compelled to crawl out of bed and throw on jeans, a sweatshirt, boots, and a coat, leave Tito snoozing on his pillow, and walk out of his apartment.

That had led him here, to an unassuming city park called Robins Park that was less than a mile from the house he'd grown up in. The park was surrounded on three and a half sides by houses, with a small parking lot on the fourth side that would hold half a dozen cars.

He climbed out of his truck, which he'd parked in the end spot, and looked out over the expanse of the park. There was the playground, the wading pool, the picnic shelter, the open field that was often used for soccer games, and the baseball diamond, none of which had changed much since he was a kid, with the exception of the playground. The baseball diamond was what had lured Cole out in the middle of this frigid night.

With a glance around at the surrounding houses to verify the entire world was asleep, he set off across the frozen grass. There wasn't much to the diamond, and in fact, from the parking lot, it was easy to miss it altogether if you didn't know it was there. There were no bleachers, no bases, no fences behind the plate or in the outfield. Just dirt patches in the appropriate places plus a bit of a pitcher's mound. Rudimentary and not suitable for an official game, but good enough for a neighborhood pickup game.

None of that mattered. It hadn't when he was seven years old and his dad had brought him here for his first father-son pitching lesson, and it didn't matter now, because Cole was seeing it through seven-year-old eyes, when the field had seemed special, the distance between the mound and the plate—a rubber mat they'd brought with them—had seemed immense, and he'd been buzzing with importance and excitement and love for his father.

He strode to the mound and gazed off to the bare spot of dirt that served as home plate and the catcher's box, overcome by nostalgia and memories. His eyes slid shut as he was engulfed by the past.

He could hear his dad's voice, first on the mound with him— teaching him a beginner's leg kick, gently pulling Cole back from his overzealous determination to do a full wind-up, explaining that would come later—and then from the plate, encouraging, coaching, praising, teaching, and catching for him. With a start, he realized he could recall his dad's smell—a hint of aftershave beneath the mint of the gum his old man had chewed incessantly.

With his eyes still closed, the years washed away, and Cole

remembered that summer day like it was yesterday. The heat of the sun on his arms, the smell of cut grass and mint, the distant sound of little kids playing on the playground at the opposite end of the park. His dad's enthusiasm when Cole picked up the basics more quickly than expected. His encouragement, his patience, his pride. His love.

He'd always known his dad loved him. Had taken it for granted for sure. Even when Cole had gotten in trouble at school or at home, even when his dad had disciplined him, there'd never been any question about whether he was loved. And always, no matter how much of a shit Cole had been, there was forgiveness.

When he felt little bits of dampness on his face, Cole opened his eyes. It was snowing. The silent, gentle flakes started out sparse, but within a couple of minutes, they'd picked up in intensity. He looked up at the sky, and it was like a 3D optical illusion with all the flakes coming at him. He wasn't a religious guy, but as he gazed upward, the concept of heaven crossed his mind, and he wondered if his dad was looking down at him.

He lay down on his back, right there on the nearly flat mound, his arms behind his head to cushion it, and felt it—a peace like he hadn't known for ages, maybe hadn't ever known. And he knew. There was no logic to it, but still, he knew—his dad *was* looking down at him, sending him a message. A dad's love forgave, and he was forgiven.

Cole lay there, the snowflakes alighting on him like the gentlest kisses and then melting, and he soaked it in. The peace. The calm. The knowledge that he could stop hating himself for that one ugly argument. For everything in his past. Because it had nothing to do with today or tomorrow, unless he let it.

When he eventually sat up, still warm inside from the memory of his dad's love, the ground around him was covered with a dusting of white, and the park had a magical feel to it. Pulling his legs into his chest, resting his arms on his knees, he breathed in the cold freshness of the air and felt invigorated by it. As if it infused him with the power to move forward, to let go of the bad stuff from his past.

He let out a low laugh at himself, realizing he'd always had that power but just hadn't wanted to move on. Hadn't wanted to let things go. He hadn't had a big enough reason, a strong enough motivator.

He wanted a future with Sierra, wanted to be the man she wanted, needed, deserved. Up until now, he'd been fighting with that, telling himself that wasn't him, but...it could be. He had some work to do, some truths to wrangle with, some actions to take. But he had two things now that he hadn't had before—clarity and determination.

Now he just needed a plan.

CHAPTER THIRTY-FOUR

The only thing black about the Friday after Thanksgiving for Sierra was her mood, and really, gray or blue was probably a better description of it.

No, she thought, there was still some black, some anger as well as melancholy and loneliness, because, when you got down to it, Cole was an idiot. He was stubborn and blind and too hard on himself and…

Dammit, she loved that idiot.

And thinking about him was doing her no good whatsoever.

She'd pushed her crew hard earlier in the week in order to enable them to take today off, but now that she'd had a full day looming over her with no family obligations, no work obligations, and nothing to do, she regretted it, for her sake. Her guys definitely deserved the extra time off, but it left her with too much time to think. That's why, at five forty-five p.m. on a day that half the known universe took as a holiday, she was still tucked in her office at the Dunn & Lowell headquarters, her laptop on the table in front of her and the space heater purring a few feet away. Because, as Kennedy had pointed out, Sierra did love her job, and pathetically, that was all she had to focus on right now. She thought she deserved credit for making it until mid-afternoon before she'd hit the office. Now she was deep into get-stuff-done mode.

Good thing, too, as she needed to see if she could book about one more project before Christmas now that they wouldn't be involved in anything related to the Eldridge mansion. That meant upping the marketing efforts stat, and she and Kennedy had come up with a way to do that before she'd gone home last night. Sierra had just gotten off the phone with her radio ad rep, having increased her ad spend for the next ten days.

She also needed to get back to working on the first quarter of next year, filling up their schedule, as it was currently a little light on projects. Those would come, she knew, but she intended to do what she could to encourage them. Of particular interest to her was a bed-and-breakfast just outside of town that was looking for a gut job. Sierra had met with the owners a couple of days ago, had toured the property, and aimed to get the meat of the proposal down on paper this evening for her next meeting with them on Tuesday.

Not five minutes after she'd pulled up the photos of the property on her computer, she thought she heard a noise in the other room. But she'd locked the door when she'd come in, so she didn't think too much about it, as it was probably the wind. There was a good two or three inches of snow on the ground, and the wind was on a tear.

When something tapped on the window right behind her, though, she nearly jumped through the ceiling. Because that wasn't the wind. That noise sounded like it was made by a human.

Her heart racing, she stood, glanced around at the room as if it could tell her what to do. Her phone was in her pocket, and she pulled it out in case she needed to call the cops. The tapping came again, *tink tink tink tink* on the glass, and yeah, that was a person.

It was dark outside and she had the overhead light and a lamp on, so if she tried to look out the blinds, she would see nothing, and whoever was out there would see her clearly. After flipping the overhead light off, she went into the next room over, the darkened meeting room, and peeked between the blinds toward the area outside her office window. Sure enough, there was someone out there, and her mouth went dry and her grip tightened on her phone.

It was too dark to tell who it was or what they were doing, but what could they be doing other than trying to break in? Which would be stupid, because there wasn't much of value in here. The workshop in back contained thousands of dollars of tools and equipment, but the priciest thing in here was probably the copy machine, and who wanted to steal one of those? She didn't have a safe, didn't deal in cash—

"Sierra!"

She let the blinds slip back together as she identified the male voice that sounded all too familiar. Or was she imagining it? Surely Cole wouldn't—

"Sierra, it's me. Let me in!" he yelled, still talking to the window in her office.

What the hell?

Apparently he would.

She didn't know whether she wanted to kick him for scaring the crap out of her, yell at him for being an idiot in general, or calmly, quietly let him in and hear what the hell he wanted, as a tiny kernel of hope took root in her heart.

Instead of heading straight for the back door, she went to the window in the main room, on the opposite side of the building, and stole a glance out at the driveway. The sight of Cole's familiar blue truck had her heart rate picking up yet again, no longer in fear. She hurried into the kitchen, dimly lit by the fixture over the sink, and to the side door. When she opened it, no one was there, and she vaguely heard him tapping on the window in the other room again.

Idiot.

"Cole!" she yelled into the brisk evening air, her breath clouding into vapor and the wind making her shiver. "Hello?"

Though she couldn't see the back side of the building from the doorway, she could hear his footsteps crunching across the snow toward her.

"Hey," he said as he came around the corner. "Finally."

"What's going on?" she asked, suddenly wondering if something bad had happened, if his mom—

"Can I come in?" He opened the storm door wider, his breath also coming out in visible puffs.

Sierra backed up to let him in, then walked farther into the kitchen to put space between them. Cole shut both doors and locked the heavy inside door, then leaned against it, shuddering from the cold.

"What are you doing here?" Sierra asked, crossing her arms over her chest as she tried to decipher his intentions. He didn't seem like there was an emergency or bad news, though he definitely looked like he hadn't been sleeping, based on the dark shadows under his eyes. Now that she looked at him fully in the light, though, she couldn't help but notice that, under his winter coat, he was wearing something she'd never seen him wear before—khakis and a button-down shirt. And he had shaved recently, which made her fingers itch to touch his sandpapery jaw.

"I need to talk to you."

"Why didn't you text me instead of nearly giving me a heart attack?"

He grimaced. "Sorry about that. I went old-school, tried knocking on the door, but apparently you didn't hear it."

"I was kind of in my zone. What do you need to talk about? Why are you dressed like that?"

He stepped away from the door, came closer, and Sierra wanted to touch him so badly, to run her hands up his chest as if she hadn't walked away from him a few days ago. To ensure she didn't, she pushed off the counter and headed to her office, where she could sit with the table in between them.

Except when she got there, she couldn't bring herself to sit. The heater was still pumping out blessed warm air, and she stood in front of it, letting it blow on her feet.

Cole sauntered in, pulled out the chair that used to be his usual one from the table, and instead of sitting on it, sat on the table itself.

"I knew I'd find you here," he said. "Tried this first, even before your apartment."

"Why?"

"Because I figured you'd be work—"

"I mean why did you track me down, Cole?" she said impatiently. Her nerves were stretched taut as he took his sweet time explaining himself.

He exhaled and looked suddenly nervous, flustered. She'd never seen him like this, not even at Kennedy's wedding, when she knew he was uneasy and felt out of place.

"I've been thinking about everything you said Monday night," he said. "Pretty much thinking about it nonstop since Monday. I was up all night, turning things over in my mind. Mason helped me realize some stuff and…" He shook his head. "Forget all that. Come over here."

Sierra frowned. Her spot in front of the heater was only about four feet away from where he sat. She wasn't sure she trusted herself to go closer.

"Please?" he said, and there was a plea in his eyes, along with something else, something she'd never seen on him before. An openness, as if he was laying himself bare.

That or she was being stupidly hopeful.

He held a hand out in invitation, and she studied the part of his body she knew so well—okay, *one* of the parts she knew well. His hands had always looked so strong and capable, even before she'd gotten involved with him. Long fingers, work-roughened skin, so much skill and talent…and yeah, she wasn't just talking about with a hammer or a power tool.

With a minute shake of her head at herself, she bit down on her lip, a reminder to keep herself in check. She took one step toward him, unable to deny that look in his eyes, and when his hand remained outstretched, she eyed it, met his gaze again, and tentatively placed her palm on top of his. He closed his fingers gently around hers and tugged her closer.

"Hear me out," he said.

"I'm listening."

"The other night you said you loved me. Did you mean it?"

"That's not something I would say unless I meant it," she said, feeling vulnerable, trying to take her hand back, but he held on firmly.

"Good," he breathed out. "I didn't want you to say it Monday, because I didn't think you should love me."

Sierra narrowed her eyes at him.

"But that was Monday," he rushed to say.

"And today?"

"I want you to love me. Because I don't want to be the only one. In love."

There was a catch in her chest. "You're in love?" She couldn't help the grin breaking through as she said it. "With me?"

He laughed out a nervous exhale. "Of course with you." He pulled her into his chest, wrapping his arms around her, and Sierra breathed out fully for the first time since she'd identified him in the snow outside her window. He buried his face in her hair and sucked in a slow, deep breath. "I love you, Sierra."

She closed her eyes and savored every bit of him, the words he spoke, the clean, arousing scent of him, the familiar feel of his muscular chest beneath her cheek.

Cole pulled back enough that he could look into her eyes. "I've never said that to another woman. Never wanted to. Still didn't want to on Monday, but"—he pressed his forehead to hers, grinning—"you got me. Whether you want me or not, you got me, and I know that telling you how I feel is one thing, but I also know that your concerns were justified, and that's what I've been thinking about."

"All night."

"All damn night. I had a lot of ground to cover, and though I'm not about to suggest I could be fixed in one night, I did figure some things out, came to some decisions."

"That you're okay with loving me?" she said, needing to hear it yet again.

"That's one thing." He blew out his breath. "There was a lot, stuff about the past, about my dad, about the future. I want you in mine, and I'm doing everything I can to think forward instead of backward."

"Like forgiving yourself?" she asked.

"Something like that. I've come to see that that one night, that terrible fight didn't define what my dad thought of me. I know he loved me, and I loved him, no matter how much stuff I screwed up. And there was a lot."

"None of that matters to me, Cole," she said, running her finger along his jawline. "I love every part of you." She eased him closer with her hand and kissed him, slowly, thoroughly, with every drop of love running through her veins for this man.

As the kiss heated up, she trailed her hands down to his waist, needing to feel his flesh under her fingers. She had to untuck his shirt from his pants, and that reminded her... "You never said why you're dressed more like Gabe than you."

He let out a lazy growl, as if he'd rather kiss than talk now. "It seemed appropriate for my visit to Nancy Callahan, one of the company lawyers and a family friend. We discussed setting up a baseball scholarship program in memory of my dad. It'll go toward things like private baseball coaching for kids who can't afford it, all ages, all skill levels. Because that's what my dad loved and what he was good at. He loved the sport, loved teaching us boys the fundamentals, loved going to our games. Baseball is the reason he opened the business in the first place. There's a lot of kids out there who might want to play baseball but don't have a dad like that, maybe don't have a dad at all."

"This was your idea?" she asked, impressed, excited for Cole, and even more in love with him than she'd been five minutes ago.

"About six a.m.," he said, "after a night on the ball diamond where he taught me to pitch."

"And you're planning to fund it?"

"With a part of my share from the company," Cole said.

"You accepted it from your brothers? Signed the papers?"

"Right before my appointment with Nancy."

She pulled him in for a tight hug. "That's wonderful, Cole. I'm so happy for you. Not because you're now loaded enough to buy the Eldridge Mansion if you wanted to—"

"I don't, unless you really wanted to work on that specific building that badly…"

Smiling, she shook her head. "You deserve what your dad intended for you to have. It's part of the North legacy he left for your family, which you're just as much a part of as any of your brothers." His acceptance said a lot about how far Cole had come, mentally, emotionally, toward making peace with himself, accepting himself.

Cole nodded. "You know what? This isn't supposed to be about my dad or money or my family. It's about me and you and how I'm going to be the kind of guy you deserve. You make me want to be a better person. You make me believe I can be."

"You're just right exactly as you are." She pulled him in for another kiss, taking care to show him how *just right* he was.

Cole lifted her up by her thighs and pulled her onto him in a straddle, his long legs stretched out from the table, her legs curling around him, feet crossing behind his back. The friction between their lower bodies was like a switch, turning on a physical ache deep in her abdomen and between her legs. He stood, forcing her to cling to him harder.

Laughing, she said, "What are you doing?"

With her wrapped around him, he walked around the desk she rarely used and set her butt down on the edge of it. "I'm going to do something I've dreamed about doing for years, right here on this desk." With all of his attention homed in on her and his erection pressing into her, he left no question about what that consisted of.

"Years?" she asked as he kissed a spot beneath her ear, sending shivers of pleasure through her.

He paused what he was doing and met her gaze. "Since the first day I worked for you," he confessed.

"Time for that dream to come true then," she whispered, peering into brown eyes that were so full of love it took her breath away.

"That and so many more." He sealed his lips to hers in a promise.

EPILOGUE

FOUR MONTHS LATER

ole leaned against the newly painted living room wall of the Eldridge mansion, watching his girl shine on camera, doing what she was born to do.

The Eldridge project—and the TV show—were hers now, as they should've been all along. A couple of weeks after the "winner" was originally announced, it was discovered that the guy had a previous business relationship with the producer of the show, or more accurately, the *former* producer, Robert Crum. Neither had disclosed the relationship, and since that went against the rules, Eldridge had gotten rid of both of them and awarded Dunn & Lowell the opportunity. Sierra was embracing the hell out of it, showing Eldridge and the world that she should've been first choice anyway.

They were filming a segment on the fireplace in the living room, and Cole was there with his family—his mom, Drake, Gabe, and Mason—to watch the filming process...or so Sierra thought. Andy, Sierra's new foreman, who was thankfully too old and too ugly for Cole to be jealous of, was assisting as she measured and installed the supports for the mantel—a thick, heavy slab of oak whose beauty came from the wood itself instead of any carving or decoration. The piece was at the center of Cole's plan.

"How much longer do you think?" Drake said in a low voice to him at a moment when the cameras weren't on.

Cole looked at his Timex and realized they'd been there for over an hour already. He'd gotten so wrapped up in watching Sierra that time had flown by. "Why? You got a date or something?" It was a Wednesday, and filming was supposed to go till six, but it was after that now. It didn't matter the time or day though. Drake usually had a date, and it was usually with a different woman each time.

"Not tonight," Drake said. "I have to pick up Ezra's little sister, Mackenzie, at the airport. She's moving back to town."

Ezra was Drake's best friend, had been for years, though the guy had some kind of jet-setting career now where he was usually doing business somewhere in the world besides the States.

"Knowing you, you'll turn it into a date before the night's over," Cole said, smacking his brother on the back.

"Nope. No chance. Ezra would bust my balls if I so much as looked at his sister. I'm just hoping I can recognize her. I haven't seen her since she was fifteen and a pain in the ass."

The camera guys signaled they were ready to roll again, shutting Cole and his brother up. As Sierra rechecked that the supports were level one last time, Cole's heart sped up and his hands started sweating as he stuck them in his front pockets. He watched Andy, who stood off to the side now, for a nod. Seconds later, he got it, and Cole hurried out of the room to the hallway through one of the two arched doorways, and Andy met him outside of the other.

"You ready for this?" the foreman asked quietly.

"So damn ready," Cole said with a smile, hoping his nerves didn't show.

Together the two men lifted the mantel, Andy closest to the living room, just feet away from Sierra, who was talking away to the camera, explaining every bit of what she was doing. They slid the long chunk of wood onto Cole's shoulder just as Sierra said they were ready for it.

Cole swallowed down his fear of being on camera, focusing

only on the woman he loved as he entered the living room, slab on his shoulder, and waited for Sierra to notice him.

"So we've already stained the mantel and done everything that needs to be done to it," she said, facing the camera, "and now we're just going to— Oh." Her eyes went big as she realized Cole was the one standing there. "Camera's rolling," she said to him in a whisper.

Cole nodded, his heart racing, only distantly aware of anything but her and the heavy-ass piece of wood. "I know. Andy asked me to step in. Let's set this down." He lowered the wood to the floor, set it on end, resting it against the bricks as Sierra ad-libbed to the cameras.

"A surprise," she said. "This is Cole, my former foreman, and he's—"

To save her from having to sputter too much other nonsense, Cole got straight to business, reaching into his right front pocket as he went down to one knee.

Sierra sucked in her breath and her hands flew to her face as she gazed down at him. "Oh, my god," she said from behind her hands. "Cole, what are you doing?"

His goddamn hands were shaking, and he hoped that didn't show on camera, but what the hell. He sucked in a breath and took one of her hands in his, the ring in his other one. "I once told you I would support you in this project in any way possible, as long as I didn't have to be on camera. Do you remember that?"

She nodded, and he could see tears forming in her eyes, which made his emotions clutch up even tighter in his throat. He fought through them, though, because he'd never wanted anything as much as he wanted her.

"And here I am," he said with a shaky laugh. "I'll do just about anything in the world for you, because I love you more than I ever knew was possible." He swallowed again and held up the ring, looked into her gorgeous brown eyes, and asked, "Will you marry me, Sierra?"

With his words, her tears overflowed and streamed down her face, and it felt like eternity ticked by before she nodded silently as she tugged at his arm to pull him up off the floor. He stood, staring into her eyes, which peered back up at him with so much love that he could barely believe his luck.

"Yes," she said on a gusty exhale. "Yes, I'll marry you, Cole."

Grinning like an idiot, he slid the ring onto her finger, his hand still shaking like crazy. He pulled her into his arms and spun her around as everyone in the room—his family, the production crew, even Eldridge himself, all of whom were in on his scheme—cheered and clapped.

He had no idea whether the cameras were still rolling and didn't really care. Before he knew it, his family was surrounding them, congratulating them, hugging them, laughing and celebrating with them. When everyone had hugged everyone else, and his mother had held on an extra-long time to Sierra, whispering things into her ear, Cole pulled Sierra back into his side and faced everyone.

"The segment might not be over," he said. "Mr. Eldridge said you'll be starting tomorrow where you left off, but for me, that's a wrap. The wrap of a lifetime."

NOTE FROM THE AUTHOR

Thanks for reading *True North*! I hope you loved Cole and Sierra's story.

Want to read more of the Lowell family? Kennedy and Hunter's story, is now available in print and ebook formats. Find out what happens when bartender Kennedy's new boss, Hunter, has her shaken *and* stirred.

You can also order *True Colors*, Drake and Mackenzie's story, available in both print and ebook. Find out what happens when eternal bachelor Drake's best friend's little sister moves back to Nashville, grown-up, independent, and irresistible.

I love to hear from readers! Please drop me a line at amy@amyknupp.com or on my Facebook author page at facebook.com/AuthorAmyKnupp.

ACKNOWLEDGMENTS

As always, though writing is a solitary pursuit, I couldn't do it without help.

Thanks to Suzanne Cox for her medical expertise and plotting help. It takes a special kind of person who knows all the hospital/medical things and can use that knowledge to help me come up with a feasible situation for my story. Suzanne is that special person, and I feel lucky to call her a friend as well.

Thanks to Jasminka Vujic for sharing her knowledge on the Nashville area and for her patience in answering my numerous bizarre character questions—as well as for being a dear friend for two decades.

Thanks to my beta readers, who offered their precious time and enthusiasm to help me fine-tune my story and improve my story-telling. Their suggestions and encouragement give me courage at that moment when I need it most, and my betas are the best!

Thanks, as always, to my family, for their love, support, and understanding that, yes, I really am working as I sit in my comfy "nest" chair with the special color-changing string of star lights twinkling around me. And to Justin, for his extra patience and his plot whispering ways. Love you always, even if you one day decide you can't listen to one more story ramble. :)

ALSO BY AMY KNUPP

<u>Henry Brothers Series</u>

Untold (prequel)

Unraveled

Unsung

Undone

<u>North Brothers Series</u>

True North

True Colors

True Blue

True Harmony

True Hero

North Brothers Box Sets:

North Brothers Books 1-3

North Brothers Books 4-5

North Brothers: The Complete Series

<u>Hale Street Series</u>:

Sweet Spot

Sweet Dreams

Soft Spot

One and Only

Last First Kiss

Heartstrings

<u>Hale Street Box Sets:</u>

Meet Me at Clayborne's

Clayborne's After Hours

It Happened on Hale Street (all 6 of Amy's stories)

<u>Island Fire Series</u>:

Playing with Fire

Heat of the Night

Fully Involved

Firestorm

Afterburn

Up in Flames

Flash Point

Fire Within

Impulse

Slow Burn

Island Fire Box Sets:

Sparked (books 1-3)

Ignited (books 4-6)

Enflamed (books 7-10)

OR

Island Fire: The Complete Series

Themed Box Sets:

Friends to Forever (Friends to Lovers Romance)

Working It (Workplace Romance)

ABOUT THE AUTHOR

Amy Knupp is an author of contemporary romance stories. She loves words and grammar and meaty, engrossing stories with complex characters.

Amy lives in Wisconsin with her husband, two teenage sons, four cats, and two box turtles. She graduated from the University of Kansas with degrees in French and journalism. In her spare time, she enjoys traveling, breaking up cat fights, watching college hoops, and annoying her family by correcting their grammar.

For more information:
www.amyknuppbooks.com